D1280138

THE BRIDGE AT ARTA
and other stories

THE BRIDGE AT ARTA

and other stories

by

J. I. M. STEWART

W · W · NORTON & COMPANY
New York · London

Copyright © 1981 by J. I. M. Stewart

All rights reserved.

Printed in the United States of America.

Library of Congress Cataloging in Publication Data

Stewart, John Innes Mackintosh, 1906–
The bridge at Arta and other stories.

Contents: The bridge at Arta—The time-bomb
—The little duffer—[etc.]
I. Title.
PR6037.T466B7   1982   823'.912   82-2228
AACR2

W. W. Norton & Company, Inc. 500 Fifth Avenue, New York, N.Y. 10110
W. W. Norton & Company, Ltd. 37 Great Russell Street, London WC1B 3NU

1 2 3 4 5 6 7 8 9 0

ISBN 0-393-01590-4

CONTENTS

THE BRIDGE AT ARTA

and other stories

THE BRIDGE AT ARTA

LADY CAMERON HAD recognized Charles Hornett at once.

It was in the departure lounge of Number Two Terminal at Heathrow. She had shown her passport, briefly resigned her handbag for rummaging, and walked through the contraption that rings a bell or flashes a light should one happen to be secreting any substantial metallic object about one's person. There was something slightly ignominious about this last manoeuvre. Perhaps it suggested to cultivated persons (and on this trip, incidentally, they would all be that) the symbolic driving beneath a yoke which in the ancient world had transformed a free man into a slave. Lady Cameron had once, in a sense, been a slave, and she hadn't liked it at all.

Yes, there was Charles—instantly known, although unglimpsed for fifty years. He was among a group of people not themselves labelled (as happens on packaged tours within the simpler reaches of society) but with the distinctive yellow and red tags supplied by Messrs Pipkin and Pipkin dutifully attached to their hand-baggage. So here was another instantaneous discovery. She and Charles were together going to do 'Sites and Flowers of Thessaly and Epirus' under the guidance of Professor and Mrs Boss-Baker.

Lady Cameron had never gone out of her way to avoid a meeting with Charles, and she had from time to time envisaged—with amusement rather than discomposure—various circumstances under which a casual encounter might take place. It hadn't, indeed, been like that at the beginning; for a long period after their divorce she would have regarded anything of the sort as quite horrible. But after fifty years! It was almost something that *ought* to take place when each had survived their disaster so long. It would not be a touching occasion, or sentimental in any way. Essentially it would be curious. They would both comport themselves properly, and that would be that.

Lady Cameron saw a number of familiar faces in the little group.

7

There was a pronounced element of reunion in the occasion for many of them. Like Lady Cameron herself, they had 'been with' the Boss-Bakers before. Indeed, if you hadn't 'been with' the Boss-Bakers before, you were apt to feel, at least at the start, a bit of an outsider in the party. So what about Charles? He was already talking fluently to two elderly women a little wedged into a corner of the lounge. But as a conversationalist he had always been quick off the mark, and it was quite possible that he was a new boy in the Pipkin and Pipkin fold.

Mrs Boss-Baker bore down on Lady Cameron with enthusiastic acclaim. This wasn't because Lady Cameron, being a baronet's widow, was likely to be the person of most formal consequence in the group. Mrs Boss-Baker was always enthusiastic, although it didn't prevent her from also being wary and alert. She had a genius for smoothing things over almost before they were ruffled. If you had been promised that your 'facilities' would include a proper bath and you found yourself fobbed off with a shower, Mrs Boss-Baker would know in advance precisely how cross you were likely to be, and proceed to action in the light of this knowledge. And nobody could call her shy. Professor Boss-Baker *was* shy. He was invariably voted, indeed, wholly delightful; he was a marvellous lecturer; and although he claimed competence only over the flowers he was a classical man by training and knew quite as much about the sites as did the young Greek archaeologists commonly turned on to expatiate about them. Only Professor Boss-Baker did have an odd propensity for simply slipping away. At one moment he would be talking charmingly and instructively to the ladies of his party on this wild-flower and that, and the next moment he would have disappeared, mysteriously and unaccountably, into a landscape that ought not to have afforded cover for a mouse. His wife, however, was always to hand.

Mrs Boss-Baker recalled former trips, and Lady Cameron made suitable replies. It gave her time to think about Charles, and also to assess as a whole the party as so far constituted. It was an elderly crowd; indeed it was possible to suppose that she and Charles, both in their mid-seventies, were going to consort with several people a good deal older than themselves. Some of them, it occurred to her, might go in for remembering insignificant social events remote in time. But the small history of Charles Hornett and herself had been very insignificant indeed, and it was only her second marriage that had made her known beyond the bounds of a single parish. So although she had met some of these elderly people on previous trips it was unlikely that any

8

of them would have a story to tell the others about Charles and herself. Which was just as well—trivial although the whole thing was. A divorced couple finding themselves fortuitously on the same tour would come under a good deal of covert scrutiny were their relationship—or former relationship—discovered and bruited abroad.

There was, of course, Mrs Boss-Baker. It was quite clear that she never set out on one of these expeditions without doing vigorous homework on the pedigree of her flock. This enabled her never to put a foot wrong. She and her husband, she would cheerfully confide to you, had to hold down the job year after year if their two sons were to continue at their public school. It was only a commendable love of Greece on the part of a small section of the English prosperous classes that stood between these youths and the horrors of comprehensive education. So Mrs Boss-Baker, although she might well know the truth, would be discretion itself.

'Charles, this is after more years than one cares to remember. . . .' Lady Cameron had decided to begin—and for the moment pretty well to end—with that. Later on, she and Charles would work it out that there had formerly been some slight acquaintanceship between them. It would be deception—but deception of a civilized sort, designed to obviate any occasion of embarrassment to other people. And perhaps she had better not turn to Charles at once. For one thing, it didn't look as if he had yet noticed her; for another, the Peppers were now in evidence, and had. The Peppers frequented the enterprises of Messrs Pipkin and Pipkin with an assiduity suggesting both uncommon physical vitality and enormous wealth. Yet they were a weedy couple, and it was demonstrably not to the 'higher' clergy that the Reverend Mr Pepper belonged. So there was something enigmatical about the Peppers, although a modicum of light was perhaps cast on it by Mrs Boss-Baker's occasional discreet reference to Mrs Pepper as coming of 'people very well known in the City'. Lady Cameron conversed for a few minutes with the Peppers. Mr Pepper, as usual on these occasions, retained his somewhat shabby clerical attire. But this effect he had a little lightened—as again was his custom—by superimposing upon it a new and therefore immaculate panama hat. Such objects, Lady Cameron vaguely believed, nowadays cost about as much as an air ticket to Athens.

And now for Charles, Lady Cameron resolved. He was still talking to the two women in a corner. But no: that was incorrect. It was the

9

same corner, but a different brace of women. And as Lady Cameron approached they moved away. It had been a shade oddly, she thought. Could they conceivably have been aware of an awkward moment as in prospect? Or was it simply that Charles *still* . . .? But there was no time for speculation, and Lady Cameron's prepared words were on her lips. They died there. Charles, planted squarely in front of her, was looking at her absolutely blankly. For a moment she supposed that this was what used to be called the cut direct; that Charles was simply going to refuse to know her. Then the truth came to her. He hadn't recognized her. He was totally failing to recognize her now. It was rather a bewildering situation. Curiously, too, it was an intensely humiliating one.

Mrs Boss-Baker was at their side. The admirable woman had sensed some *contretemps* from afar and on the instant, and now she was performing an introduction.

'Lady Cameron,' she said, 'may I introduce Mr Hornett? Mr Hornett has not been with us before, but has travelled extensively in the Far East. Mr Hornett, this is Lady Cameron, who has been President of the Alpine Flower Society.' Having thus provided two little spring-boards towards acquaintanceship, Mrs Boss-Baker departed on some further diplomatic mission. She would keep it up untiringly until their flight was called and they had all been settled in their seats.

'How do you do?' Charles said with the perfunctory air (which Lady Cameron well remembered) of one getting through a useless preliminary. 'I'm afraid I know nothing about alpine flowers. But I can tell you something I remember about my tactics when I decided I had as much information as I needed about the plans I had been working on when I was in Persia.'

'In Persia?' It was in a tone of well-bred interest that Lady Cameron contrived to respond to this prolix remark. Inwardly, she was overwhelmed. Charles *was* just as he had been. And how could it be otherwise? Leopards don't change their spots, nor bores their blotches. Her former husband's egotism, so mysteriously masked during their brief courtship, had calamitously revealed itself in the earliest days of their marriage. And now (if the thing were possible) he was even more of a monomaniac than he had proved to be fifty years ago.

'Of course I hadn't believed a word they told me,' Charles was saying. 'I'm not a fool, and it was as simple as that. I didn't believe a word of it.' Charles's tone had now become aggressive, resentful, aggrieved—although what he was embarking upon was plainly an anecdote designed to show how he had triumphed over enemies. 'I rather fancy I always know just where I stand when I find that it's with cattle of that sort that I have to deal.'

Charles continued in this vein without any sign of stopping. It was all hideously of the past, and yet present here and now. She had been buried under this, stifled by it, crushed by it as by a cartload of stone, when she had been no more than a young bride. But now there was a bizarre superaddition to the burden. He still hadn't a clue about her. He still believed her to be a stranger—an empty pot, a blank sheet or *tabula rasa*, for the reception, for the remorseless inscribing or incising, of all this compulsive self-absorption.

Lily Cameron had been a beauty. She liked to believe that people still spoke of her as a handsome woman. Was she in brutal truth an unrecognizable ruin? Charles wasn't. Age had not withered him nor custom staled his infinite monotony. And again she had that dreadful sense of humiliation. Feebly, she told herself that his eyesight might have become defective—and his hearing, surely, as well. But that was a wholly unnecessary conjecture. As a young man his self-regard had been a literal thing. Even on their bridal night he probably hadn't really *seen* her. So why should he be seeing her now?

Nor, presumably, had he ever thought of her after they had parted, or acquainted himself with her subsequent fortune in any regard. Her second married name would mean nothing to him. Hence this strange situation. There seemed no reason why it should not continue through the fortnight that lay ahead. That, certainly, would be the most comfortable thing: that when they parted here at Heathrow he should be in the same state of ignorance as held him now. But would playing it that way be quite—well, spirited? Ought there not to be, at some time during their trip, a *dénouement* to this small absurd episode? Lady Cameron, who owned a sense of style, was not at all sure that it oughtn't to be so.

The flight to Athens was called, and the Pipkin and Pipkin party—individually scurrying or at leisure according to their degree of experience as pilgrims—made their way down the long sloping corridor leading to their plane. Lady Cameron, it need scarcely be related, secured herself a seat comfortably remote from Charles Hornett.

'Sites and Flowers' didn't, as it happened, begin too well. Athens duly appeared below them, and the Acropolis was glimpsed. Both disappeared; a little later both turned up again; and a little later still they were plainly over nowhere in particular. Then the captain's voice announced with careful indifference that there was trouble at Alexandria, and that Athens was in a bit of a fuss as a result. For the time being, in fact, Athens would have nothing to do with them. So they were now on their way to Salonika, which it was to be hoped would prove more hospitable, as their endurance was running out. This last was an ambiguous expression, since it might refer either to human patience or to aviation fuel. Mr Pepper, who had a map, announced that Salonika appeared to be about two hundred miles away.

In circumstances such as these the English are not, indeed, tight-lipped, since anything of the kind may indicate nervous strain. Rather they are low-keyed. The Pipkin and Pipkin party, although their ears were alert to catch the first spluttering of an engine which would draw upon them an Icarian fate in the Aegean now so unexpectedly expansed beneath them, conversed quietly from time to time on indifferent topics. Or they all did this except Charles Hornett—who conversed, or rather monologized, unintermittedly and in a penetrating voice to the two unfortunate ladies of his first acquaintance. His subject, being that of a battle fought with a recalcitrant Inspector of Taxes in the previous year, could have been only of a somewhat confined interest to his hearers, but this didn't prevent Charles from according it a saga-like breadth of treatment. Mrs Boss-Baker (who had just been constrained to announce to her charges that tea and biscuits had run out on the plane, but that drinking-water was still in moderate supply) must already have been aware that in Mr Hornett (widely travelled in the Far East though he might be) she had a first-class problem on her hands.

Salonika made no bones about receiving them, and after half-an-hour even permitted them to disembark—although it then immediately incarcerated them in an enormous glass box. The acoustics of this were notable as combining great resonance with the qualities of an echo-chamber of the kind favoured by the BBC when in quest of eerie effects. It was just right for Charles, who lived up to its opportunities for something under three hours. The party was then embarked again, flown back to Athens, given a meal in a restaurant distinguishably over-taxed and appalled by their arrival, and then driven for three hours in a coach through magnificent scenery which was unfortunately invisible. Finally, at two o'clock in the morning, they tumbled into bed in a hotel which the less bemused or better informed understood to be in the neighbourhood of Delphi. For a few quite appreciable periods during this Odyssey Charles was out of action. He owned the enviable faculty of being able to fall asleep at will, and to wake up fifteen minutes later, restored and alert for new exertions. During this nocturnal journey, too, he made the happy discovery that the coach in which the succeeding twelve days were to be largely spent was half as big again as the Pipkin and Pipkin crowd required. This meant that he could move round the vacant seats in turn—'chatting' (as he would have outrageously expressed it) to a succession of small captive audiences.

On the following morning the party, to a man (or woman) heroically declaring itself refreshed and fit for anything, paid a visit to Hosios Loukas. Professor Boss-Baker, declaring himself wholly uninstructed on early Byzantine art, in fact knew at once which were the most approved mosaics, and was charmingly perceptive, if also a little whimsical, in front of them.

'He means business, you know,' Professor Boss-Baker said of the Christ of *The Harrowing of Hell*. 'You can see he won't let go of Adam easily. Eve is expected to look after herself. And as for David and Solomon—I'm told it's David and Solomon there on the left—they're quite clearly just you and me. So you can see how amazement and gratification are expected of us—and quite right, too, of course.'

There was a murmur of appreciation among the Pipkins—evoked partly by this important artistic object itself and partly by the Professor's lightness of touch in hinting the propriety of mild reverence before such strange old things. Mrs Pepper ventured to explain with agreeable diffidence why the sun and moon were simultaneously present at the Crucifixion, and her husband translated the inscriptions on several of the mosaics. It was in the middle of this that Charles's voice was again heard, addressing an unwary individual who had strayed from the company.

'And he had the damned cheek,' Charles's voice was heard by all to declare, 'to propose raising an assessment under Schedule D.'

Lady Cameron slipped out of the *catholicon* into the warm sun. Here in mid-April there was already the scent of lemon blossom in the air, and across the groves and orchards the eye travelled to the foothills of Helicon. ' "Where Helicon breaks down in cliffs to the sea," ' she murmured to herself. But she wasn't feeling poetical. She was feeling

13

ashamed. She knew—although she was now almost certain that none of her present companions were aware of her as having been Charles's wife—that she was going to feel her heart sink every time she heard him speak. It would be her impulse always to edge away from him, as one used to edge away from a rashly-chosen school-friend when she proved liable to talk shaming nonsense.

On the following day the party 'did' Delphi, but Lady Cameron cried off. She had been to Delphi before, and could recall being properly awed by the undeniable numinousness of the site. She had been told, however, that it was now much commercialized. ('"Not here, O Apollo, are haunts fit for thee," ' she pronounced, returning to Matthew Arnold's poem.) And of this she made an excuse to herself for a get-away plan. She ordered sandwiches and summoned a taxi—for she was a capable woman—and proposed to spend the day in solitude on the plateau of Mount Parnassus. But quite this was not to be. Mrs Boss-Baker appeared as she was about to drive off—a Mrs Boss-Baker all conspiratorial fun.

'Please, can I come too?' Mrs Boss-Baker asked childishly. 'Oh, I am wicked! Here's only the second day, and I'm dying for a little time off.'

Lady Cameron produced the necessary cordial acquiescence, although inwardly she was inclined to be annoyed. Just because she was seventy-four this interfering woman was judging her unfit to go off for a day's ramble by herself. It was totally insufferable! But then Lady Cameron remembered those two boys at Rugby—paid for year by year at the cost of this sort of eternal vigilance on their parents' part. If the Boss-Bakers lost a baronet's doddering old widow over a precipice it was quite certain that Messrs Pipkin and Pipkin wouldn't be too pleased. So Lady Cameron's heart warmed towards Mrs Boss-Baker, and they got on excellently together throughout the day.

There was a lake and there was a deserted village. ('Goldsmith in Phocis,' Lady Cameron said—to the bewilderment of Mrs Boss-Baker, who was not literary.) They walked through irises and tiny forget-me-nots and sheets of blue veronica; chats and pipits and buntings enlivened the immediate scene; falcons and vultures hovered; in the distance the Muses' haunt lay under brilliant sunlit snow. It was a perfect day, and ought to have been totally absorbing. Yet for Lady Cameron it wasn't quite that. Ought she to have stuck it out? She asked herself the question again and again as it returned to her from its hiding-place half-a-century back. Had she hung on, could she have broken through the dreadful prison of self-absorption that Charles had constructed for himself? Its walls had thickened over the years, and were certainly impregnable now. Even at the time of her first horrified realization of his malady—for it was certainly that—she had judged it to be already so. But she had been very young—and might she not have been wrong? And to have stood before an altar with a man, taking tremendous vows—and then to have divorced him merely because he was a bore! And that had been it. Not, of course, in law. Only in queer places in America could you at that time have parted with a husband for such a reason. She had detected poor Charles in sporadic low amours—and had hardly blamed him in the least. It would have been unfair to do so, since her own going to bed with him had proved mutually unrewarding. But it was something upon which she was entitled to seize, and she *had* seized upon it— unscrupulously, she now told herself. It had, naturally, all been very uncomfortable. In those days any sort of airing adultery in court had been very uncomfortable indeed.

Thus did Lady Cameron, sharing her sandwiches with Mrs Boss-Baker on the slopes of Mount Parnassus, meditate a distant past. She knew that it wasn't a very effective meditation, in the sense of being one that might lead to a changed course of conduct. She knew that she couldn't have done other than she had done, and that if it could all happen again she would do it again. And she *had* stuck it out—for quite long enough to *know*. Why, for two whole years it was almost literally true that she had been reduced to silence—since from dawn to dusk there had scarcely been an opportunity of getting a word in edgewise! And how different it had been with her second husband. She and Donald had been endlessly interested each in the other. They had chattered together like happy children through a long married life.

Mrs Boss-Baker did not intrude upon these periods of abstraction on the part of her companion. From time to time their conversation strayed from the birds and flowers to one or another member of their party—sometimes not without amusement, but predominantly on the proper note of cordial regard. Mrs Boss-Baker said nothing about Mr Hornett. Was this because he was fast becoming such a pain in the neck (Lady Cameron had a brother who would have used this phrase) that any reference to him had tacitly been voted taboo? Or was it because Mrs Boss-Baker had indeed done her homework only too well? Lady Cameron didn't much mind. Only she was coming to feel a little sorry for Charles. Surely through the terrible bars he had forged for himself he sometimes peered out and was aware of the figure he cut? Yes—she told herself again—she might have done something about it once, but it was too late now. The weird fact of his continued failure to identify her surely spoke of a pathological condition of a formidable sort, not to be resolved by amateurs.

The taxi reappeared, and in half-an-hour restored the two wanderers to their companions. Mrs Pepper, it seemed, had taken a photograph of the Castalian Spring, but was apprehensive that she had superimposed it upon one of the Sanctuary of Athena Pronaea. Another lady was triumphing in the discovery of an unfamiliar bee-orchid, pronounced by Professor Boss-Baker to be quite a surprise in this habitat. A third had stolen some bay leaves, and was inquiring whether it would be a further misdemeanour to smuggle them into England. Lady Cameron joined the group she judged likeliest to suggest a preliminary glass of *ouzo* before changing for dinner. Fortified by this, she ventured to speculate anew to herself on what would happen were she to confront Charles with the revelation that she was his former wife. She decided that it would be merely wounding and bewildering, and therefore a wicked and silly thing to do.

It was the agreeable custom of Professor Boss-Baker to spend half-an-hour or so after dinner talking about the following day's prospects to any members of his party who cared to gather around. He did this with the most casual air, but in fact was contriving to keep a cunning balance of interest between one sort of activity and another. Everybody was going to get a fair share of their sort of thing. The botanical ladies (who were in a majority) would be afforded ample scampering grounds for hunting down the rarer flora of the region. But the archaeologically minded, and those who (like the Peppers) were deeply versed in the Glory that was Greece, and again those more modish persons who were becoming well-seen in Byzantine art: all would be catered for in the most accommodating fashion. Professor Boss-Baker performed this task in a slightly throw-away manner which—as has been recorded—was judged very delightful in an overpoweringly learned man.

He mounted such an occasion on the evening before their arrival at Arta. Arta, it seemed, was stuffed with history—mainly of the ecclesiastical order. There were little churches all over the place, acting as a kind of supporting chorus to one big one. The Panagia

Parigoritissa—which somebody had told him meant the Virgin of Consolation—was a very rum thirteenth-century effort indeed: so rum that they mustn't mistake it for a bank and try to cash their traveller's cheques in it. Once inside the unlikely cube they would be in the presence of a naked architecture which was quite breathtakingly strange. There would be a guide who would have a great deal to say about it. In fact what with cyclopean walls, and the palace of the Greek metropolitan, and mosques and synagogues thrown in, they would be hurried round for the whole day after their arrival if they cared to be. So it had occurred to him that it might be a good idea to drive straight to the bridge before going to their hotel.

'Is it an *important* bridge?' one of the botanical ladies asked. Bridges were not her thing, but she had been brought up to respect objects adequately starred in Baedeker or Michelin.

'It has a certain historical interest,' Professor Boss-Baker said mildly. 'The river, you know, is the ancient Arachthos. Not long ago—or not long ago as one reckons time in these parts—it marked the frontier between Greece and Turkey. It's a Turkish bridge, although that fact is probably ignored locally. But it was treated as neutral ground, and what happened when it required repair, I don't know. It's a handsome and picturesque structure—on nine semicircular arches, if I remember aright.'

'But isn't there a legend?' Mrs Pepper asked. 'I'm sure I've read somewhere about the legend of the bridge at Arta.'

'There's certainly a legend, and it's even older than this particular bridge is. Like the trade-winds, such things move with the sun from country to country, changing a little as they go.'

'Like ballads,' one of the botanical ladies said with a flash of erudition in an unexpected field.

'Just so. And it's in a Greek folk ballad—not, I believe, a particularly ancient one—that the legend hitches on to the bridge at Arta. But it's a slightly macabre affair, I'm afraid.' Professor Boss-Baker glanced round his auditory—which was, of course, predominantly female—in a hesitant way. But this was a merely teasing manoeuvre, since he had every intention of telling his story. 'The bridge-builder got into trouble every time his work neared completion. At the final and critical moment, when the principal keystone was just about to be slipped into place, the whole affair fell down. It kept on happening until one night along came a raven and had a word with him. The raven was some sort of tutelary spirit, I imagine, and it told him just what to do. He must immure in the foundations—alive, needless to say—the first living creature that came in sight. This might have been a goat or a donkey, I suppose, but as things turned out it was the builder's wife. So there was no help for it. Professional success and duty were paramount, and in she went.'

'How extremely horrible!' one of the botanical ladies said.

'Well, yes.' Professor Boss-Baker was delighted at having elicited this reaction. 'And it wasn't, if the ballad is to be believed, any sort of sharp and short occasion. There is some difficulty in lowering the unfortunate woman into position, and she makes a long and lugubrious speech while the job is going on. One gets the impression of a somewhat insistently talkative person. She enters, in fact, on a good deal of family history. Two of her sisters, it seems, were married to bridge-builders, and precisely this fate overtook them. It seems improbable, one must admit. But that sort of thing is constantly happening in ballads the world over, is it not? I believe it's known as the technique of incremental repetition. However, the bridge got completed; it's there to this day; and we're all going to stand on it and meditate the tale. I don't know whether it can be said to have a moral.'

'I rather think it has,' Mr Pepper said. He had perhaps observed that some of the ladies were really shocked by Professor Boss-Baker's recital, and aimed at offering some droll comment upon it. 'Prudent wives will keep clear of their husbands' work. For my part, I deprecate the suggestion. Long may my own wife continue to find time and inclination to cast a critical eye over my sermons.'

From Mr Pepper, this was quite a sally, and it was strongly approved of. Lady Cameron, however, was among those not much amused by the story—or rather by the slightly morbid notion of a kind of tourist attraction having been manufactured out of it. She would have been glad enough not herself to have to visit the bridge at Arta. But this, she saw, could not be, since the coach was going to take the whole party straight there at the end of their next day's run. She glanced across at Charles, whom as usual on these after-dinner occasions she had contrived a little to distance. He had actually listened in silence to Professor Boss-Baker's narrative. He even appeared to have been much struck by it.

Perhaps because of the build-up it had received, the bridge at Arta proved rather a flop. Unlike Delphi, or Dodona, or even the charming

island where Ali Pasha had lived so unspeakably scandalous a life
(and which is still in the charge, most improperly, of half-a-dozen
extremely personable young men), the bridge and its environs were
by no means heavy with the spirit of place, whether numinous or
otherwise. The Arachthos flowed in a rapid but well-conducted way
beneath its arches; on its banks there were a few old men fishing and a
few young couples making not particularly passionate love; at one end
there were some broken-down farm buildings and a low pot-house of
the most unpromising sort. But the parapet was of a height convenient for leaning upon and its stone was warm from the sun. People lit
cigarettes, or took photographs, or talked about English gardens. The
more elderly exchanged information about ailments or grandchildren. Nobody much thought about the bridge-builder's wife.
There was perhaps a slight impatience to board the coach again, be
driven on to their hotel and discover whether in Arta bathrooms had
baths or not.

Lady Cameron did again think of the ballad. Professor Boss-Baker
had told her that, although there was almost certainly no woman's
skeleton imprisoned beneath her feet, it was likely enough that some
member of the brute creation had been unkindly done by at an
appropriate stage in the bridge's fashioning. She disliked the idea of
such a ritual, and as a consequence walked the full length of the
structure and got on innocent earth again. It was possible to follow
the farther bank for some way down-stream to a point from which the
bridge would appear at least pleasingly picturesque. In this interest
she strolled on, not much regarding the time, or reflecting that she
had injudiciously sundered herself from her fellow-travellers. But this
she suddenly found was not entirely so. Immediately in front of her
the figure of a man had emerged abruptly from behind a tree—
perhaps having withdrawn there for some trivial private purpose.
And this last circumstance absurdly lent a small additional edge of
unease to the disconcerting fact that the man was Charles.

'Oh, Lady Cunningham!' Charles said in his perfunctory way. He
hadn't bothered to acquire more than random approximations to the
names of any members of the party. 'I wonder whether I left my
camera on my seat when I got out of the bus. And I happened to have
an eye on the driver and I don't think I saw him lock the doors as he
ought to have done. I can tell you something about how I came by
that camera in a way I'm rather proud of.' Charles didn't sound
proud; he sounded, as he always did, immensely aggrieved about

something that he would communicate to you in due course. And *that*—Lady Cameron suddenly remembered—had really been it. It had been the constant note of discontent and self-commiseration accompanying Charles's solipsistic maunderings that had put the final lid on things. And this had continued, like the drone on a bagpipe, through all the varied exigencies, whatever they had been, of the past fifty years of his life! It was a horrible thought: much more horrible, even, than the thought of a woman buried in a bridge.

Lady Cameron tried to think of something to say. So far, she had been very successful in avoiding Charles, and this sudden encounter with him in near solitude almost frightened her. Tête-à-tête like this, it was surely impossible that he shouldn't recognize her at last. She felt, too, as she had not felt before, that on her own part it was demeaning to continue concealing her identity as if she were ashamed of it. She even wondered how she had conceivably justified the deception to herself in the first place. Yet she knew that this was only a matter of a momentary failure of nerve. Why should she take any step that involved having more to do with Charles than the odd coincidence of their both being on this Pipkin and Pipkin affair made necessary?

'I think we had better go back to the coach,' Lady Cameron said.

But in the very moment that she uttered these words, Lady Cameron realized that they proposed something no longer possible of fulfilment. Beyond the bridge the roof of the coach was visible above the small tumble-down farm building. And it was evident that the vehicle was in motion.

'I suppose the fellow's just turning round,' Charles said, having himself become aware of what was happening. But he spoke without conviction, and it quite clearly wouldn't do. The coach was gathering speed. The coach disappeared in the direction of Arta.

'I've known Mrs Boss-Baker do it before,' Lady Cameron said, with a casualness she didn't actually feel. 'She's extremely careful, but she does occasionally count the heads incorrectly. It must be very easy to do.'

'But I can't believe she'd fail to see I wasn't yet on board the damned thing!' Charles exclaimed indignantly. 'It's impossible! It's an outrage! I'll have the woman sacked.'

'I don't think we ought to take it too seriously, Mr Hornett. And we had better return over the bridge at once. It's probable they'll turn back in a few minutes. They mayn't miss me, but they're certain to miss your voice.'

'I bloody well hope so.' Charles had been conscious of no barb in his companion's words. 'But if they don't miss me until it comes to allocating the rooms in the hotel, they mayn't come back to pick me up for more than an hour.' Charles paused, broodingly. 'Or you,' he added as an unexpected afterthought.

'Let us hope it won't be as long as that.' Lady Cameron now felt that it quite probably would be. Her former husband did, after all, take those fifteen-minute naps on board the coach. So her small witticism hadn't meant much. 'For I rather think,' she said, 'that it's going to turn chilly.' This was undeniable. As they reached the apex of the bridge a cold wind caught them. She regretted that she had left her overcoat in the coach. For that matter she had left her handbag as well, which wasn't at all her habit. This meant that she was penniless. It wasn't important, but it was a shade vexatious. The town of Arta was invisible, and might be several miles away. The anglers and the courting couples had departed, and the surroundings now registered a back-of-beyond effect which was far from pleasing. There was nothing but the pot-house they were now approaching, and it was no more than a low hovel with a couple of dirty benches outside. Lady Cameron disliked the effect of dependence on Charles which all this engendered.

'I'd say it was a pub of sorts,' Charles announced. 'I dare say I can get a drink. I'll ask them for an *ouzo*.' He glanced absently at Lady Cameron, and it was as if a vague memory of the usages of civilization stirred in his head. 'What about you, Lady Cunningham?'

'A *café grecque*, perhaps.' Lady Cameron had been so surprised that she sat down abruptly on one of the grubby benches, although it was something she had just decided not to do.

'Ten drachmas.'

It was not the habit of Messrs Pipkin and Pipkin's pilgrims to be perpetually standing one another drinks, but in the present circumstances this demand was decidedly peculiar.

'My purse is in the coach,' Lady Cameron said briefly.

'Ah, yes.' Charles spoke as if this settled the matter, and departed. When he emerged again from the hovel he was carrying a single glass. It wasn't a matter, his former wife told herself, of brutish bad manners. Charles wasn't exactly like that. It was much more that the very existence of other people in the universe was a fact continually slipping from him even between one second and the next. Strictly regarded, much of his monologue was really pure soliloquy. And now, when he had sat down with his drink in front of him, he was actually silent for some time. Any attention that he did pay to the external world appeared to be directed towards the bridge, close to which they were still sitting. Lady Cameron was silent too; she felt rather like one of those bespangled females whose function is to disappear opportunely on the stage of an illusionist. Once or twice she detected Charles as producing a sound which she had very little memory of associating with him: a kind of semi-internalized laughter. He seemed to be tickled by the bridge.

Then something very disturbing happened. Charles ceased gazing at the bridge and gazed at her instead. He was actually gazing at her with genuine, if fleeting, curiosity. And he was looking puzzled, as well.

'I'll tell you an odd thing about myself,' Charles said abruptly. 'It has come into my head that you remind me of somebody.'

'Indeed, Mr Hornett?'

Lady Cameron had offered this convention of mild encouragement automatically. She still didn't in the least want to encourage or coax her former husband's pathologically defective memory. But clearly the thing now had to come. There was no point in attempting diversion or delay.

'Only I can't remember who it is. Perhaps it will come back to me later. Of course it can't be of any importance to me, can it?'

'Almost certainly not, I should imagine.' Lady Cameron produced this reply with some relief, and at the same time she looked anxiously in the direction of what she supposed to be the road from Arta. There was always the possibility that a relief expedition would heave into view. And now for the moment the crisis had passed. Charles's attention had wandered again. It was once more engaged with the bridge.

'I call that a damned good yarn,' he said. 'Sensible chap, eh? And resourceful, too. I'll bet he made up that raven.'

'Perhaps the whole story is made up. It's not a particularly agreeable one.'

'Depends on how you look at it. And I'll tell you another interesting thing about myself, Lady Cunningham. I had a wife just like that myself. Never stopped chattering at me. I tell you I just could not shut her up. But this chap managed that in the simplest and most literal manner. Piled up the rubble on her, eh? Stout fellow! I drink to him.'

Charles Hornett raised his glass and drained it. He showed no awareness that the woman vaguely known to him as Lady Cunningham was staring at him in naked horror. And even when she had a little recovered herself she didn't attempt to speak. The strangeness of this neat and convinced reversal of historical fact was too much for her. For the present, at least, she simply wanted to get away, to be released from a nightmare at once absurd and insupportable.

And release was at hand. Suddenly as if by magic, the coach had appeared and was drawing to a halt beside them. It contained only the driver and Mrs Boss-Baker—who was already lavishly signalling rescue and apology.

'Well, thank goodness for that,' Charles said. 'I was getting damned bored, sitting outside this God-forsaken pub and talking about nothing at all. At least I shan't be late for my dinner.' He stood up, glancing blankly at Lady Cameron as he did so. Or glancing, so to speak, at where she was. For it was reassuringly evident—she somehow knew this—that her former husband wouldn't give her another thought during the remaining course of 'Sites and Flowers of Thessaly and Epirus'.

THE TIME-BOMB

I

GILBERT PILLMAN AND Francis Gethin shared digs. They were in their early twenties, and among the most junior of the junior lecturers in a provincial university. Their resemblance to one another stopped short just there. Pillman had taken his first steps in learning at a small Midland grammar school and considered himself (or thought he ought to consider himself) lucky to have got where he had. Apart from being clever there was nothing remarkable about him except his being very good-looking, which he was in a rather distinguished and (so to speak) unexpected way. People regarded him as being good natured and as not incapable of being good fun.

Gethin was the son of an eminent philosopher and the grandson of a peer. He just couldn't believe that Winchester and Oxford had vanished from his ken and that here he was in this absurd place. Along with this intolerance and fastidiousness there went, oddly enough, a great deal of modesty and diffidence. His acquaintances accounted for this by remarking that, as a physical presence, he was distinctly pinched and meagre. *Chétif* was his own word for himself when he became intimate and confiding. But this he didn't do at all readily. In fact in all Nessfield it was only his room-mate Gillie who was allowed much glimpse of a gloomy and self-tormenting Franco.

Neither of these young men was particularly keen on his job. Pillman's subject was English literature (capital 'L' literature in professional contexts), and he wasn't very clear as to what one did about it. He could run up quite amusing lectures surprisingly rapidly—which was just as well, since he was required to hold forth on a dais four times a week and had as yet no stock of the wretched things in a drawer. But, to get on, it was essential to be a scholar. You found something to edit, or somebody whose humdrum life you burrow into, or books which could be speciously represented as 'influenced' by other books. 'We come on quite an interesting line of derivation here,' he would say from that dais. 'It's odd how big dogs

24

go for little dogs' vomit. You'd expect it to be the other way round.' And he'd get a not very comprehending laugh here and there from the captive audience ranged in front of him.

Gethin was a mathematician. It was the very bloodiest thing you could be, he declared, if you happened to be *not* a mathematician. He had recently counted up and found that there were at present six mathematicians in England. He himself was not among them.

So here was something more the two had in common, after all: a morose comfortable grousing was agreeable to them both. They'd hold sessions for this of an evening, sitting on either side of a smoky little fire in their shared sitting-room, drinking cheap burgundy (and it was really cheap in the nineteen-thirties) out of a flagon shaped (Gethin said) like a po.

Pillman was quite fond of Gethin. He approved of a distinct tendency in Gethin to admire him: something the more gratifying in that Gethin seemed indisposed to admire much else. Pillman felt it to be his role to jolly Gethin out of his glooms; even to rag him mildly at times. They had become Gillie and Franco to one another in the first week of their association.

'He's quite too absurd,' Franco would say of his professor, whose name was Shuffrey. 'It's hard not to intimate one's sense that he ought to have a little shop somewhere. Rather a shady little shop, with French letters kept under the counter.'

'How very coarse. And I don't believe, Franco, you'd know a French letter if you saw one.'

'Oh, shut up, Gillie.' For some reason Franco disliked this quip very much. 'And do you know? He refers to his children as the kiddies. It's unbelievable.'

'I suppose it would be unbelievable in your class of society, my dear infant. But even men who beget kiddies are also God's creatures. And I rather like your Professor Shuffrey. His finger-nails keep mine company, I suppose. Pass the bottle.' Franco during the previous week had commented unfavourably on Gillie's notion of adequate cleanliness in this regard. Public school standards of uncompromising candour were among the few things he felt he could assist his friend to a command of.

'Look not on the third glass, Gillie.'

'Bloody well look on the third glass when it's three lectures on *Samson Agonistes* that lie ahead. Three lectures on *Samson Agonistes*! It's straight murder.'

'You'd better get started.' Gethin himself had recourse to the third glass. 'We don't seem very cheerful, do we?'

'No.'

'Nor shall be when we've become professors in some awful hole in Wales or the Middle East. Nor when retired and seventy.'

'Perfectly true, Franco. Sighing that only one thing has been lent to youth and age in common: discontent.'

'I suppose you chuck those stale old poetical tags at your undergraduates.'

'Students.'

Franco was falling into the habit of staring at Gillie quite a lot, but in the course of this exercise he usually switched on a frown of disapproval. He did this now.

'Students or undergraduates,' he said, 'they're a dreary crowd.'

'Oh, some of them aren't too bad.' Pillman in fact rather liked many of his pupils, and particularly three or four of the prettier girls. In bed at night, and before he went to sleep, he commonly put in time accomplishing the seduction of one or another of them. They weren't, after all, much younger than he was, and were certainly above what one read of in the newspapers as the age of consent. Unfortunately it seemed you could be sacked for sleeping with a member of the university *in statu pupillari*—which you couldn't be for going with some stray girl down in the town. Not that Pillman had ever done this. It was one of his few secrets that he was a virginal youth. Possibly Gethin was too. Gethin would sometimes describe a man as a 'womanizer' in a tone of chilly contempt, but without enlarging on the topic.

'I suppose I'd better get cracking,' Pillman said. He struggled out of a creaking basket chair, crossed the room, and glowered at the typewriter on his small work-table. ' "Oh dark, dark, dark, amid the blaze of noon." Why was it Samson's hair that Dalila cut off? I could tell them it's what psychoanalysts call an upward displacement. Like inserting a foreign body in old King Hamlet's ear.'

'If you've only got rubbish like that in your head, Gillie, you'd better leave it until tomorrow.'

'I can't. I'm going to Notton Grange tomorrow. It's going to be a regular Saturday assignment for quite some time. A great opportunity for me, Hedger says.' Hedger was Pillman's professor.

'Hell, Gillie! What about our golf?' For a moment Gethin was pale and furious. The two young men had recently taken to playing singularly bad golf on the municipal links. 'And what's this Notton Grange, anyway?'

'It's Lord Furlong's place. He's a local grandee.' Pillman told himself that 'place' was pretentious, as being what some other sort of person would say, and that he ought to have said 'house'. Much reading in Eng. Lit. had given him a lot of information about U and non-U usage, although these actual terms had not yet been invented. 'I'm going to have the run of the library.'

'What absurd person had taken to concealing himself behind that cognomen? Another prosperous brewer, I suppose.'

'Quite right. The family name's a bit odd. It's Eatwell.'

'Eatwell?' Repeating the word, Franco raised his eyebrows in a deprecating way, and then dropped them into a frown. 'I once knew an Eatwell. It was in a juvenile society, in which he suffered for it. Justly, of course. One ought not to allow oneself to be born to such a *bizarrerie*.'

'Well, here's an Eatwell who has escaped from it. You'd be damned glad to become a first baron, or whatever it is, yourself if you'd been born Francis Eatwell instead of Francis bloody Vere de Vere.' Pillman grinned amiably as he delivered himself of this. He knew that Franco quite liked being the recipient of such crude banter. On this occasion, however, Franco did not respond, but spent some minutes staring sombrely into his glass. Then he roused himself.

'Tell me more about this nonsense, Gillie,' he said abruptly.

'Well, Lord Furlong has this library—starting from scratch, and buying every volume in it himself.'

'Himself?'

'He has agents, no doubt. And he has a librarian. The Furlong Librarian. A chap called Bounce. I've had a letter from him, signed just like that. "C. Bounce, Furlong Librarian".'

'Ye Gods!'

'Quite so, Franco. And now his lordship has been going in for manuscripts as well as books. He has discovered, much to his surprise, that you can pay even more for stuff written by hand than for real printed books. So he has told Bounce to go ahead. I expect Bounce will take to calling himself "C. Bounce, Furlong Librarian and Archivist".'

'Your ridiculous subject does seem to be taking you among queer cattle, Gillie.'

'Hedger has discovered there's a lot of eighteenth-century material, including a batch of letters by Shenstone.'

'Shenstone?'

'Do quit that silly trick, Franco. I've told you about Shenstone. Hedger says nobody much seems to be working on Shenstone, so here's my chance. Shenstone has a social tone you might rather admire. Poems upon Various Occasions. Written for the Entertainment of the Author, And Printed for the Amusement of a few Friends, Prejudiced in his Favour. What do you think of that? And Shenstone was a country gent. He entertained himself with landscape gardening as well. It might be quite entertaining to get up all that. Only there are several rather good books about it already. You should read Christopher Hussey's. It's the best one for beginners.'

'I'll have a look. I'm bloody ignorant, I know.' Gethin was suddenly lapsing into his diffidence. He was also looking at his friend with unguarded pleasure, presumably at being in the company of so cultivated a character. 'Just to keep up, I never dare take my nose out of maths. All figures and squiggles. It's utterly barbarous.'

'Nonsense, Franco. Numbers first began our might. There's Yeats's word for it. And look at your father. He takes maths in his stride and weaves it into the most profound philosophical speculations.'

'So they say. I never made anything of my father— not any way on. I must have gone in for just having a mother right from the start.'

'I suppose some chaps do. My father made himself felt. With quite a heavy hand.' Pillman found himself tapping at the keys of the typewriter in front of him. Franco had never talked about his family before, and there was something a little uncomfortable about it now. 'They let you play on that course on Sunday afternoons,' he said suddenly. 'We might have a go then.'

'So we might.' Gethin had faintly flushed, as if aware of having been made an object of consideration in an unwonted and not wholly agreeable way. 'Yes, let's say Sunday.' And he put the cork in the burgundy flagon as a sign that he was going to bed.

Left to himself, Pillman tapped on for a few minutes on his boring machine. 'The date of the composition of this sombre non-drama,' he tapped, 'is in dispute among the learned. So is the merit of its leaden versification.' He stared at this and saw it wouldn't do. It was half-baked throw-away stuff, which wouldn't even raise a smile. So he ripped the sheet from the machine, crumpled it up, and went off to bed himself. As he climbed the staircase he selected, rather half-heartedly, his bed-time girl for the night.

Notton Grange had been acquired by Lord Furlong from a nobleman of somewhat more ancient lineage who had run out of money, packed up, and departed to the South of France. It was a big house but not big enough for Lord Furlong, who had caused various bits and pieces to be added to it. These embellishments included two curved colonnades each terminating in a pavilion. The pavilions were understood to be 'ornamental' (which meant twiddly) in a manner relieving the general severity of the main design. The house was in fact a plain double cube. In the centre of one cube there was a very grand staircase lit by a lantern into which you could have fitted quite a commodious cottage. The centre of the other was an open well across which there stared at one another the windows of numerous bedrooms and offices of inferior consideration. The single and eccentric lantern thus lent the august building a lopsided and incongruously comical effect, like a creature with one ear cocked and the other invisible on a picture-postcard of humorous intention. Notton Grange was sufficiently imposing, all the same, and if it had once *been* a grange, with farm buildings grouped comfortably around it, all evidence of the fact had been obliterated in the interest of various formal gardens of one sort or another. William Shenstone, who had believed in a great deal of duskiness in the Salvator Rosa manner, together with an ample provision of grots and groves appropriate for the use of hermits, would not have thought much of it.

Gilbert Pillman tried to persuade himself he didn't think all that of it either. He had already heard a good deal about it, and about its supposed bibliographical treasures, from more senior members of his faculty whom it had pleased Lord Furlong to entertain for the purpose of demonstrating how his Library was coming along. The Library (capital 'L' as in English Literature)—or if not the library then his lordship's relation to it—was what Franco would at once have termed, in one of his favourite words, an absurdity. Lord Furlong had perhaps never read a book in his life. He had been brought up in a household in which 'book' meant 'magazine'. So, for that matter, had Pillman. Only Pillman, undistracted by the task of turning a little brewery into an enormous one, had come a long way from that in the brief twenty years since he had mastered the alphabet. He hadn't come far enough, however, to take Notton Grange quite in his stride, as Franco would have done. He knew that he was going to be a little defensive amid its grandeurs—even scared, perhaps, now that he was there on his own. Moreover he had a lurking sense that he had come in quest of small beer—the phrase being metaphorical and having nothing to do with the Eatwell family commodity. Who the hell was Shenstone anyway? He represented the fact that in the academic profession you were expected in every way to begin at the bottom of the ladder. From Shenstone you might scramble up to Sheridan, and from Sheridan to, say, Swinburne, and from Swinburne to Shelley. That sort of *gradus*. What would be fun would be to know that what you were going to be handed was a copy of North's *Plutarch* (1579), copiously annotated in a hand which you would triumphantly identify as Shakespeare's, as that supposedly exists in *The Booke of Sir Thomas Moore*. This immodest fantasy (more exciting, really, than those bed-time fantasies) was in Pillman's head as he parked his car.

He parked his car on what he supposed might be called the sweep. This followed the curve of one of the colonnades, and the battered little second-hand Austin Seven looked uncommonly incongruous there. Even so, it had been a rash purchase, ventured upon during the euphoria that results from the receiving of a first pay-packet, and he now knew that he could keep it going only if Franco and he could come to some arrangement about sharing it. The fact was that there was no money in learning. He'd be doing better for himself perched on a stool in one of Lord Furlong's counting-houses.

But now he had to decide how to present himself. 'Is Mr Bounce at home?' didn't sound right, since it wasn't Mr Bounce's home but Lord Furlong's. 'I have an appointment with Mr Bounce' might be better—or he might even say 'My name is Gilbert Pillman and I've come to work on William Shenstone'—rather as if William Shenstone was the gas or the drains. Deciding it would be best to speak on the spur of the moment, he mounted a short flight of steps and rang a bell. At this the front door was opened so immediately that he wondered for a moment whether Lord Furlong kept a footman permanently on the other side of it, perhaps in one of those wicker-work affairs like an up-ended coffin. Then he found himself confronted by a young woman in a neat uniform, whom he took to be a parlourmaid.

'Oh, hullo,' the young woman said—and gazed at him rather round-eyed. 'Are you the one from the university?'

Pillman now saw that the uniform was a school uniform—from which it followed that he was being greeted by a schoolgirl. And there was a fairly firm further inference that here was a Miss Eatwell, in fact a Hon. Miss Eatwell, which was surely a particularly bizarre thing to be. It might almost be called a shame. She was a nice-looking girl, and it was in the slightly boyish way which can sometimes assist a young man to achieve, without undue alarm, a hitherto uncompassed relationship with a member of the opposite sex. Pillman judged her quite as pretty as any of his selected nocturnal companions—and with the substantial additional advantage of being three-dimensional. She seemed, too, very much of the same age. She must be in the Upper Sixth, or something of the kind, and ready to take wing for a university. But not for his university. The proprietor of the Furlong Library would have seen to it that she was to be taken on by Oxford or Cambridge.

'Yes,' Pillman said. 'That's me. Gillie Pillman.' Encouraged by a sense that this familiar reply had been quite dashing, he added boldly, 'Miss Eatwell, is it? How did you know about me?'

'I'm Diana Eatwell, all right. Daddy said something about your coming before he went off to London, so I decided to keep a look-out for you. You do teach poetry, don't you?'

'Well, yes—I suppose I do in a way.'

'I write it.'

'Oh, good!' Pillman couldn't think of any more adequate response to the information thus afforded him than this rather inane exclamation. Diana Eatwell had decidedly an air of not being disappointed by what she had opened the door of Notton Grange on. Presumably she had seen at once that here was an intellectual and competent person, who could set her right on Rupert Brooke and other fellow-practitioners. 'I haven't come about poetry,' Pillman added—perhaps not felicitously. 'Or rather,' he went on in what he recognized in himself as deepening confusion, 'I suppose I have, in a way. I've come after a chap called Shenstone, who wrote poems of a sort. Poems upon Various Occasions for the Amusement of a few Friends.'

'I know about that.' Miss Eatwell now had a pleasing appearance of knowing she was in the presence of a scintillating wit as well as a scholar. 'And I'll take you along to Mr Bounce presently. He looks after the books and things, as you probably know. Did you ever hear such a ridiculous name as Bounce?'

Pillman might have said, 'Well, yes,' again, but felt it wouldn't be tactful. Instead, he resolved to get on 'Diana' terms as quickly as possible. It was a pity, he thought, that her father was a mere baron and not an earl. Otherwise he could have started in on 'Lady Diana' straight away.

'Do call me Diana,' Miss Eatwell said clairvoyantly. 'And I'll call you Gillie, even although you are a professor. You're very young-looking, among other things. You can't really be much older than me.'

'I'm twenty-four, Diana—and in my first university job. So I'm nothing like a professor, and I hope I don't look like one.'

'I shan't tell you what you look like, Gillie.' Miss Eatwell said this in a fashion that alarmed Pillman. Or perhaps it was less a matter of her tone than of the way she glanced at him as she spoke. It was almost as if she had some impulse to take his clothes off—mentally speaking, of course—and this would have been a much more proper impulse on his part towards her. Men, he believed, are sanctioned to do this with a pretty girl in a perfectly wholesome way, whereas the opposite process was surely unmaidenly. Then he told himself that it was, after all, he who was being libidinous in thus interpreting what was no doubt a regard of merely friendly (if also admiring) interest. It was simply his being hitched on to poetry that attracted her warmth of feeling. She was probably dotty about the stuff as adolescent girls sometimes are.

'But first I'll make us some coffee,' the Hon. Diana said firmly. 'I have a den of my own, you know, where nobody else is allowed to come. That's only civilized, don't you think?'

Pillman had no difficulty in subscribing to this view, although 'den' struck him as a shade ominous. Would Lord Furlong approve of his daughter's thus proposing to carry off a totally strange young man into seclusion? What would old Hedger think of it as a way of starting in on Shenstone? And—and here was the real point—what about the girl herself? It was nice being so unexpectedly received by a nubile young person with such evident pleasure and even excitement. But what if it turned out to be excitement of a decidedly sexual sort? That ought to be O.K. too. All young men in novels went bang after that when it came along, and in a mild way he himself had a creditable record of hopeful flirtations when the chance of it had turned up on him—in the university book-stacks, for instance, or at dances and other social occasions when the girl students expected some prestige-according response of the sort from junior members of the faculty.

Despite all this, with Miss Eatwell, and in so intimidating a house, he was undeniably apprehensive. He even had a passing thought that

Diana might be nymphomaniac—a word he had only recently discovered implies desire on the part of nymphs and not for them. For a morbid moment he had a wild vision of being pursued through Notton Grange in a Maenadic fashion by this probably perfectly chaste young woman, who might well be as virginal as her namesake.

What they were actually doing was moving through a kind of marble hall ornamented with marble statues in niches. There was at least nothing erotic about the statues; they were mostly of elderly men in senatorial robes and had obviously come with the house and commemorated former proprietors who had achieved eminence in church or state. And now they were going up the great staircase side by side—which was proper enough, since it would have accommodated half-a-dozen people walking abreast. It was rather like being in a Hollywood film of high life in England.

'Who's your *favourite* poet?' Diana demanded suddenly.

'Wordsworth.'

Had this bald question been pitched at Pillman by one of his pupils, he would probably have answered 'Villon' or 'Valéry' or even 'Verlaine' or 'Verhaeren' simply by way of asserting the superior reach of his reading. As it was, he spoke the truth. And this was a great success.

'Oh, how *marvellous!*' Diana breathed. 'He's mine too. Gillie, I'll always remember this. Always.'

The assertion, although it didn't seem pregnant of anything in particular, at least confirmed the fact that the poetry-bug had indeed got the girl. This was at once reassuring and rather disappointing. Of course there was the hazard (or off-chance) that he and Diana would presently find themselves sitting on a window-seat with an amatorious book between them, like Paolo and Francesca in Dante's poem and Rossetti's painting—and with similar consequences. But the notion was no doubt far-fetched. Pillman now found himself quite looking forward to the den.

It struck him that the enormous house seemed oddly deserted. He had imagined that in such places there would always be a few flunkeys or at least scurrying housemaids on view. As it was, Notton Grange might have been a museum shut up for the day.

'Are you a large family?' he asked. 'I mean, have you brothers and sisters, as well as parents?'

'Oh, no, Gillie. There's only Daddy and me. My mother died years and years ago. I had a twin brother, but he died too.'

'I see. I'm sorry.' Pillman said this awkwardly. It occurred to him that Diana might lead rather a dull life, and that this would account in part for the warmth of her reception for him. 'Where do you go to school, Diana?'

Diana answered this question in some detail as they walked down a long broad corridor. It seemed that she was at rather a grand girls' public school—which perhaps accounted for her having nothing of what Franco might have called the whiff of beer about her. But it was as a weekly boarder, and she always came home on Friday evening or Saturday morning.

'I've just got back,' she said. 'That's why I'm still in these idiotic clothes. We're made to travel in them. They're supposed to be a protection.'

Pillman almost heard himself saying, 'They won't protect you from me'—which showed that he was really in a very confused state by this time. Instead, he ventured on, 'I think they're rather nice', and had a sense that this had gone down quite well.

'I'm going to show you my poems,' Diana said. 'Or some of them. You see, I do feel I need advice. Daddy's very encouraging. But it's not quite his sort of thing—even if he has stacks of Shenstone and all that in his library.'

'Does he regard Shenstone and all that chiefly as an investment?' Here was something that Pillman—like other scholars, old and young—was genuinely curious about. Nobody knew why Lord Furlong had set up to achieve one of the finest private libraries in England.

'I don't really know. But I think Mr Bounce may have had something to do with getting him going. Bounce originally had a job with books in the city library. I believe he carried them around.'

Pillman knew the last fact already, so had received no fresh enlightenment on this small Eatwell mystery. And now they were in the den. It was at least den-like in being quite small and cosy. Or it would have been cosy to Pillman's sense had not everything it contained been a good deal more expensive-looking than anything he was accustomed to. Had he been required to give a guess as to what an eighteen-year-old girl's room would contain he'd have plumped for group photographs of hockey teams and the like, a further photograph or two of what were called matinée idols, and perhaps a romantic print in washy sepias with some such title as *A Lovers' Tryst*. In fact there was only one picture on display, and it turned out to be a nocturne by

34

Whistler. The furniture was what he vaguely thought of as 'French', and two or three of the chairs looked as if they couldn't safely support more than a cat. There were a lot of books—some of them lying carelessly around, but most of them displaying ornate bindings through protective walls of glass. It none of it seemed quite right, somehow, for a healthy sixth-former, and in fact rendered what might be called the poor-little-rich-girl effect. He suspected Lord Furlong of being a dominating character (you couldn't have arrived at pouring millions of gallons of beer down British throats without being that) who threw his weight about at home as well as in the office. Having just one daughter, he insisted that everything should be slap-up around her.

'Do you know how to make coffee?' Diana demanded.

'Well, yes—I suppose so. I put the stuff in a jug and pour on boiling water.'

'I make *café filtre*,' Diana said, and disappeared into a small pantry-like room next door. Pillman (who was inclined to be impressed by this degree of sophistication in one whom Professor Shuffrey might still have called a kiddy) looked round for evidences of literary work in progress. Sure enough there was a typewriter—an elegant little affair that looked as if it was carved out of ivory—and there protruded from it a sheet of quarto paper betraying what certainly looked like metrical composition. Presumably Diana did her poems straight on to the machine: a technique which he understood to be quite the go at the time. He conscientiously refrained from attempting to read the effusion currently on hand. It looked as if this poetry business might be embarrassing. Once or twice at the university young women had advanced upon him after a lecture, manuscript at the ready, and demanded criticism—but clearly feeling that nothing short of encomium would fill the bill. It had been a situation not too easy to handle. 'It reminds me of *Prufrock*,' he would say after due scrutiny—or 'I think you must have been influenced by Isaac Rosenberg'. He somehow didn't see himself saying that sort of thing to Diana Eatwell.

She turned out to be rather shy about it all, and they had finished the coffee before the subject turned up. He was astonished that when it did so it was through the production of a printed book. This was again of the slap-up order: typography by Bruce Rodgers, Van Gelder paper, stencilled decorations by T. L. Poulton, bound in vellum. And on the cover, in elegant gilt, it said *First Poems by Diana Eatwell*.

Pillman had the good sense not to make a to-do about all this refinement, and nerved himself to open the volume at an early page.

'No,' Diana said decidedly. 'You must just take it away, and read it only if you want to. And please remember it's only *juvenilia*. Daddy had it made for me as a sixteenth-birthday present. Books are always a thing with us on birthdays.'

'Very well.' Pillman wasn't slow in agreeing to this arrangement. 'I'll be extremely interested,' he added—not wholly mendaciously. What if the girl were a prodigy: a kind of female Rimbaud or Chatterton? That would be more exciting than acres of the familiar correspondence of William Shenstone on boring topics like the scooping out of hermits' grottoes at the Leasowes in eighteenth-century Worcestershire.

'And now I'll take you to Bounce,' Diana said briskly. Her nerve had perhaps a little failed her in this early crisis of her literary career. 'But I come home *every* weekend, you know. So we're going to have lots of quiet confabs here, Gillie.'

'I do hope so,' Pillman said. He was wondering whether Lord Furlong went up to London every Saturday.

The Furlong Library—in the sense of a chamber or chambers holding a collection of books—was less overwhelming than Pillman had expected. The Duke of Devonshire, he told himself, owned something a good deal more imposing at Chatsworth. Here was simply a very large room, with books all round it and more books jutting out in bays on either side, and what was chiefly remarkable about it was simply the fact that everything looked so very new. No end of the books, of course, must be as old as the hills, but everything in their setting seemed so recent an exercise of the slap-up sort that it was hard to believe that even the sixteenth-century folios hadn't just been unpacked from the straw. Indeed, something of very much that sort appeared to be going on. Half-a-dozen large packing-cases stood open down the centre of the room, and it looked as if an army of librarians must have knocked off for elevenses while coping with them since all of them seemed to be disgorging more books than they could really contain. Pillman thought of those fake Christmas hampers you saw in the windows of expensive shops, spewing out hams and haggises and bottles of champagne. Two or three of the cases contained nests of steel boxes of the sort held at that time to be essential for the safe preservation of manuscripts. What if some of them contained a fresh flood of epistolary correspondence by William Shenstone? What if

Shenstone proved to have been as maniacally compulsive a letter-writer as, say, Horace Walpole? Pillman had a momentary nightmarish vision of himself as condemned to labour for years on end in this poshed-up place—like a character in some farcical savagery by his contemporary Evelyn Waugh. Diana, meantime, would have been locked away in her den by Lord Furlong: more inaccessible to him than Miranda to Ferdinand when he was condemned to heaving logs.

And now for the moment, at least, Diana was sundered from him. She had handed him over to Mr Bounce and departed—presumably to her own superior labour of poetical composition. Mr Bounce had shaken hands with him, and though Mr Bounce was about five feet tall it had been in a decidedly condescending way. Although without first-hand acquaintance with academic life, Mr Bounce knew a junior lecturer from a professor when he saw one.

'Delighted to help you, Pillman,' Mr Bounce said (with intolerable familiarity). 'Delighted to give you a leg up. Of course—and as you can see—we have a great deal of work on hand. The accessions are coming in rapidly, very rapidly indeed.' As he said this, the Furlong Librarian glanced round the packing-cases in perplexity, as if some supernatural agency had deposited them only that moment within his view. 'The cataloguing is becoming very onerous, I assure you. I might have you help out a little one day. Pocket-money in your spare time, eh? Once you had learnt the ropes, of course. I've devised a very effective system: much in advance of the Bodleian, or any place of that sort. Each card is eight by six, suspended filing, instantly removable, with all the technical stuff on the recto, and on the verso biographical particulars, and selected critical appreciations by his lordship and others. You'd get the hang of it, and be quite useful, with a little hard work.'

'Thank you very much,' Pillman said (concealing outrage). 'But I've come about Shenstone, as a matter of fact.'

'Ah, yes—I remember. Well, Shenstone will be *Poetry: Late Romantic: Miscellaneous Minor*. That must be in the fifth catalogue cabinet. We'll see what we have.' For a moment Mr Bounce's confidence and self-satisfaction flickered. 'Or at least we can try.'

It would take a very raw freshman indeed, Pillman thought, to suppose that William Shenstone (1714–1763) was a late Romantic. As a ripe scholar Mr Bounce clearly had his limitations. Still, it wouldn't do to alienate the man. About Shenstone Pillman couldn't in his heart of hearts care less. But now Shenstone had become, as it

37

were, the gateway or passport to Diana Eatwell, who was (he realized with some amazement) extremely attractive to him. So he must treat this tiresome man with circumspection if there were to be any more of those quiet confabs.

'I'll be most grateful,' he said. 'Just as I am to Professor Hedger for fixing me up with you. The Professor has a high regard for your work, Mr Bounce.'

This remark (although it was surely impertinent as well as untrue) went down well. Nearly an hour was taken up with various false casts, but at length the batch of Shenstone letters was run to earth. Having done his homework, Pillman was able to discover almost at once that none of them had ever seen print. And there were a great many of them. The job of transcribing them on Saturday mornings could be spread over months and months. He just hoped that it wouldn't occur to Bounce to present him with the whole lot on microfilm with his lordship's compliments. But that wasn't likely. Lord Furlong was known not to be too liberal about his possessions. And he supposed that Bounce really had an eye on him as something going cheap on the labour market as an occasional harmless drudge. He spent the rest of the morning making a start on getting the things—which were all higgledy-piggledy—into a chronological series.

II

Francis Gethin listened attentively to Gillie's account of Notton Grange. He had an odd way of doing this even when he seemed not at all interested in what Gillie was talking about.

'But you didn't see the fledgling lord?' he asked.

'Furlong? He was away in London, and I don't know whether he'd have bothered to see me anyway. I only saw this daughter, Diana.'

'Who did the honours of the ancestral home.'

'Well, she did the honours of what she called her den. I thought her rather nice, as a matter of fact. In a childish way, that is.' Pillman didn't know quite why he added this not particularly honest qualification. 'She's still at school, so she can't be more than a bare eighteen.'

'I suppose the girl *can* be very nice, if she's bare and eighteen.' Franco frowned, apparently in disapproval of having made this feeble and not very characteristic joke. 'Did you say something about poetry?'

'She writes it. And her father has had some of it printed for her in a classy way.'

'They call that vanity publishing, I believe.'

'Yes—but of course it's her father's vanity and not hers. She seems quite a sensible girl. Anyway, I've promised to read the stuff and offer remarks.'

'Good God, Gillie! It just shows what whoring after Shenstone leads to. Is your Diana a creature inspired, like Mrs Hemans and Mrs Browning?'

'I don't think so—although I've only just looked at some of the poems. I doubt whether there will really be much to say about them.'

'Probably the less the better.'

'Oh, I don't know about that. They seem quite nice really.' Pillman saw that this was not a particularly incisive remark. But it was fair enough in its way. Diana's verses didn't recall *Prufrock*. The influence of Isaac Rosenberg was not to be detected in them. They were, in fact, Wordsworthian—surprisingly so, considering the distance between Notton Grange and Dove Cottage. Of course their harmless pastiche would certainly not bear much analysis. Curiously enough, this didn't perturb him. He had a feeling that, poems or no poems, he was going to get on with Diana Eatwell entirely agreeably.

'Talking of women,' Franco said, 'I heard today that my sister's coming.'

'Your sister, Franco? I didn't know you had one.'

'Louisa. We call her Lou. She's staying with people about twenty miles away, and she's coming over to inspect us. You might quite like her, Gillie.' Franco was looking his gloomiest. 'I don't know that I do, particularly. Lou's a year younger than I am, but a bit bossy.'

'You mean she's coming to inspect you—or us, as you say—in these dismal digs?'

'That's up to you, Gillie. I could go it alone with her, and take her out to lunch. But I've an idea she wants to meet you. It seems to be a way girls have. Look at this Diana of yours, panting for the arrival of young Adonis.'

'Diana didn't have anything to do with Adonis. That was Venus.' Pillman had produced this pedantic correction because Franco was vaguely puzzling him. 'I shouldn't have thought your sister would ever have heard of me.'

'I've talked about you, I suppose, Gillie. I've no snobbish impulse, you know, to conceal my low connections.'

'Well, of course I'll like meeting Lou. Let's take her out to lunch jointly.' Pillman was still slightly at sea. That last crack about low connections hadn't been quite in the common tone of the banter he and Franco exchanged. But it seemed to knit up with a way Franco had, when at all perturbed, of saying something quite opposite to what was in his head. Indeed, it had something to do with the fact, obscurely understood by Pillman, that Franco thought much better of his room-mate than his room-mate (in decently modest moments) knew he deserved. The idea of this meeting, he decided, had been Franco's, not Lou's. Franco wanted to show off the wonderful friend he had so cleverly gained for himself from a quite alien social milieu.

Nothing of this annoyed Pillman, or even much held his attention. He was too pleased with himself for having successfully (as the Americans said) dated a girl. For that was what it came to. Regular Saturday dates, with Daddy well out of the road! As for Louisa Gethin, whether bossy or not, he knew he wasn't going to give twopence for her. For one thing, she'd probably be like poor old Franco: far from being anything much in the physical way.

It turned out that there couldn't have been a worse guess. When she turned up for the luncheon engagement Louisa Gethin proved strangely to combine a strong family resemblance to her brother with being quite staggeringly beautiful. Or so Pillman in the first moment of seeing her judged her to be. Not that he was at once bowled over by her. What he chiefly felt was that he had come by a piece of information. A woman can be something to which neither the word 'pretty' on the one hand nor 'handsome' on the other has any applicability, and which is at once a straightforward ocular phenomenon and completely mysterious and beyond the scope of analysis. This, he told himself, must be what 'beauty' is—and as he hadn't met it before there couldn't be very much of it around. And it struck him—for he was really quite a thoughtful young man—that the effect was probably not one that often produced the response known as love at first sight. That is something provoked by some identifiable irregularity or idiosyncrasy of form or feature for which, for some reason, one has all-unconsciously been waiting around. With somebody like Lou one had to cope with absorbing a purely aesthetic experience before getting on to anything further. He found himself wanting to look at Lou Gethin quite a lot. But it wasn't, so far as he could detect, in any concupiscent way.

Quite early in the meal he got the impression that Lou, on her part, wanted to do a certain amount of looking at him. But this wasn't concupiscent either. And although he was aware of himself as being quite good-looking he knew that he certainly wasn't beautiful, so it seemed improbable that she was emulating him in the field of detached aesthetic contemplation. What she seemed to be doing was sizing him up to the limited extent that the eye can size up a total stranger. He was inclined to suppose that this was a purely social thing; that it had to do, perhaps, with his choice of clothes and the way he wore them; that she was working out whether this intruder from the Midlands, picked up by her brother at his outlandish place of employment, was to be admitted to the category of 'possible' acquaintances. It was no doubt significant that she kept on addressing him as 'Mr Pillman'. This was a formality still just possible at that time even between quite young people. It was consciously distancing, all the same—just as it was when Franco persisted in saying 'Smith' or 'Jones' to colleagues of his own standing. Pillman had too much self-confidence to be riled rather than amused by this, and every now and then he said 'Miss Gethin' in a courteous and at the same time almost avuncular way, as if he were speaking to a child recently out of the nursery who would relish this solemnity of address.

As for Franco, he had an air of controlled distaste which might have been occasioned either by the fare in the pretentious 'French' restaurant of the local posh hotel upon which the young men were expending injudicious sums in Miss Gethin's honour or by the situation more at large. If this last was the correct supposition he was surely being rather unreasonable, since the original initiative in the affair had been largely his. But then Franco was quite good at being unreasonable from time to time. It wasn't, however, that he was washing his hands of the encounter, or at all suggesting that pitching Gillie at Lou or Lou at Gillie was necessarily a bad and ill-considered job. He didn't say much, but at least he was being sharply observant of any signs indicating how his sister and his friend were hitching up. This was so obvious at times that an obscure suspicion—perhaps gratifying in itself—was set lurking in Pillman's head.

'You're not quite as I imagined you, Mr Pillman,' Lou said easily. 'But then I've had nothing to go on but the brief word or two about you that Francis has let fall from time to time.'

'Anything he says needs interpreting.' Pillman found that he did resent this 'Francis' business. His friend, in reply to the early question

'What do they call you when they want to take the chill off?' had replied that they'd always called him Franco at home—and that it had nothing to do with 'the reactionary character who later bobbed up in Spain'. So Lou's 'Francis' was another bit of distancing.

'I suppose you're attracted to one another through having contrasting temperaments,' Lou went on. 'It's said to be a good basis for tolerance and even affection. But what would you say you have in common?'

'Our lowly and inconsiderable station in the academic world,' Franco said, unexpectedly breaking in. 'And we listen to quite a lot of music together. It's something of which Gillie is totally ignorant, but it seems to help him through to the close of the day. And then he sleeps like a pig. I can hear him snoring in his sty from mine next door.'

'Do you mean you're not sleeping properly again?' Lou demanded sharply. 'That you lie awake trying to solve hopeless equations?'

'I don't want my health asked after, thank you. Even if you are a sucking doctor.'

Franco had said this quite savagely, and Pillman found the incident curious. For one thing, Franco had never even hinted that he lay awake at night, whether doing sums or not. For another, he'd been reminded of something he'd been told already: that Lou was a medical student at a London hospital. He didn't know why he should find this at all out of the way. Perhaps he had got her so firmly in his head as the grand-daughter of an earl that he was forgetting something that went for Franco equally with herself. More immediately considered, their background lay in a kind of top rank of professional people, in fact the intelligentsia. Franco, who found it unbelievable that an educated man should call children kiddies, invariably professed himself as holding his own aristocratic ancestry in particular disesteem. It was true he would equally have scoffed at the term 'intelligentsia'. But he had lately taken a fancy for 'clerisy', recently revived as a vogue word and blowing around quite a lot. He probably believed that, really and truly, a sacred bond united the absurd Professor Shuffrey and himself. Reflecting on this, Pillman again found himself suspecting something that might be hovering in Franco's head.

'Tell me about Shenstone, please,' Lou said, making an abrupt change of subject after this slightly awkward moment.

'I'm afraid he's not terribly glamorous.' Pillman knew by this time that he was always going to sound an apologetic note about the owner of the Leasowes. 'He wrote something called *The School-Mistress. A Poem.*'

'An eminently poetical theme,' Franco said.

'It's an imitation of Spenser. He didn't seem to realize there's quite enough of Spenser already.' Pillman wasn't very pleased with this. It might have come from one of his feebler lecture-giving jollities.

'However,' Franco went on, 'Shenstone has led Gillie to enchanted ground. Notton Grange. There he has found a mistress—although not a school one. The fair Diana Eatwell, and a poet herself.'

'Don't be so bloody silly, Franco.' Pillman was suddenly quite furious with his friend. He was also a little upset at having said 'bloody' in Lou's presence, since there was here a small semantic uncertainty in his head. He could name the few words, freely chucked about between young men, that they wouldn't employ in the presence of a woman not intimately known to them. But he wasn't quite sure about 'bloody'.

'Francis *can* be bloody silly,' Lou said calmly. 'But tell me about Miss Eatwell.' Lou, for some reason, was now looking at Pillman very consideringly indeed. He found this elusively exciting, but at the same time he didn't like it a bit. He was quite clear that he wasn't going to produce lunch-time chat about Diana. But at least Diana did now come into his head. And this produced an astonishing discovery.

He couldn't *see* Diana. He couldn't—sitting, as he now was, opposite Franco's sister—see Diana at all. He could see that den. He could see those school clothes. He could even taste the flavour of *café filtre*. But Diana's features were a blur.

'She's Lord Furlong's only child,' he said, 'and she was home from school for the weekend. She gave me some coffee—a good deal better than we're going to get in this place—and then she took me along to the man Bounce.' And Pillman addressed himself firmly to elaborating a ludicrous narrative of his encounter with the Furlong Librarian.

Lou didn't renew her demand for information about Diana—which showed, Pillman thought, that she could take a hint. Franco didn't mention her again either. But his little bit of raillery about Gillie's having found himself a girl at Notton Grange seemed to have cheered him up, and he took a fuller part in the conversation than he had done at first. It did come into Pillman's head that poor old Franco was pleasing himself with the notion that he had been very cunning. For Pillman had now managed to confirm himself in that suspicion which had occurred to him earlier. What Franco was up to on his contrived occasion was a stroke of match-making, and he had judged it tremendously clever to bring in a mention of Diana as likely to add a useful component of jealousy to his design. His admiration for his friend must be even livelier than that friend had supposed, so that he had decided he wanted him as a brother-in-law. Pillman, like the many of his generation who had made deep studies in the wonderful world of Freud, seemed to remember that there was some sort of syndrome or complex associated with behaviour of this sort. Chaps were continually planning to marry off their sisters to their friends. You saw it happening at those university dances, and he had been told it was a positive mainspring of those grander affairs of the same sort at what were known at Oxford as Commem Balls. It was, of course, a suppressed incestuous impulse that was involved. You weren't allowed to lay your sister yourself, so you proposed to get a kick out of doing it, as it were, by proxy in the person of some intimate friend with whom you could 'identify'. There was a great deal in the notion of identifying. Children were doing it all the time in their imitative play, and it was axiomatic in this as in other matters that we all remain children to the end.

Of course Franco could have no notion of the mechanism at work. Even with all his sophistication, he would be revolted if it were put to him. And it was rather comical really. Pillman was so pleased with his own perspicacity in the matter that he began, half-way through the meal, to enjoy himself enormously. In fact he must have been putting on quite a sparkling turn, for he suddenly perceived—or thought he did—that something like Franco's familiar admiration for himself was now being evinced by Franco's sister. Lou was looking at him in a new way. Indeed, she was behaving in a new way. There was nothing crude about it, but he was aware of it as holding a distinct affinity with the occasional comportment of simpler and less well-mannered girls towards the tail-end of courageously uninhibited student parties. Lou Gethin was actually making passes at him! He could hardly have said how it was being done. But there could be no possible doubt about the fact.

Pillman's head swam a little as he realized this. And it was precisely making his head swim that the girl must be after. She wanted a sign or a response from him; wanted, you might say, the release of appropriate chemicals into his bloodstream. He could hardly believe it—particularly as it was with so deft an unobtrusiveness that it was being done. And she succeeded. Just what sign he gave, he didn't remotely know. Perhaps it was a gulp or gasp or a moment's heavy breathing. Whatever it was, it had happened.

And then, quite suddenly, Lou switched off. It was over. The thing had vanished. He had a momentary weird vision of his family doctor (and Lou was going to be a doctor, after all) tucking away in his black bag the little mallet with which he had tapped you expertly just below the knee and elicited the reassuring involuntary jerk.

Lou had picked up her handbag. Franco was frowning over the bill, and had been doing so for several minutes—so it was possible that he had been quite unaware of what had occurred. Or was it the position that brother and sister understood one another very well? Was it possible that Lou knew that a first step towards a grotesque species of arranged marriage had been going forward, and that as part of the exploration had wanted to assure herself that those chemicals were there at all? Pillman couldn't bring himself to believe quite this. It was too absurd, and the plain fact must be that he had been imagining things. Yet he had a sense—and it was to be a haunting sense—that his speculation had, as it were, got within a target area.

They saw Lou to her car—a smarter car than Pillman's—and she drove off. Walking back to the university, Franco had a good deal to say about that doubtful bill.

III

Several weeks after the mysterious occasion just described, Pillman decided that, since Franco had introduced him to his sister, he ought himself to introduce Franco to Diana Eatwell. There was no particular logic about this. It was simply that Diana and Lou were linked in his mind as the only two young women he knew who existed substantially in the flesh. Pop either on a weighing-machine, and the dial would register at once. Dream-girls weren't like that at all.

There was no difficulty—except with Franco himself—in arranging something. Lord Furlong was still quite regularly an absentee on Saturdays: in fact Pillman had not yet set eyes on him. So Bounce had only to be told that Pillman had a friend eager to view the wonders of the Furlong Library, and that this friend happened to be the grandson of an Earl of Westcot, and the visit was fixed up at once.

At first Franco was definitely recalcitrant. He said he had no taste

45

for beer, and when he had to mention Diana he referred to her not by name but as the poetess, which was even more rude than it would have been for Pillman to call Lou the leech or the sawbones. But, at the same time, the project seemed to hold for Franco a fascination to be felt as of an obscurely masochistic sort. And this Pillman was aware of as entirely in his character; Franco was a dab hand at going through with disagreeable assignments; when he was invited to tea by the Vice-Chancellor's wife—an appalling woman with a drawing-room full of little gilt chairs as in a chichi tea-shop, Franco said—it never occurred to him to intimate a previous engagement.

So the two young men walked out to Notton Grange together. Their route took them through a long stretch of back-to-back slum-like dwellings (from which a few of their pupils came) and then through a further stretch of mean, tidy suburbs (from which all the rest came) and eventually landed them, quite suddenly, in open country. And there, beyond a broad stretch of rising ground and embosomed in trees, lay Notton. Viewed from this distance, William Shenstone would have thought quite highly of it. Franco, pausing to take stock, muttered that here was where the lion and the lizard keep the courts where Jamshyd gloried and drank deep. Being a mathematician and not a literary character, he was unaware of the distressingly banal character of this quotation.

'And what they drink *now*—' he began.

'Yes, yes—Eatwell's Entire. Don't worry, Franco. You won't be offered any.'

Just as on the occasion of Pillman's earliest visit, the front door of the Grange opened instantly upon the first peal of the bell. Diana had now settled for waiting for Gillie's arrival in this gratifying fashion, and wasn't going to change it upon a particular occasion just because there was another young man. But she wasn't in school uniform this Saturday, and a practised eye might have detected her as having given some thought to her dress. Pillman, had he been aware of this, would not have attributed it to the notoriously fickle nature of women. He would have supposed—and probably quite rightly—that Diana simply wanted to show Gillie's friend what a nice-looking girl Gillie had gained the regard of, and that this might be termed in essence a Gillie-orientated impulse. But at least Diana looked at Franco curiously and at once. What she saw was a fine-featured but distinctly meagre young man in a state of considerable confusion.

'This is Franco,' Pillman said robustly. 'He's pretending to have come to see Bounce's bumper books, but what he really wants to see is you.'

'And I haven't had to wait long.' Franco brought this out in a jerky fashion which, although in fact quite normal with him, suggested even more disquietude than he had immediately evinced. 'It's awfully good of you,' he added with sudden almost chilly formality. And he made a stiff little bow such as would have been appropriate had Diana been not an English schoolgirl but a French or German lady of mature years.

Pillman, who was always being amused by Franco, was amused now. Diana was less amused than pleased, and it was immediately clear that she was prepared quite to take to Gillie's shy and rather distinguished friend.

'Have you really got to do the bumper books at all?' she asked.

'I suppose so—although I'm not in the slightest degree interested in them, I'm afraid.' Franco, who was quite composed again, had assumed his severest frown and his most incisive manner of utterance. 'Gillie, you see, has mentioned the thing to Mr Bounce, so some civil show of interest is essential.' As he said this, Franco removed his gaze from Diana—apparently not without effort—and glanced around the delicately ornate hall with its august marble presences. It was an environment that seemed yet further to restore his ease. It struck Pillman that his friend was well-accustomed to finding himself in such places, although not perhaps in the ownership of people like Lord Furlong. He told himself that if later that day Franco made any more snooty remarks about beer he would collar him and most vigorously scrag him. This was a juvenile form of behaviour which these two academic persons privily indulged in from time to time, and Franco in particular found entertainment in it.

'I thought we might lurk in the den for a bit,' Pillman said. 'And that then I'd take Franco over to Bounce, and do a token stab at Billy Shenstone while he's being shown over the works. Then we'll come back and we can all wander around until it's time for us to make off again. Perhaps we could get right round the park and chat up the deer.' Pillman enjoyed thus showing his friend that he had become rather largely at home at Notton. But he did a little wonder what Lord Furlong would have made of it.

'Lurking in the den for a bit' involved, of course, Diana's *café filtre*. Pillman, having an exaggerated sense of the degree of expertness required for the quite simple operations involved, took satisfaction in

47

showing her off at them. Franco, although his attention was inclined to waver, seemed anxious to comport himself well. He received the eventual concoction with gravity and produced some proper murmur of appreciation when he had tasted it. So for a time it was quite a solemn business, rather as if these three had been Japanese persons involved in a ritual tea-drinking. But Diana and Gillie, at least, had a lot to say to one another—or at least they felt this to be so—and they were soon chattering animatedly enough. While this was happening Franco withdrew into little more than a listener's or spectator's part. He even took to letting his glance wander around the den more absently than one might have expected in so very well-mannered a young man. It was almost as if he was looking for something that wasn't there. Perhaps—Gillie thought when he happened to remark this—what Franco found wanting was another girl. As things were, he was slightly in the position of a gooseberry, a position only too likely to be ungrateful to so sensitive a young man. Gillie, who had so recently discovered that a seriously regarded girl-friend was essential to the sane conduct of life, thought that Franco's recurrent glooms might well be attributable to a deficiency in this regard. Franco's customary severity of manner, he very well knew, masked a great deal of diffidence, and it was possible that so shy a chap had never succeeded in getting going with a girl at all.

Diana—the clairvoyant Diana—eventually proved to have arrived at some such conception herself. She had heard about the Sunday-afternoon golf, and presently got round to making mild fun of it. It was essentially a diversion for elderly business men, she said, and must be particularly dismal when prosecuted on a jaded municipal golf-course. So why didn't they both come to Notton and play tennis instead? She could easily scratch up another girl for mixed doubles. She could do that, in fact, for the very next day. And it was high time that the student of Shenstone should meet the owner of that fascinating batch of Shenstone's letters. Her father was always at home on Sundays.

Gillie was all for this idea at once, but Franco was at first no keener than politeness required. He was no earthly good at tennis, he said, and would be no more than a drag on the whole thing. But he offered this objection while looking at Diana in considerable fascination. It was, it was true, in a kind of puzzled fascination not easy to interpret. But there was at the same time something so definite about it as to set Gillie momentarily thinking on fresh lines. Having along another girl for Franco to muck in with was a wholly admirable idea on Diana's part. But what if Franco took it into his head to prefer Diana herself? Nothing could be more reasonable, Diana being what she was. It might lead to considerable awkwardness, all the same.

Nevertheless the plan went through. Diana picked up her telephone (there was even a telephone in that well-appointed den) and fixed things with a girl called Judy there and then. A time was arranged, and then Gillie carried off Franco to be presented to Mr Bounce.

Later in the morning the three young people went out to inspect the tennis court, and then they walked round the park. During their perambulation Franco became abstracted again. So Gillie decided that it would be a good idea if, at least for five or ten minutes, Diana had his slightly elusive friend to herself. This was an altruistic notion, and he approved of himself for having thought of it. The manoeuvre was quite easy to manage. They were wandering around informally, and he had only to drop behind for a little as if particularly attracted by Lord Furlong's deer beyond their ha-ha, and then not be in too much of a hurry to catch up again.

It thus came about that, for an appreciable span of time, Gillie had Franco and Diana in view some thirty yards ahead of him. They were quite out of earshot but he could see them very clearly. They seemed to be talking a little, but not much. Then something happened which Pillman had reason to judge slightly odd. Franco had half-halted for a moment and turned towards Diana as if he suddenly had something of moment to communicate. For a fraction of a second he hesitated and then, as if he had changed his mind, walked on. When they had gone no more than a dozen paces further, precisely the same thing happened. Franco, that was to say, had twice been on the brink of uttering words he had then thought better of.

There was nothing remarkable about this in itself. In fact it was a habit of Franco's, and almost like a nervous tic. It usually happened in circumstances suggesting simply that he had been overcome by a sudden sense of the appalling triviality of some remark he had been on the verge of making. Gillie was used to it. He had decided it was part of the misdoubting of himself that went deep into Francis Gethin's character.

But what if it hadn't been quite like that this time? Perhaps Franco had been about to say something like 'I think you're the most marvellous girl I've ever met', or even 'Diana, it's no good; I must simply tell you I'm madly in love with you'. It would be dreadful if Diana found she had to cope with such a wild aberration on the part of Gillie's close friend.

But all this was surely nonsense. It was a minute incident of the sort that comes under somebody's observation, usually in a shrubbery, in Jane Austen's novels. The aberration, Pillman decided, had been entirely his own. Probably Franco had intended no more than to offer another depreciatory remark about his tennis, and had then very rightly decided that it would be fussy to do so. Pillman hurried forward and made resolute light conversation about anything that came into his head. Later on he would probably tell Franco—again lightly—of what had been a simple impulse of jealousy on his own part. Franco would be embarrassed, since he always shied away from talk about sexual feeling. But that would merely add to the fun.

The tennis party on the following day was quite a success. The only snag was that Franco's game proved to be a class ahead of any of the others'. He tried a little to dissimulate the fact at first. But that doesn't really do, and when the girl called Judy, who was his first partner, became suspicious he dropped the attempt at once, and went right ahead. It was all rather amusing. Even Lord Furlong, who was the only spectator, was amused. And he didn't seem to be a man who would often condescend to anything of the kind.

Pillman found himself not much liking Lord Furlong, who was physically imposing in an alarming way, and at the same time the kind of man one of Pillman's uncles would have been had he flourished tremendously in the sphere of sanitary plumbing. And Lord Furlong, although he was civil, perhaps didn't greatly take to Pillman in return. He did, on the other hand, take to Franco, and this was patently because Franco was hitched to the peerage in a much more distinguished way than his lordship himself was. Lord Furlong was much too intelligent not to understand that sort of thing. Franco in his turn was much too perceptive to remain unaware of the fact, and it might have been expected to infuriate him. But Franco got on quite well with Lord Furlong, as he sometimes tended to do with people to whom he gave high marks for absurdity. Gillie felt his friend to be mistaken in this particular instance. Lord Furlong was too formidable a man to be treated as a joke. He hadn't been created a baron because he collected books. He did that as another man might

collect postage stamps or butterflies. His real weight lay quite elsewhere.

'I gather, Mr Pillman, that you work in my library every week,' he
said in a break between sets. 'I suppose you ran into my daughter
there. You must have, since she has invited you to come and play
tennis.'

'Yes, Lord Furlong.' Pillman thought it prudent to let this serve as
an answer to both these conjectures. It startled him a little to gather
that Diana had said nothing to her father about the Saturday confabs
in the den.

'Diana is studiously inclined, and is very fond of books. Mr Bounce,
of course, helps her to find her way about. He checked her poems for
the spelling and so on before I sent them to the printer. Are poems
your line, Mr Pillman?'

'Well, yes they are, sir, in a way. But I'm working—'

'You will find I have a great many of them—perhaps more than any
other man in the country. And I see no reason why some of you
university people shouldn't have the turning over of them now and
then.'

'It's most generous of you, sir.'

'I believe, you see, in encouraging the universities. They have a
part to play. Between you and me, Pillman, this country is facing very
severe industrial recession. It's a result of the Americans having made
such a mess of things. And the universities, I repeat, will have their
part to play.'

'I believe the Economics Department at ours, sir, is quite tip-top.'

'Economics? All nonsense. The stuff merely makes confusion worse
confounded. What the universities will do is keep young men and
women off the labour market for three or four years at comparatively
inconsiderable expense. I favour more universities—and I am reliably told you can run one up within eighteen months. But there's your
tennis again. Your friend's too good for you at it, by the way. I don't
say he's much to look at. But that thoroughbred strain counts.'

'You and I must do what we can, sir.'

Lord Furlong stared, being unfortunately quicker to recognize
impertinence than his guest had reckoned on. It had been extremely
rash in Gillie—potential suitor for Diana's hand as he hoped to
be—thus to imply that Eatwells and Pillmans were much of a much-
ness in point of social origins.

'I hope that you and Mr Gethin will stay to luncheon,' Lord

Furlong said—suddenly with the frigid courtesy of one of ancient lineage.

'I'm sure Francis and I would like to very much.'

Lord Furlong inclined his head with a senatorial dignity that would have done credit to any of those marble noblemen he had taken over with the house. But his final words for the moment were not quite in keeping with this.

'And now,' he said, 'go back and make a fool of yourself again on that court.'

IV

The tennis party was repeated on two or three subsequent occasions during the university's summer term, but stopped short of becoming a regular thing. This wasn't because Gilbert Pillman and Lord Furlong had been rather rude to one another. Lord Furlong clearly judged Gillie to be an inconsiderable person who needn't be much thought about, and Gillie was perfectly prepared to put up with Lord Furlong in general society on Sunday provided he continued to be an absentee the day before. As for Diana Eatwell, she liked her tennis and was improving her game quite fast, since she practised hard at it at school. Her friend Judy (whose other name Gillie either kept forgetting or never picked up) seemed to be short of access to young men, and simply clocked in whenever this particular opportunity for it arose. It was Francis Gethin who wasn't keen, or who at least wasn't consistently and reliably so. Franco was becoming rather a puzzle to Gillie. It was understandable that he should find it boring to have to play with three people markedly below his own form, yet he seemed to look forward to these occasions almost with impatience. When they arrived, however, he changed to being irritable and baffled by them. This had something to do with Diana, and in the circumstances it was natural enough. If Franco had become interested in Diana (as he seemed to have done) he would obviously take a poor view of the fact that she was now so definitely Gillie's girl. But this wasn't quite the feel of the thing. Franco, Gillie thought, was at times like a man who sees some enchanting prospect straight ahead of him, makes a dash at it, and bumps his nose against a sheet of plate glass. This odd state of affairs, however, was to be resolved in a peculiar manner quite soon.

And Gillie didn't think much about it. He was far too absorbed in his Saturdays. These were now weaving a kind of magic carpet for him. His attendances in the Furlong Library became shorter and shorter (a fact of which the Furlong Librarian fortunately failed to take notice) and the confabs became correspondingly longer and longer. They hadn't turned into what could vulgarly be termed spooning matches or petting parties. In fact anyone coming in on them would have judged himself to be in the presence of something wholly edifying: a species of mini-seminar in English poetry. Gilbert Pillman, that promising young tutor and lecturer, had found a pupil equally promising in Diana Eatwell, and was bringing her along at a great pace. They read a lot of standard verse, particularly Wordsworth's, to one another, skipping the boring bits and allowing plenty of time for cogent exposition on Gillie's part. Gillie, needless to say, had entirely ceased to think of Diana as a schoolgirl with a silly pash for the stuff; he had honestly decided that she had talent as a writer which it was his business to educe and fortify. In other words his manner of falling in love with her was by that sort of imaginative and seemingly unsensual route which is apt to have sudden and explosive consequences.

Wordsworth, like Milton, is all very well if one simply wants the patently top-class article. But nobody (or not in Gillie's view) is going to get far by making a direct model of them. Contemporary poetry had to come in here, and Gillie worked out a little reading plan from the beginning of the decade. They had a go at Wystan Auden's *Poems* (1930) and then at Stephen Spender's *Twenty Poems* (1930) and then Gillie cast around for a third volume of the same date. He found it in Richard Aldington's *A Dream in the Luxembourg*.

The shade of Dante, if present to witness Gillie's opening this book, might well have trembled. No chronicle of how love constrained Lancelot could be quite so potent a nostalgic performance. The bereft young Troilus, waiting in vain for his lost Cressida as the watch-fires pale at dawn before the tents of the Achaeans, is scarcely better calculated to unlock the callow heart than is Richard Aldington's dreamer in a Parisian garden. The moment came when Gillie's voice trembled and the overwhelming thing happened. The lovers would have read no further in that book that day even if Lord Furlong (at home and in a bad temper because of a touch of gout) had not walked into the den to find his daughter and the obscure young man from the university locked in a first passionate embrace.

In the ensuing scene, which was very brief, Gillie was assisted to a certain semblance of dignity by a consciousness of virtue. The instantaneous mutual avowal had happened, the book had dropped from his hand, only a very few minutes before. If Diana's clothing had somehow become a little disarranged his own had not. Although unpractised in such situations, he was sufficiently sensitive to understand the substantial improbability outside fiction of matters having taken a more definitive turn that day, even without this luckless interruption. For as well as loving Diana dearly did he not also respect her very much? Unfortunately it did not occur to Lord Furlong to view the matter in this light. Containing himself only until the wretched youth had withdrawn his hands from cupping Diana's breasts, he uttered a roar of rage, and glanced wildly round the den much as if in the expectation of finding in it a conveniently disposed horse-whip or cane. Gillie got to his feet, prepared for respectful but not craven speech. Lord Furlong, abandoning the thought of castigation, turned to the technique of ejection instead. Striding forward (despite the gout) and with a sudden exercise of physical strength totally unnerving in one of his years, he grabbed Gillie, whirled him around, seized him by the collar and the seat of his pants (yes, even that, as in a comic strip!), and pitched him through the door which he had left open behind him. Then, only briefly taking breath, he fell to bellowing again. Gilbert Pillman was being bidden to leave his house instantly and never again venture to enter it.

It was an impossible, it was a nightmarish situation. He couldn't attempt, in a daughter's presence, to retaliate upon the man—and it didn't look as if any such effort would be crowned with much success anyway. He was in the man's own house. He was even, since William Shenstone was no longer the honest occasion of his visits, in the man's own house under false pretences. The uncivilized old ruffian hadn't given him the slightest chance of apology, profession of honest intentions, promises of discreet and open courses in the future. There was nothing for it but to leave. And between him and Diana Lord Furlong barred the way. All he could do was to call out, incoherently enough, what were designed to be words of encouragement and pledges of enduring devotion. Then he left. At his last glimpse of her his beloved (a shade disappointingly, somehow) had straightened up on the sofa which had been accommodating them, and had begun to cry.

By this misadventure Gilbert Pillman must be described as a good deal cast down. He could think of nothing he could do about it, so his suffering was of that passive order which has been held to be particularly painful since it falls short of the stir and struggle of tragedy. He did, indeed, make one or two attempts at action. He rang up Notton Grange and asked to be put through to Miss Eatwell, but was told at once that she was not at home. He wrote Diana a long letter which he was quite sure would not be delivered to her. He wrote almost as long a letter to her father, but got no reply. The notion of boldly presenting himself again at the front door of the mansion had to be abandoned when he considered how certain it was that somebody would have been instructed to unleash a cry of hounds at him were he to do so. It was perfectly clear that Lord Furlong, a doting father in some regards, was an atrociously tyrannical father in others. And Diana, after all, was only a schoolgirl, and he supposed that an outraged parent could banish her instantly at will to one hideous doom or another. She was probably even now on her way to some ghastly convent or 'finishing school' in France or Switzerland. Of course Diana had enormous courage; she must have, since all conceivable virtues were hers; nevertheless it must be considered that she was a spirit too finely attuned easily to resist the buffetings of a universe which had turned fiendishly cruel overnight.

There were also embarrassing professional complications. Gillie was involved in them, if not up to the neck at least well above the ankles, with regard to beastly Shenstone. He had even staked out a kind of formal claim on the man through the 'Work in Progress' column in an appropriate learned journal. What would Hedger say— Hedger who had ordained that his assistant should, after many years of labour, attain to the position of a world authority on the productions and personality of this trivial scribbler and garden-maniac? Hedger had fixed him up at Notton; how would Hedger take the news that Notton was suddenly not on at all? Gillie Pillman almost howled aloud as he detected himself perpetrating this weirdly involuntary pun. He would be lucky to keep his job, were Hedger to penetrate to the inward occasion of the catastrophe. At best, he believed, he would now remain a junior lecturer all his days, on a salary generously subject to an increment of fifteen pounds every second year.

At this particular point in his miseries, indeed, he did bethink himself of Sir John Suckling. It was distinctly within his recollection that on one occasion Hedger had debated with him the rival claim to current attention of this Caroline character. Suckling, it seemed, was almost as much in need of a leg-up as was Shenstone. Perhaps Gillie could brazenly tell Hedger that he had belatedly yet firmly opted for this alternative learned resource. So he got out of the university library a volume declaring itself to be *A Collection of all the Incomparable Peeces written by Sir John Suckling*, and read it through between supper and breakfast. There was a play called *Aglaura*, in which it appeared that the actors were clothed in lace hammered out of real gold and silver, but which was distinctly lacking in dramatic interest. He decided that only a sucker could fall for Suckling. So he took the book back to the library and faced despair.

It was at this nadir in point of Gillie's nervous tone that Franco perpetrated his strange indiscretion. Gillie had told Franco nothing at all about what had befallen at Notton Grange, since the thing was simply too painful for speech. But Franco had of course marked his dejection, and since his own disposition was at least intermittently melancholic he must have fabricated the notion that he and his room-mate were thus more in some sort of spiritual harmony than usual. It was a moment propitious for avowal. So it came about that one evening, as the two young men sat in front of their now empty grate without even the flagon of burgundy between them, Franco made Gillie a declaration of passion. And Gillie was still gaping at his friend in mere bewilderment when he found that Franco had cast himself down at his feet, wildly declaring his willingness, if better might not be, to settle for a kiss.

It is not possible that Gilbert Pillman can have been without at least an occasional fleeting glimpse of something unsettled in Francis Gethin's sexual inclination. But, if so, he had put it down to some insignificant hang-over from his friend's schooldays. He was totally without first-hand experience of any such course of action as Franco was urging, perhaps because he hadn't himself been at the right sort of school. Moreover there was much in their recent experience together, and notably at Notton Grange, that seemed incomprehensible in terms of what was now, so to speak, on the carpet. Hadn't Franco quite plainly been a bit hooked on Diana? As this thought came into Gillie's head, as the image of Diana rose before him, he felt a sudden quite uncontrollable revulsion before the scene now transacting itself. He jumped to his feet, punched the kneeling Franco on the jaw, and ran from the room.

He spent a wretched night—the more wretched because at one point he believed he could hear Franco quietly sobbing in the next room.

First Diana and then Franco: he was spreading behind him a trail of woe. And he knew that with Franco he had behaved very badly indeed. He had behaved like a thug in the street! The more he thought about his motives, the more beastly did he see himself to be. For one thing, there had even been injured vanity behind that brutal blow. He had believed himself to be liked and indeed admired by Franco on account of his cleverness, his various acquirements, his cheerfulness, the dash and vivacity of his general make-up. And what he had really been in his friend's eyes was a sexual object! Yes, there had been this absurd and unbeautiful resentment operative (he now realized in the small hours) in his manner of rejecting the strange homage Franco had been offering him. But there was worse than this. It came to him that, in that utterly unexpected and utterly naked moment, what had motivated him was the fact that in no conceivable circumstances could Francis Gethin ever have turned him on. He could perfectly well imagine himself, at least when a good deal younger, getting quite something out of sporadic homosexual behaviour. But it wouldn't have been with Franco. It just happened that for him, although not in the least necessarily for other people, whether male or female, Francis Gethin was rather the reverse of physically appealing. And Franco, in that horrible revealing moment, had known this. Gillie now found himself wishing that, if only for seconds, he had felt himself *tempted* by Franco, or even that he had consented to go through some mild ritual of love with him. Nothing lasting would have come of it; it would just have been embarrassing; since he was himself in love in an ordinary sort of way it would probably have been a bit revolting as well. And it was certainly true that most men who happened to be much attached to a virtuous girl would react pretty sharply to being suddenly pro-positioned in an irregular fashion. He ought to have managed some-thing more civilized with Franco, all the same.

They *were* civilized, both of them—in the useful if imprecise sense of the word which was coming into vogue at that time. It might have been expected, therefore, that on a basis of reciprocal candour and good-will relations would have been patched up, or even repaired, on the following morning. It didn't happen. Gillie's contrition was en-tire, but he couldn't convincingly announce a change of heart and mind so hard upon having hit out at his friend so wildly. Franco's key was not contrition but abjection; his apologies were for his very existence as the vilest and most worm-like of men. It was evident that he believed this unwholesome nonsense, or believed that he believed it; at the same time Gillie perceived that where he himself had felt that sense of injured vanity Franco was choking down something much more formidable: an injured pride. Franco was ashen with distress, but Gillie wondered whether it was not with anger too. Nobody abasing himself like this to you, he told himself, is going to be other than your enemy for life. So Franco, of whom he had really become rather fond over the past year, was going to be as lost to him as Diana was.

Later in the morning, however, Franco revealed that something of the sort was going to happen in any case.

'There's a thing I heard about last week,' he said, suddenly at his most nervous and diffident. 'Only I haven't mentioned it, because it's all going to be rather a bore. Some people in Cambridge—'

'What do you mean—some people in Cambridge?' It was now apparent to Gillie that he and Franco would henceforward talk to one another in a perfectly commonplace way, although never with intimacy again. 'Do you mean they're finding you a job there?'

'Well, yes. I wrote a couple of stupid papers last year, and they were published in some rag or other a few months ago. And these people have taken it into their heads that I can do sums in a fashion after all. So they've offered me a Fellowship, and I suppose I'd better go.'

'Franco, that's absolutely splendid!' It was difficult, Gillie found, to get the right note of congratulation into this: partly because Franco was treating what was in fact dazzling promotion as if it were one of the sadder incidents of life; and partly because it meant that they would not have to suffer the embarrassment of one another's company for more than a few days longer, since they were already in the last week of the summer term.

'Perhaps it's just as well, since I've made such a filthy fool of myself.' Franco was going to be abject again, but he was also lurkingly mutinous. 'I can't think how I imagined things about you. I can't think how I was led to. After all, I could take a good guess as to how you felt about the girl out there at the beer hall.'

'Let's drop it, Franco.' Gillie remembered that he had promised himself to scrag Franco—possibly tumbling about on the carpet with him—the next time he talked that offensive rubbish about beer. It was an unthinkable diversion now. 'And it's all over, anyhow, that business. Lord Furlong won't have me in his house ever again. I'm not enough of a gentleman for him, I imagine. So you can have a go there yourself, if you bloody well want to try commonplace girl and boy.'

This unpremeditated savagery had come from Gillie to his own immediate complete dismay. It seemed to betray a feeling in him about Franco and Franco's late solicitation and Franco's coming Fellowship which was not at all agreeable to contemplate. And now Franco was looking at him with what he took to be a moment's overt hostility. But there was nothing of this in his tone when he next spoke.

'I'm frightfully sorry about Lou,' he said. 'It was terribly awkward, but I just couldn't help it.'

'Just what was terribly awkward?'

'Our giving Lou lunch like that. In that rotten restaurant.'

'I don't know that it was awkward particularly. But it was certainly bloody mysterious.' Gillie didn't quite know why he wanted to sort this out. 'Why on earth, Franco, should you chuck Lou at my head, or her at mine, if—' Gillie hesitated, and then turned almost brutal again, '—if, all the time, you had other views for me.'

'It was none of it my idea, at all. Lou insisted on it. She was interested in you, just as I said.'

'I can't see why she should have been, since she'd never before set eyes on me. But I admit she was making passes at her brother's friend before the meal was over. And I did, come to think of it, find that a bit awkward.' Gillie didn't make this last comment with much conviction. In fact a certain complacency might have been detected as attaching to his memory of certain aspects of Lou Gethin's behaviour.

'I don't think it was quite as you're imagining, Gillie.' For the first time during this dreadful morning Franco managed a faint smile— which might have cheered Gillie up a little had he not imagined it to be malign rather than friendly. 'Lou was being an ambassador,' Franco went on. 'Or it might be better to say a spy.'

'I can't think what you mean. It sounds merely crazy.'

'It's not exactly that. My family get worried about me, you see. I suppose you can understand that?'

'Well, yes, if they know—I mean—'

'Quite so. They have a notion that I ought to make wholesome friends. Husky heteros. Lou was sent to look at you, and to report if you turned out to be another fancy boy. Of course I saw her stirring you up a bit. Lou's good at it, wouldn't you say? I was quite proud of her. It was all a put-up thing, you see. But she had you fairly panting for it, hadn't she?'

'What utter balls! Of all the revolting—'

'Don't be a hypocrite, Gillie. There you were, fresh from the embraces of the trusting Maid of Notton, getting a kick out of an ogling match with a girl you hadn't known the inside of an hour before. So you'd been vetted and proved O.K. A manly little chap.'

'Do shut up, Franco. All this is no good at all.' Gillie was on the verge of losing his temper. What he had just heard was uncommonly humiliating in itself, he felt, without having nasty half-truths added to it.

'I'm sorry. I'm a beast. I wish I had the guts to shoot myself.'

'Franco, I do want—' Once more, Gillie broke off in mid-sentence, since 'I do want to help' sounded impossibly patronizing. And as he hesitated, Franco jumped up and ran from the room. But within five minutes he was back again, pausing in the doorway and staring at Gillie from under his most tremendous frown.

'I think I ought to tell you something else,' he said, abruptly and huskily. 'It's rather confusing, really. Well, I suppose not. But it did confuse me.'

'What on earth are you talking about this time, Franco?'

'I'm talking about Diana Eatwell's brother—her twin brother, I think he was. He died, you know. I expect you've heard about him.'

'Yes, I have.'

'He was the Eatwell I knew at my prep school—the boy they didn't treat too well. But it just didn't occur to me to connect up until I saw Diana. She's the split image of Tony.'

'Tony must have been a good deal younger than you.'

'Yes, he was. He was a new boy in my last year. He was marvellously beautiful, and I was very fond of him.'

'I see.'

'No need to be horrified. Nothing came of it, you know. Not even five minutes' misconduct in the boot cupboard. In fact it wasn't like that at all. I was thirteen, and it was first love. That's something painful but to be recommended, Gillie. You may find the right girl and run into it one day.'

V

A few days later Francis Gethin packed his bags and departed. Since his destination, eventual if not immediate, was Cambridge, his going was regarded with some awe by a good many junior members of what this provincial university called its staff. Gilbert Pillman, whose own academic prospects now seemed so dim, was conscious of a certain envy of the blissful security of tenure which his late room-mate was now to enjoy. Franco's new job could under almost no conceivable circumstances be terminated during the next forty years or so. Envy of such a condition was natural enough. But Gillie also felt (so strangely mingled is our clay) a distinct pang of jealousy when he reflected that in his new college Franco would certainly find himself surrounded by numerous highly agreeable young men. And who was going to admire Gillie now? There seemed to be nobody at all who was in the least inclined to do so.

In this dismal state, and with no particular plans for the vacation, Gillie had little to do except think about Diana. And he had one very uncomfortable thought. Although Lord Furlong could intercept, or cause to be intercepted, any letter addressed to his daughter, he could scarcely prevent the passage of a letter in the opposite direction. It couldn't be believed that he had actually locked up Diana—like a heavy father in some mouldy eighteenth-century play or novel—and forbidden her all communication with the outside world. So why hadn't Diana written to him? As day succeeded day, this became a very dark mystery indeed.

Perhaps Diana was ill. Perhaps the shock of that horrible scene in the den had cast her into a fever of an obstinately delirious sort. Perhaps she was dead! This last possibility so haunted him for a time that he actually raked through the notices of death in the local newspaper. Then he was horrified that he had done this. Only some dire death-wish complex could account for so morbid an activity. Gloomily, he played Wagner to himself on his portable gramophone. But no clarification of his state succeeded upon this. He only became further confused. He told himself that he loved Diana but that Diana didn't love him. He told himself that Diana loved him but that he didn't really and truly love Diana. Into things that Franco had said he read a disparaging estimate of the seriousness of his and Diana's mutual attachment. Hadn't Franco said that he, Gillie, might fall in love one day? And love did seem to be something that Franco—if in a peculiar fashion—knew about. Gillie felt his confidence to be ebbing from him in every direction.

And then all this—or nearly all this—cleared away. Not only a letter arrived from Diana, but a parcel as well. On the outside of the parcel was written: *Do not open this parcel until you have read my letter.* He felt at once that there was something childish about this. Diana *was* childish. It was part of her charm—not that 'charm' was at all a nice or adequate word when you had thought about it. Probably Romeo himself had viewed Juliet as on the childish side. There was absolutely no harm in it. Gillie opened and read the letter.

Darling Gillie,

I've only just been able to discover where you *live*. You never told me! And I've thought that if I wrote to you at the university my letter would probably be opened and *read* by some horrid secretary. But now I've found out, ever so cunningly, from that stupid Bounce. Now, for a start, I'm sending you a *birthday present*. Don't open the parcel till your birthday—which is next week, isn't it? I'll only tell you it's *books*. Haven't I told you how books and birthdays go together in this family? There's something in one of them—the books, I mean—I hope you'll like them for. xxxx (Kisses)

Darling, darling Gillie, I think we must *wait*—just for a little. Daddy will come round—particularly if I'm obedient even when his ideas are quite horrid as they are because he's sending me away today to some relations even although it isn't the end of the school term yet. Of course I don't mind about school because I'm fed up with it anyway. But I hate being made a *parcel* of myself!

I'll write to you again quite soon, darling, darling Gillie. I do so love you, darling, darling Gillie. In haste in case he comes in.

DIANA XXXXXX

P.S. Give my love to Franco. He's rather funny but I like him very much because he's your friend. DIANA XXXXXXXX

Gillie was overjoyed at receiving this letter. When he had read it over five or six times, however, he found it to be capable of prompting some unexpected reflections. He suddenly saw Diana as a considerable responsibility. She probably wouldn't be this in the financial sense which he knew so formidably faced many of his contemporaries in the university: the dubious prospect, when contemplating marriage, of raising a mortgage and that sort of thing. Lord Furlong, if he came round at all, would come round to the necessity of substantial subsidy. The burden of responsibility he apprehended was something more difficult to define. It had to do with his feeling that whereas he himself was at least more or less grown up Diana was rather far from being anything of the kind. It was true that Diana, with all her poetry reading and poetry writing, *was* just a kid, with a character almost wholly fluid and unformed. Somehow or other, her letter suggested this quite strongly. When the thing was honestly confronted it was difficult to feel that she was ready to embark upon so serious a business as marriage.

If Gillie was discomfited by these thoughts it may have been partly from a dim sense that they spoke of something immature and unconsidered in his own condition. But he clung to the idea of Diana as his eternal beloved, and he even clung to her birthday present—which he wasn't going to open until the proper day, but which he meanwhile took to carrying about with him. When he went to work in the university library, intending to prepare some lectures since he had nothing better to do, he propped it up in front of him in the little tin cubby-hole, rather like the inside of a filing-cabinet, which was his very own to labour in. And here he was found one day by Professor Hedger.

Professor Hedger, who had a professorial and therefore slightly larger cubby-hole three or four cubby-holes away, came to a halt and looked at Gillie suspiciously. Gillie felt that he even looked at Diana's parcel suspiciously, as if imagining it might conceal an explosive device with which this disaffected young man was proposing to blow up the very core of the university's centre of learning. It was so universal a rule that those junior lecturers as yet unencumbered by wife and child invariably put several counties between themselves and the scene of their professional endeavours on the very first day of a vacation that Hedger certainly regarded young Pillman's continued haunting of the place to be alarmingly unaccountable in itself.

'Ah, Pillman!' Hedger said heavily. 'Busily occupied with Shenstone, no doubt.'

So here it was. Such was the degree of Gillie's intellectual and moral disarray at this stage that the book open in front of him was, in point of fact, *Fanny Hill: or, Memoirs of a Woman of Pleasure*, a work of culpable diversion known to a select few to have escaped the vigilance of the university librarian, and therefore to harbour in a dusty corner of the book-stack rather than in the library's strong room. Gillie wondered whether, at a pinch, he could represent it as having been among Shenstone's favourite books, and therefore proper to be read in the interest of advanced research. But he was a little doubtful about the dates—and dates were things that Hedger was known to be very hot on. So Gillie closed the volume as if courteously signifying that his

63

full attention was to be given to his professor. Its back cover, at least, afforded no clue to the agreeably distracting salacities that lurked within.

'I'm giving Shenstone a rest for a few days, sir,' he said. (Franco had judged it peculiarly absurd that in his wretched place of employment one was expected to address professors in this fawning way: at Cambridge, no doubt, different conventions obtained.) 'I'm getting up a few lectures, as a matter of fact. I always try to remember that the teaching must come first.'

'Ah!' Hedger seemed not particularly to approve this blameless profession. 'It's a moot point, my dear Pillman. Decidedly, it is a moot point. We are not schoolteachers, remember—although I am bound to admit that some of us are little qualified to be anything else. Radically regarded, our function is to transmit the knowledge which we are granted the leisure to make. I hope you are getting along well with the worthy Bounce—although the man is no scholar, I fear.'

'No, sir. He hasn't a clue to much of what he has got in the Furlong Library, for one thing.' Gillie saw a hopeful diversion in this. 'The accessions, in particular, are all at sixes and sevens. He busies himself with a pretentious catalogue. It's quite pitiful, bibliographically re-garded. He seems to think he ought to turn it into a kind of dictionary of received opinions. What Sir Edmund Gosse thinks of Sir Thomas Browne. That kind of thing.'

'Gosse—dear me!' Professor Hedger had frowned at the mere mention of this successful but insufficient person. 'But tell me how Shenstone is going, Pillman.'

'Well, sir, there is a difficulty.' (Here it was again.) 'I've discovered there's an American professor who's doing a good deal of work on Shenstone, and I wouldn't like to be duplicating the research of a much more senior man. In fact I think I may have to rethink things a bit.'

'I see.' Hedger said this so weightily that Gillie felt the confounded man's suspicions to be on the up-grade again. 'Well, keep me in-formed, Pillman. The Committee on Advanced Studies will want a preliminary report at the beginning of next term, you know.'

'Yes, of course, sir.' The existence of the Committee on Advanced Studies was news to Gillie. 'I'll bear it in mind, sir.'

At this, Hedger went away. Gillie made guilty haste to restore Fanny Hill (who now seemed a symbol of his own shocking disinte-gration) to her hiding place on the shelves. He felt quite desperate again. His distress increased, moreover, whenever, as frequently happened, he found himself ceasing to think for a time either of William Shenstone or of Diana Eatwell and thought of Francis Gethin instead. He didn't suppose he'd ever see Franco again, and for that matter he didn't feel he particularly wanted to. But he had wounded Franco as well as punched him, and it had been in a way that Franco could surely never forgive. He took Franco's resulting enmity for granted, and hated the thought of it. This wasn't really very sensible. But it was a notion that did firmly lodge itself in his head.

And then something transforming and at the same time bewildering occurred. His birthday arrived and he opened Diana's parcel. It proved to contain two leather-bound volumes, plainly of the eighteenth century. He opened the first on the fly-leaf, to find inscribed on it in browned and faded ink:

Wm. Wordsworth 1791

Gillie stared at the signature unbelievingly for a minute, and then realized that this was why Diana had thought he would like her present. Hadn't she said at their first meeting that she would never forget his having said 'Wordsworth' when she had asked him who was his favourite poet? He turned to the title-page of this two-volume work and read:

Observations on Man, his frame, his duty,
and his expectations

That Wordsworth should have possessed David Hartley's treatise was, Gillie knew at once, extremely curious. He began to turn over the pages. It was to find that, over and over again, their broad margins had been copiously annotated in Wordsworth's hand. The discovery was entirely staggering, and it told him two things at once. These volumes must have a high monetary value, and it had been extremely rash of Diana to raid the Furlong Library and simply steal for him—for it came to that—so costly a present. But there was more to it than this. For certain learned reasons with which Gillie was perfectly familiar, what he had in front of him was likely to prove the greatest Wordsworth sensation since there had erupted into fame the poet's love affair in France with Annette Vallon, and as a consequence his having fathered an illegitimate daughter. Poor Diana could have no notion of what she had unearthed. Nor would anything at all be known about it by that pretentious ignoramus Bounce.

Gilbert Pillman sat quite still for a long time as he contemplated these facts, and it is to his credit that his first conviction was of the paramount necessity of not giving Diana away. He must somehow conceal how these volumes had come to him. But they *had* come to him. Suddenly he felt that the finger of destiny had pointed at him, and it was not for him to take evasive action. It would not be as an authority on William Shenstone (or Sir John Suckling either) that Professor Pillman would make his name.

He turned back to that fly-leaf. *Wm. Wordsworth 1791.* Now, where was Wordsworth in that year? Gillie's eyes rounded and his breath quickened as he found the answer. He wrapped up the books again and went back to his digs. But on the way he called at his bank and drew out all but a few shillings of what he possessed there. And that afternoon, with high enjoyment, he wrote a note to Professor Hedger.

Dear Professor,

When I saw you the other day, and you talked to me so kindly about Wm. Shenstone, I forgot to mention that I have it in mind to take a short holiday in France. The châteaux of the Loire attract me, beginning at Blois, and I think I may also visit Orléans. I feel that I shall come back in a better state to get some effective work done.

With kind regards to Mrs Hedger and the Misses Hedger,

Yours sincerely,

GILBERT PILLMAN

When Gillie had posted this letter he felt so relaxed that he went to see a Russian film at the local cinema, and then dined out. He marvelled at himself—a scholar of such potential distinction—for having sought solace with Fanny Hill in that shamefully juvenile way. Morally considered, he was now a man regenerated and made new.

VI

When Gillie returned from his holiday the first thing he looked for, very naturally, was some communication from Diana. And a letter proved to be waiting for him, perched on the mantel-shelf at his digs and bearing a French stamp. It was odd that he and his beloved, without knowing it, had been in France simultaneously. For a moment he liked the idea of this, and then it came to him suddenly that the French stamp was ominous. Diana had certainly been immured by her unspeakable father in that convent or finishing school he had himself foreboded for her. He didn't doubt that it was a perfectly frightful place, little short of what might be called a house of correction. The nuns, or whoever they were, probably strove to chasten her rebellious spirit by keeping her on bread and water, or even scourging her in front of an altar. Unbelievable things, he was sure, happened in such places, and their perpetrators thought nothing of them.

But Diana proved to write from Biarritz, and she really was staying with relations. They were her dead mother's relations, who were clearly wealthy people and wholly upper-class as well—in this latter regard being singularly remote from Lord Furlong, at least in point of his origins. The letter was a somewhat inconsequent affair, wandering between professions of undying love and a recital of numerous social occasions. Biarritz seemed to be a place in which a large and floating cosmopolitan society put in all its time living it up no end. To Gillie Pillman the presented scene seemed excruciatingly vulgar in a glossy Edwardian way, but it was evident that Diana was quite bowled over by it. She certainly wasn't thinking of Wordsworth, or remembering that love is to be found in huts where poor men lie. Gillie saw that what he was faced with was a fiendish cunning on Lord Furlong's part, and that a whirl of gaiety was much more likely than an old-fashioned paternal severity to drive his daughter's late adolescent infatuation out of her head.

He felt that he ought to hasten to Biarritz at once. But it lay in a discouragingly remote corner of France, and moreover he felt that, without a penny in his pocket, he would appear at some disadvantage amid Diana's new surroundings. And of course the empty-purse factor went further than that. He would have to hitch-hike all the way from Calais, a distance which an old *Guide Miche* told him was 1032 kilometres. It just wasn't on.

In addition to which, he had something else to do.

'There was this bookshop, you see,' he said to Professor Hedger.

'*A* bookshop, Pillman,' Hedger said severely. 'The intrusive use of a demonstrative pronoun is, to my mind, less a colloquialism than a vulgarism.'

'I couldn't agree less, Hedger. To *my* mind, "this" has a small but legitimate rhetorical function. However, in Blois there was a bookshop, if you prefer it that way.' Gillie paused, and was gratified to observe that Hedger was already a little shaken by the brusque familiarity with which he had been addressed by his subordinate. 'It's odd that in France they call bookshops libraries, more or less. Well, this bookshop is near the cathedral and just above the *Jardins de L'ancien Evêché*. You probably know it.'

'No, I do not. I've never been to Blois.'

'Well, you should drop in there some day. Your wife and daughters would find the Château quite marvellous. Well now, this bookshop is a dusty old place, almost entirely antiquarian, with a mass of stuff that mightn't have been disturbed for centuries. I poked around for quite a long time, mostly in a small and completely neglected English section. I picked up a couple of things I thought I'd rather like to have—miscellanies in duodecimo which I'll be delighted to show you one day—and then I came on these two volumes of Hartley's. I've always been a bit interested in Hartley, because his ideas look forward to Pavlov, you know.'

'Pavlov?' Hedger repeated suspiciously.

'He's a Russian who has some dogs. However, the point is that I came away with those four books—and as quite a bargain, too, as you'll see if you glance at the bill.'

Not very willingly, Hedger glanced at the bill. It duly recorded the sale, in the Rue du Ht. Bourg at Blois, of *quatre tomes* to an unnamed purchaser.

'Well?' he demanded.

'When I got back to my hotel I discovered that the Hartley had belonged to Wordsworth. The first volume has his signature on the fly-leaf. Here it is.'

'Most interesting.' Hedger said this a shade testily. He'd have quite liked to own a book with Wordsworth's signature himself. 'But it's probably a forgery,' he added hopefully. 'One is constantly coming across such foolish impostures. As you will find, Pillman, when you gain a little more experience than you at present possess.'

'I rather think it's not a forgery.'

'Then you ought to think harder,' Hedger said—now definitely with bad temper. 'Of course Wordsworth spent some time at Blois during his liaison with that young woman. But Hartley's is a most unlikely book for him to have possessed—either then or when he was older.'

68

'Oh, come, Hedger. There's no end of Hartley's associationism in *The Prelude.*'

'My dear young man, he picked up scraps of that sort of vocabulary from Coleridge. Even your pupils are likely to know that. He himself had no interest in philosophy whatever. When he died his library didn't contain a single one of the philosophical classics.'

'That's true. I see you have a very fair working knowledge of Wordsworth.' Gillie paused again, this time to allow himself the pleasure of hearing Hedger breathing heavily. 'It makes it all the more interesting that he owned Hartley's *Observations on Man* in 1791, and that he annotated it so extensively.'

'That he *what?*'

'Look for yourself.'

Professor Hedger did look for himself—and in a progressively disorganized state.

'If he put in all this work on the thing,' he said, 'I don't see he could have come to leave it behind him, either at Blois or anywhere else.'

'It was the French Revolution, wasn't it?' Gillie offered this prompting in the encouraging tone he might have adopted to a dull or diffident pupil. ' "Bliss was it in that dawn to be alive", and so forth. Still, he probably felt one day that he'd better beat it quick, or he'd be bowling along on a tumbril in no time.'

Hedger had no reply to this, and resumed his dubitative scrutiny.

'And you *own* this book?' he asked at last.

'Yes, of course—and I'm going to edit the stuff. It's true the annotations, since they've never been published, are copyright still. But I'll fix all that. And no end of people are interested. Professor Beatty, for instance. Of course you know his *William Wordsworth, his Doctrine and Art in their Historical Relations*. It's a great thrill for Beatty. And there are one or two other people I must drop a line to. Old Legouis, for instance. And Ernest de Selincourt. The Coleridge crowd are interested too. I've had a delightful note from Livingston Lowes.'

Professor Hedger (who was an entirely obscure professor) was suitably daunted by this august roll-call. He acknowledged to himself that he was in the presence of a coming man, and no doubt heartily wished that he was a going man as well. The late neophyte in Shenstone studies, he was bound to be feeling, had got well above himself.

'And I gather,' Gillie said, 'that the British Academy will be inviting me to give one of those annual lectures. When they do, I'll see that they send you a card.'

'That's very kind of you, Pillman. I'm sure it will be most interesting.'

There could be no doubt about it. Professor Hedger was a broken man.

Gillie enjoyed all this very much. He enjoyed it the more, perhaps, because in another department of life things were so clearly not going well. As the weeks went by it was progressively harder not to resign himself to the condition of a thwarted lover. A second letter from Diana in Biarritz was just like the first, and moreover it made very little reference to a letter he had addressed to her. He had to face the fact (he told himself) that what had occurred between them had been rather tenuous, after all; that as her declared and accepted lover he had enjoyed a tenure to be estimated as between three and four minutes; and that this had to be regarded as on the brief side for establishing a lasting relationship. He also discovered with some surprise that he came short of any sharp and specific wish to possess Diana. If he *was* a thwarted lover, what he was thwarted of was obscure at the centre and hazy at the edges. It didn't come at all easily to him to imagine himself in bed with Diana, although he conscientiously exercised himself in this way. In fact he was constrained to begin whispering to himself that what lay behind him was a boy-and-girl romance. What lay in front of him (in another sense) was William Wordsworth's copy of Hartley's *Observations on Man*. It looked very much as if Diana's birthday present to him was going to be her farewell present into the bargain.

He was very worried about the Hartley (as he well might be). Working away like mad to get up Hartley's theory of the mind (since it was going to be necessary that he should have mastered it completely), he was haunted by a sense of guilt which arose partly from his feeling that he was being feeble about Diana and partly from the fact that he had involved himself in a risky deception on her behalf. Yet it had to be admitted that it was on his own behalf as well. Had he returned Hartley's work to Bounce, or confidentially to Lord Furlong himself, saying that he felt Diana to have been led through ignorance to make him a gift of something quite inappropriately valuable, it was very unlikely (offending as he had done) that he would have received permission to remain in on the discovery in a scholarly way. For a time he had been so pleased with the perfect success of his ploy at Blois that no doubts had assailed him. Even now he couldn't see that he had done anything enormously wrong. He hadn't stolen the volumes; they'd been given to him. He hadn't forged Wordsworth's annotations; he could no more have managed such a feat than he could have flown to the moon. He had merely manipulated things a little in the interest of protecting the reputation of a confiding young gentlewoman. Yet coming back to this theory of his conduct didn't much reassure him. He told himself that he hadn't fully confronted what would happen to him if somehow or other he were found out. To claim that he had bought in a French provincial town what had in fact come to him in a more than dubious way from the Furlong Library could probably be regarded as a criminal offence. He might even be put in gaol! It was true that if that threatened Diana would certainly come forward with the true story of her rash behaviour. But if that kept him out of the Scrubs it would be far from keeping him in the academic profession. He had to face it. He'd be finished.

For a time Gillie contrived to feel quite injured and indignant about this disagreeable fact of life. What he'd done—he told himself—wasn't far removed from the kind of ingenious and high-spirited learned hoax that jokers did occasionally get away with. If he himself now promptly exposed and exploded the Grand Blois Deception perhaps he'd be forgiven.

Unfortunately he was too hard-headed to believe this for more than five minutes at a time. So what were the chances of the whole affair blowing up on him? He addressed himself urgently to this question. There was no record—he was now tolerably certain—of the annotated Hartley ever having passed through a sale-room or appeared in an antiquarian bookseller's catalogue. In its early days in particular the Furlong Library had been built up on purchases made more or less by the yard, and these two volumes had almost certainly tumbled into it that way—and had remained as unknown to the ridiculous Bounce as to Lord Furlong himself. It was Diana herself who had come upon them, and all that meant anything to her would have been Wordsworth's signature; of the annotations, if she had noticed them, she would have made nothing at all. So the main secret he didn't share even with his beloved—or late beloved. It was his alone.

Yet this didn't take him quite out of the wood. He was now committed to publishing his discovery. It was true that Diana was highly unlikely ever to become aware of such an activity. She admired Wordsworth's poetry, but was as ignorant of anything to be called Wordsworth scholarship as an unborn Hottentot. Only if she happened to divulge to some informed person the title of the work which she had so fondly filched and presented to her lover was there the slightest chance of disaster.

But the chance existed. Conceivably other chances he had failed to think of existed too. As Gillie Pillman sat in his lonely digs and contemplated these facts it was almost as if he heard beneath the floor-boards the ticking of an infernal machine. He had to resign himself to living with a time-bomb.

VII

The passage first of several months and then of several years gradually diminished but never wholly dissipated Gillie's sense of living dangerously. David Hartley, that proto-Pavlov, had functioned as a tremendous spring-board for his career, and before he was thirty he had been rocketed or catapulted into a Chair at very much the sort of university in which he had been so humbly employed along with Francis Gethin. He had worked very hard, and partly because of this had remained unmarried, perhaps subscribing to the view that he travels fastest (and furthest) who travels alone. His celibate state was certainly not due to any undying memory of Diana Eatwell. He did sometimes fall into the paradox of telling himself that she never came into his head. Yet it was almost true. He had virtually censored or repressed her image as one does censor or repress painful, or even merely uncomfortable, recollections. Quite apart from her association with the terrific risk he had taken in fabricating a bogus provenance for Wordsworth's copy of *Observations on Man*, her memory made an awkward bedfellow. The crucial moment in that love affair (he now told himself when he thought about it at all) had come right at the start. No man can hope to recover in his mistress's regard from having been taken by the seat of the pants and chucked out of a room. If he did ever decide to marry he would take care that nothing of the sort happened again in the early stages of his engagement.

He had no notion of what had eventually become of Diana. Perhaps she had got married to one of that Biarritz Ritzy crowd. And Franco had passed entirely out of his life as well. He had, it was true, no reason to censor Franco. He no longer had any reason to be envious of Franco in his Fellowship. Being a professor in a provincial university was not quite so glamorous, somehow, as being a Cambridge don, but it was a good deal better paid. In fact Franco's memory wasn't in the least painful to him except in one regard. His room-mate's enamourment struck his mature sense as having been innocent and rather touching. Perhaps it had been no more than a startling instance of the hung-up state these public-school chaps were liable to for a time. The only nasty thing about it had been his own immoderate reaction. Because of this he remained sure that they had parted enemies. He had once ventured, quite early on, to send Franco a message of goodwill by a common acquaintance. There had been no response. It was possible that so casual an injunction had been neglected or forgotten about, and the signal never passed on. But Gillie decided that Franco had simply not wanted to restore their relationship even at such a harmless remove.

A day came, however, on which he chanced to run into Franco's sister. He was staying in London, doing some work in the British Museum. It was June, and he decided to take an afternoon off and amuse himself by watching tennis at Wimbledon. He had watched a whole set before suddenly becoming aware that Lou Gethin was sitting next to him. She was unaccompanied—and even better-looking than he remembered her as a medical student. It was conceivably this latter circumstance that prompted him to take a plunge.

'Good afternoon,' he said as the players were changing sides. 'I don't expect you recognize me. I'm Franco's friend, Gillie Pillman.'

'Of course I recognize you, Mr Pillman—and it's not really such a very long time since we met. It's a splendid match, don't you think? Franco would enjoy it. He's rather a good player himself, surprisingly enough.'

'So he is.' Gillie hoped that this acquiescence didn't exhibit him as endorsing the sisterly candour touched in by the last part of Lou's speech. It was, of course, true that there was something surprising in any sort of athletic prowess in anybody so physically skimpy as Franco. But that particular aspect of his former admirer was one that Gillie specially disliked remembering, since it was obscurely involved with his own bad behaviour. 'We used to play—' he began, and then checked himself, since those occasions at Notton Grange were also on the list of things he didn't care to recall. 'We used to play a bit of golf too. But Franco was no better at that than I was.'

'They're beginning again.'

Lou had thus briskly indicated that they had better give their attention to the game, and Gillie did his best to do so. But he found it hard to concentrate on the play, and every now and then he stole a glance at his companion. There was no doubt about her beauty. It was precisely as he remembered it. Nobody looking at Helen of Troy could so much as call up another woman's face. Lou was just like that. He managed to catch a glimpse of her ungloved left hand. She wasn't wearing a wedding-ring. This somehow seemed incredible in face of such attractiveness, and the sudden thought came to him that Lou perhaps shared her brother's sexual inclination. He had become of an increasingly tolerant mind in such matters, but for some reason this particular notion horrified him. Then he remembered the odd kind of mission which Lou had been engaged on at that luncheon party long ago. She'd hardly have undertaken that, he supposed, if anything of the sort were true of her.

He realized that in the casual exchange they'd so far had Lou had certainly studied him with some interest. There had been almost the same sort of sizing-up scrutiny that he remembered from long ago. This, if perplexing, was gratifying too. He wouldn't have expected Lou Gethin to take the slightest interest in a middle-aged (for he was beginning to feel himself that) provincial professor.

The current game ran to several long rallies, so Gillie had plenty of time to reflect on his situation, and to wonder whether he mightn't take some step to place his renewed acquaintance with this stunning girl on a less transitory footing. But now the game was over, and the players were going through their ritual mopping and sipping and vigorous towelling of their racket handles. This time, it was Lou who took the initiative in speaking.

'How does Shenstone come along?' she asked.

'Shenstone?' For a moment Gillie was actually at sea. 'How odd that you should remember him.'

'You told me about *The School-Mistress. A Poem.*' Lou sounded amused, and Gillie wondered whether he was being made fun of. But perhaps the idea of a learned person as engaged with something called *The School-Mistress. A Poem* was funny in itself.

'So I did. But I dropped Shenstone, more or less.'

'And took up with something else?'

'Oh, yes—one thing and another.' It was evident that Lou Gethin was no more given than Diana Eatwell to following the course of

Wordsworth studies. Gillie wasn't offended by this ignorance of his academic fame; in fact he was delighted to be now engaging Lou's attention at all. At the same time he was conscious of a certain uneasiness as besetting him. He could even believe that Lou had glanced at him in a peculiar way. But the plain fact was, of course, that the whole region upon which they had happened to touch was still capable of producing at least a mild paranoid reaction in him. At times he was capable of believing that a postman or a bus-conductor knew more about him than was wholesome. (The time-bomb, in fact, still faintly ticked.)

The next game began, and it seemed likely to be the last in the match. Gillie felt that if Lou wasn't going to vanish permanently from his ken swift action would be required. Match point came and brought its customary hush—which lasted, however, only for a moment since the issue was decided by a brilliant ace. Both players bounded forward and shook hands vigorously across the net amid general applause. Gillie had to wait until this had subsided, and when he was able to speak his mind was made up.

'Do you live in London, Lou?' he asked. (Lou had said 'Mr Pillman', so there was a bit of bold initiative here.)

'Yes, Gillie.' (This was marvellous.) 'I'm a Senior Registrar in an East End hospital.'

'I'm going to be in town until the middle of next week. I wonder whether you could possibly lunch with me one day?'

'I'd like to very much.' Lou was gathering up a light coat she had shed during the heat and excitement of spectatorship. 'Only it's rather difficult, since just at present I have to be on call rather a lot.' She glanced at Gillie consideringly. Gillie felt rather dashed, since this sounded like a polite preliminary to declining his invitation. Nothing of the kind, however, followed. 'But look,' she said, 'could you perhaps come to dinner with me one evening? My flat's quite close to the hospital, you see, and I'm at the end of my telephone there. Would Tuesday be possible?'

Gillie, whom a long period of somewhat unsatisfactory sexual life perhaps rendered particularly susceptible to altogether superior possibilities, felt that he had seldom heard more enchanting words. Lou seemed to be proposing something much more intimate than he himself would have dared to do.

'That would be quite lovely,' he said. 'Let me get down your address, Lou.' And he fished out a pocket-book.

*   *   *

75

The next few days passed in a dream. Gillie sat in the North Library of the B.M. in such a state of idle reverie for the most part that the elderly man who gave out the books took to looking at him disapprovingly, as if he had come in to shelter from the rain and was improperly occupying accommodation which ought to be available for some more genuinely enquiring person. When he went out to lunch in the little Greek restaurant in Coptic Street he was as unconscious of what he ate as the most abstracted scholar frequenting the place. And at the end of the day he fell into so deep a muse on the Underground that he was carried far beyond his proper destination to the mysterious region of Ealing Broadway.

He found that he couldn't remember nearly as much as he wanted to about his brief encounter with Lou at Wimbledon. Just how had she been feeling about him? Why should she feel about him at all? Had she been responding to his mere looks as quite casual girls did from time to time? They had exchanged very little of what might be called hard information. He had been sufficiently possessed by the uncomfortableness of the past to have failed to enquire properly about her brother. And she hadn't volunteered anything on that front. He wondered whether Franco was still a respectable Cambridge don, or whether his unfortunate constitution had carried him in some direction making easy chat about him difficult. Whatever the situation, it was probable that at a tête-à-tête dinner she would be more communicative. He wondered whether Franco had ever told her as much as he knew about the wretched conclusion of the affair with Diana. And he wondered at his own boldness in venturing anew within the whole Eatwell-Gethin network. There even lurked a disturbing thought prompted by this image. The lure of Lou Gethin was proving so potent that he could almost think of himself as a helpless fly being drawn insensibly into a spider's web. He found himself behaving in an absurdly juvenile fashion over the forthcoming engagement. Walking down Piccadilly on the day before it was to take place, he dodged into the Burlington Arcade and bought himself a new tie.

Lou's flat, when he entered it, proved to be a single large sitting-room, to which a bedroom and adequate offices were presumably attached. There was an agreeable smell of cooking, and Lou made equally agreeable haste to offer him a glass of sherry. What was not so agreeable was his immediate awareness of a dinner-table laid for four people. So it wasn't going to be a tête-à-tête occasion after all. Gillie had barely digested this ungrateful fact when the door opened without ceremony and the two remaining guests walked into the room. For a moment he couldn't believe his eyes. Yet there wasn't a doubt about it. The couple confronting him were Franco and Diana.

And they *were* a couple. Not only were they husband and wife; in the most matter-of-fact fashion they took it for granted that Gillie was aware of their condition, just as he would have been of the married state of any other two people whom he knew fairly well. And Lou, whether disingenuously or not, evinced exactly the same attitude. All this emerged in seconds and during greetings entirely unaccompanied by the suggestion of any surprise. Gillie himself, although to be described as left gasping, was for some reason reduced to wild dissembling. Eventually he was told, as something he might *not* yet know, that Diana Gethin had lately borne her second child.

Gulping a second glass of sherry, Gillie asked himself whether Lou had deliberately and of malice contrived for him this peculiarly devastating *coup de théâtre*. She was certainly glancing at him from time to time in a considering or quizzical way of which the other two were entirely innocent. But then Lou had the habit of something of the sort. Franco had the appearance of taking the occasion without effort in his stride, although he did sometimes frown at Gillie in a forbidding manner. But that of course had been Franco's habit of old; he could even contrive the appearance of a kind of contemptuous coldness towards Gillie when presumably his feelings weren't cold at all. As for Diana, she was not without a slight air of confusion in face of this meeting—which was natural enough upon being once more in the presence of her one-time adorer of the den. She was certainly very proud of Franco. So, no doubt, was the old ruffian Lord Furlong, who'd be as pleased as Punch at marrying off his daughter to the grandson of an earl. Gillie now remembered, with a certain irritation, having heard long ago that if an uncle of Franco died without an heir, as he appeared likely to do, Franco's father the philosopher would succeed to the title—which would mean Franco's becoming Viscount Something-or-Other straight away. Diana would probably be quite pleased about that too. As for the Gethin crowd, they'd probably been far from upset when a son whose proclivities had been prompting family anxiety fell for a girl who was the sole heir to an enormous brewing concern.

Gillie wondered how on earth Franco and Diana had hit up with one another. He also wondered whether Diana knew that she had reclaimed or diverted her husband from peculiar courses, or whether she was entirely without knowledge of them. He had read somewhere—probably in Proust—that inverts make particularly good husbands. If this was true they probably made particularly good fathers as well.

But there was a much more urgent riddle that required an answer, although Gillie didn't at all see how he could with any discretion arrive at it. Had Diana ever happened to tell her husband about that birthday present—mentioning not only the business of Wordsworth's signature but the title of the work in which it was inscribed? If so, had Franco then tumbled on the truth? Franco wasn't at all a literary character, but Gillie remembered that he did have the habit—as he described it—of 'glancing over the booksy bits in the public prints'. So he might well have come across the fact that Gillie had presented the world with what the young Wordsworth thought of *Observations on Man*, and he might similarly have read some reference to the manner in which Gillie was supposed to have come upon the book in a shop hard by the *Jardins de L'ancien Evêché* at Blois. Franco, in fact, might be possessed of the whole dire secret—and be the only person in the world, apart from Gillie himself, who was so. Or he might even have told his wife about it, so that she knew too. Realizing this, Gillie experienced a moment of sheer panic. It completely destroyed for him the pleasure he would otherwise have taken in Lou's distinctly superior *boeuf en daube*. Francis Gethin *was* the time-bomb. It was as simple as that.

'What are you working at now, Gillie?' Franco asked. He put the question in his most diffident way, as if Gillie's labours were so likely to be vastly increasing the world's stock of knowledge that the outer profane should scarcely venture to mention them.

'Gillie is busy with one thing and another,' Lou said (surely with a faint mockery?). 'That's how he put it to me the other day.'

'Quite right,' Gillie said. 'Just bits and pieces—chiefly by the Romantics. Lou, this is an absolutely delicious *daube*. Do tell us how you make it.'

'Including Wordsworth?' Diana asked quickly. She had pricked up her ears (one of which Gillie remembered, in those delirious minutes, having managed to kiss).

'Well, yes. Wordsworth among others. There's a lot coming to light about the composition of his *Ecclesiastical Sonnets*. It's most interesting.

78

Is there fennel in it? I imagine I can taste fennel.'

'Gillie and I used to read Wordsworth together,' Diana said. 'Franco, I've told you about that.'

'So you have, darling.' Franco seemed amused. He even glanced at Gillie as if he expected Gillie to be amused too. 'And, later on, Gillie discovered something marvellous about Wordsworth's reading. Isn't that right, Gillie?'

'More or less.' Gillie wondered whether the perturbation he felt was reflected in his voice. Franco was smiling at him as if enjoying some private joke. But was it, this time, a smile that could be described as embodying a sadistic component? He was sure that Franco knew or suspected something, but was entirely in the dark about Diana—or, for that matter, Lou. He had a sudden irrational glimpse of a long vista of years ahead during which Franco would amuse himself by appearing on the verge of betraying the dire secret of Blois as if it were no more than a funny thing that had once happened in the past. Yet Franco, if he knew the story, must also know what the true consequences of its gaining currency must still be.

In fact (he told himself) what Franco proposed was nothing less than a cat and mouse game, and this dinner-party was a kind of family rehearsal for it. They were all joining in to torment him. Gillie now remembered all Franco's glooms, his bouts of arrogance or cold contempt over this and that, his unstable psychosexual constitution—and, above all, that horrible and unforgivable punch on the jaw. Professor Gilbert Pillman decided that, sooner or later, it was going to be all up with him.

But now something very odd happened. The conversation drifted away just as if Gillie's Wordsworth studies were far from being of consuming interest; were certainly not nearly so interesting as Lou's Grassy Corner Pudding, which she had prepared in rivalry with the kitchen of her brother's Cambridge college, where the delectable concoction had apparently been invented. During the discussion of this Gillie simply sank back exhausted. And then, suddenly, the meal was over. The point had come at which, in a former time, the women would have withdrawn, leaving the men to linger over their wine. What happened now was that the women stayed put while the men went into a little kitchen to wash up. Gillie nerved himself for a plunge. He would challenge Franco to come clean.

But it was Franco who, whipping up detergent in the sink, spoke first.

'Gillie,' Franco said, 'it's tremendous fun meeting again like this. Were you awfully surprised when you heard I'd married Diana? And did you forgive me? Say you did.'

'I never heard anything about it. Not until tonight.'

'Good Lord! I know you must find it unexpected. But people do change, you know. And I always terribly wanted kids.'

'Kiddies.'

'Yes.' The allusion to Professor Shuffrey's plebeian vocabulary seemed to escape Franco. 'And it was all quite simple. I just fell tremendously in love. It began at those tennis parties. You remember what Diana's brother had meant to me when I was quite immature.'

'I see.' Gillie was utterly bewildered—so much so that he almost dropped the plate he was drying.

'And you *do* forgive me?'

'About marrying Diana? Yes, of course.'

'Hurray! I do so enormously admire you, you know. About all that business we were talking about. The Wordsworth nonsense.'

'Nonsense?'

'Your taking such a big risk in fudging up that story about the bookshop in Blois. I was staggered when I tumbled to it—which was quite some time after Diana told me about her birthday present to you. It was sheer chivalry. And just because you thought it might get her into a row with her father! And the irony of its not being necessary! That does really get me.'

'What do you mean: the irony?'

'The whole Furlong Library has been Diana's sole property for years. Legally, although in a hush-hush way. It was one of my rascally father-in-law's dodges for mitigating death-duties, of course. Diana could have given away anything she pleased. And the old boy wouldn't have minded a bit about some books, anyway.' Franco grinned happily. 'It was the disposal of his daughter he was worried about. Lucky for me, I suppose.'

A bemused Gillie Pillman dried another plate, this time with the greatest care. It was slowly dawning on him that, from the start, the time-bomb had contained nothing but sawdust. But, no: that wasn't quite true.

'Does Diana know?' he asked.

'About Blois? She doesn't, as a matter of fact. I thought she might be upset by it. By your having put yourself so much at risk, I mean.'

'What about Lou—does she know?'

'Well, yes. I did tell Lou.'

'She won't gossip?'

'Certainly not.' Franco was suddenly and sharply offended. Lou, he might have been saying, was a Gethin—and that was that. 'You and I, Gillie—and Lou—are the only people who will ever know about Blois. I understand it might be misconstrued by your professorial crowd. What an honourable thing you'd done, I mean.'

After this, they finished the washing up in silence. Gillie had a lot more to digest than Lou's admirable dinner. Everything, he told himself, was now in the clear. Only, as he glanced from time to time at Franco, he became faintly uneasy on a wholly different account. Franco *did* admire him—and not wholly on the score of his supposed quixotry over the provenance of William Wordsworth's copy of David Hartley's *Observations on Man*. He couldn't be certain that a trick of the old rage might not rekindle in the reformed Francis Gethin. It might be fancy—he was himself, after all, considerably overwrought by the strains of the past hour—but he wasn't quite sure about a fugitive glint in Franco's eye. It was decidedly time to rejoin the ladies.

An hour later, when he had taken his leave, Gillie endeavoured to compose himself by walking all the way back to his Bloomsbury hotel. He thought what a nice chap Franco was. He thought what an escape he'd had. And once or twice he thought, although not very hopefully, about the enchantingly lovely Lou.

THE LITTLE DUFFER

RICHARD HOWLAND HAD the reputation of being an excellent worker. He was married to a sensible woman, had three children who would soon be grown up, and had long ago been promoted from labouring on the home farm to the position of head gardener at the Park itself. It was said that Howland had always been something of a favourite with old General Alford, and that he owed his exalted position at Thorley more to this than to anything that could be called high horticultural ability. Nevertheless everybody respected him. There had been some trouble when he was a small boy, but the report of this, as happens in the handing down of village legends, had assumed such a variety of dim versions that nobody much attended to it. Another point about Howland—perhaps not one regarded, at least by the younger people, as particularly in his favour—was his being much involved with the church. Of course the church was so entirely an annex of Thorley Park, and the tombstones surrounding it merged so imperceptibly into General Alford's lawns and rose-gardens, that it was natural that the head gardener (rather than the vicar) should have charge of it. Howland saw to the heating (which was excellent, the late Mrs Alford having been of a rheumatic tendency), rang the bell, and took the collection. On a very special occasion, connected with a Royal Jubilee, Howland and not the General had been called upon to read the first lesson. The congregated gentry judged his performance entirely creditable.

Howland's principal notion of the duties of a head gardener was to see that everything was kept extremely tidy. Mowing and clipping and weeding were the activities he chiefly set his two young assistants to. He himself was particularly good at bonfires—perhaps because 'burning up' is the most definitive part of the tidying process. He could get the most unpromising pile of garden refuse blazing in no time, and then kept completely under control. No vagrant smuts ever reached the linen hung out to dry on the green behind the laundry. If General Alford, and his widowed daughter who lived with him, ever chanced to observe this operation through the high Georgian windows of the drawing-room (Georgian in style, although almost the entire fabric now was quite modern) it was with the knowledge that no single waft of smoke would drift their way to cloud the panes. On the other hand if the Loamshire Hunt had met, and the pack had come lumbering and slavering and senselessly yelping through not only the park but even the gardens as well, and the General knew that his neighbour the M.F.H. would treat any complaint with an irritating good-humoured off-handedness, Howland would go to work to different effect. Thorley Park was planted almost on the verge of its demesne, and so, as it chanced, was Sir Charles Apperley's house, Chesney Lodge. There was a bare two hundred yards between them. Howland would bide his time, attending on the winds, and would meanwhile make large collections of well-chosen combustibles. The day would come when the weather-vane above the stable clock at Thorley Park pointed dead at Chesney Lodge. Then the match would be applied, and almost within minutes Sir Charles Apperley and all his household (including numerous hounds in honourable retirement) would be enveloped in mephitic vapours. But because these two elderly landed proprietors had been at school together, and because each was the nearest conversational resource of the other, this peculiar warfare generated no ill-feeling. The two men between them had come to run the village, and much else for miles around.

It was to be remarked, too, that Sir Charles, although he well knew whose was the hand responsible for those punitive visitations upon his nostrils, always had a civil word for Richard Howland when he encountered him. This was because, like the General, and unlike the majority of his more rustic neighbours, he retained a clear and undistorted memory of this sober gardener's early history. That history is the subject of the present brief narrative.

General Arthur Alford had at one time been the youngest field officer in the British army: a dedicated professional soldier who was tipped to go far. When this promotion came to him he was already the owner of Thorley Park, since his father had died in early middle age. Having been as precocious in the marital as the martial sphere, he was also married and with several children. So a new and spacious home was a welcome accession in itself. He had at once decided, however, that he would not allow this responsibility to interfere with his military career, and this meant that for a long time he was something of an absentee landlord. His family saw much more of Thorley than he did. When he did get down to the place, and moved about the estate, it was almost with the feeling of being a visitor. The house had not been his boyhood home, since his grandfather had predeceased his father by only a few years. It had, however, been a regular holiday resource, and when it eventually came his way he was already decently fond of it. He tried to get to know his tenants and the local people generally, and he found a little time for squirearchal activities of one sort and another. As the years passed and his seniority rapidly increased, he found that he could be influential in various ways. Ten miles away there was a minor public school; he was helpful about its OTC, making sure that it was a decent chap who was sent down from the War Office to cope with Cert. A, and that the right things were done when the General Inspection came along. He gave a similar leg-up to the Territorials. He accepted some titular rank or other with the Boy Scouts of the county. It was as a Boy Scout—or perhaps as a boy aspiring to be a Boy Scout—that he first became aware of his future head gardener.

He had gone for an evening walk with his wife and his daughter Anne, who was home from school on her half-term holiday. It was already dusk, but the air was warm after an autumn day of steady sunshine. The Alfords strolled through the gardens, and then straight ahead through two lines of beech trees which would have constituted a long avenue had any roadway ever been laid down between them. Old prints showed that there had never been anything of the kind, but only a broad ribbon of grass opening upon a level pasture where the trees came to an end. This transition however was marked by two imposing stone columns, crowned with elaborately carved cornucopias tumbling out flowers, fruit and corn—no doubt by way of symbolizing the productivity of the region. The wrought-iron gates which these pillars were designed to support had disappeared long ago, and before that can never have supplied any useful office, the whole affair having been designed merely to lend consequence to the vista commanded from the terrace in front of the house.

The Alfords paused at this point, turned, and in silence surveyed Thorley Park. It was no sort of gem of the guide-book order, and like the lady in the song perhaps looked best in the dusk—as now—whether or not with a light behind it. The fabric had come slowly into being in bits and pieces over several centuries, and not every part was even approximately congruous with the whole. But a building that has thus changed through processes of accretion, demolition and re-edification through many generations renders, perhaps paradoxically, a strong impression of permanence. It was a satisfaction to Arthur Alford, standing between his wife and daughter and keeping his thoughts to himself, to reflect that this gracious and essentially unassuming place would be the home of Alfords yet unborn.

'Just the right distance, this,' he said to his wife—much as if that song from *Trial by Jury* had actually been in his head. 'You could never tell it all needed a good lick of paint. But it may be possible to get going on that now. There ought to be a bit of leisure to give my mind to it.'

'I think it's wonderful news—quite wonderful.' Mrs Alford, who didn't often say things like this, emphasized her words with a brisk nod. And it was true that, earlier that day, something extremely agreeable had happened. Her husband had received word that a tour of duty overseas which appeared to lie directly ahead of him had been cancelled so far as he himself was concerned by a stroke of some august pen, and that his own position was at once to become a much more exalted one on the Imperial General Staff. For some years ahead, his place of domicile during the greater part of the year could be entirely of his own choosing. There would be high-level conferences in plenty. Below that, the chaps from the Dominions and so on would simply be invited to Thorley, and his own subordinates would be summoned there, and great matters would be settled in the course of modest country-house entertainment. General Alford (for he was now to be the youngest General in the British army) told himself with some complacency that the Empire's strength lay very much in that sort of approach to things.

'Shall we go round by the Long Spinney?' he asked. 'We'll have plenty of time before it's anything like dark.'

'And see the magic cottage,' Anne said. She had given this name in an arbitrary manner to a commonplace little structure, in fact a lambing hut, which stood in a shallow coomb beyond the spinney and at no great remove from the group of cottages connected with the home farm. 'The necromancer may be at home.' Anne Alford was not a particularly fanciful child, but from near-infancy she had been provided with what were judged the appropriate books for the decade or so after the mere dawn of life. This had led her conscientiously to people the environs of Thorley with fairies and similar supernatural creatures of the adult imagination.

'If the necromancer is there,' General Alford said, 'we can have a little chat with him.' The General was feeling well-disposed to all the world this evening, and took pleasure in indulging his daughter's charming nonsense. So they walked on to the lambing hut. It was a solid stone structure, like a very small ancient barn. The remains of its roof, which had long ago fallen into decay, had been removed some years before on the instructions of Colonel Alford (as he then was) when he had heard that the village children sometimes played there and might be endangered by it.

The Alfords negotiated a stile and emerged from the spinney. There, the dusk had been deepening, but over the pasture now before them there seemed to lie no more than a first twilight. The hut itself, although shadowed by a great elm, stood out clearly enough as a grey wall pierced by two black holes: a small one where there had formerly been a window of sorts, and a larger one where there had hung a door. They were already moving towards it when there momentarily appeared through both these apertures a flicker of light. A few seconds passed, and the flicker was repeated.

'Glow-worms!' Anne exclaimed with a correct excitement. Glow-worms went with fairies, being much in demand among them as an illuminant of festive occasions. It was very probable that necromancers similarly employed them when boiling up toads in kettles.

'We must investigate,' General Alford said. He rather wanted to add, 'You two wait here, while I nip over and see.' This was because he had at once decided that what the lambing hut sheltered was a tramp—a tramp taking comfort from lighting up an evening pipe. If it were so, he would send the fellow about his business: again because of the village children who might conceivably come larking here in the gloaming. A tramp can frighten small children, and he wasn't going to have anything of the sort happen on his land. Of course he would give the man five shillings and address him with proper politeness; nevertheless he would somehow prefer not to perform this slightly heavy-handed action before his womenfolk. But by this time his wife—an active woman whose rheumatism still lay in the future—was half-way to the hut, with Anne skipping gleefully beside her; General Alford was suddenly a little irritated by Anne. Anne was much too old to skip gleefully. And—what was more—the gleeful skipping was a turn, put on because the child thought her parents still expected it. General Alford, who was a highly intelligent man (as you must be if you are to become the youngest general in the army), had really tumbled to this about the fairies and so on some time ago. The truth about his daughter was that she owned a thoroughly rational cast of mind. And this, after all, was something to find satisfaction in, since it distinguished her from the majority of her sex. It would similarly have distinguished her, he thought, had she been a male and become an army officer. General Alford, a modest man, when contemplating his own meteoric career sometimes reminded himself that in the country of the blind the one-eyed man is king.

He lengthened his stride, and they all three arrived before the lambing hut together. Meantime there had been two more flickers of light, and their character was such that there could be no doubt now that it had been the striking of a match that had occasioned them. The tramp must be having difficulty with his pipe. The General felt in a pocket for his tobacco pouch. He'd add to his effect of firm benevolence the little grace note of inviting the old chap to have a fill.

He entered the hut first, as was proper where there was an unknown situation. It was a square, bare place, and there was no tramp in it. The matches were being struck by a small boy. He was alone, and his occupation so absorbed him that he remained for a moment unaware that he was now pursuing it in the presence of spectators.

'Three!' the boy said to himself aloud. 'It mun be *three!*' And in apparent despair he threw his match-box into a litter of twigs on the earthen floor of the hut.

Although the light was poor, it was possible to see that the boy wore a scarf and a bleached khaki shirt with a couple of small badges sewn on one of its short sleeves. General Alford took in the situation at a glance.

'Aha!' he said. 'Practising for your next test, eh? What's your name, boy?'

'Dicky, sir.' The boy had turned and was staring, wide-eyed and apprehensive, at the intruders. But he had answered as a properly drilled village child should.

'Dicky Howland,' Anne said informatively. Anne was well-briefed on the village, having frequently gone round with her mother on charitable and disciplinary missions. 'From the pub,' she added.

'Yes, of course.' The General, although not so well acquainted with the locals as he would have liked to be, knew that it was a fellow called Howland who kept the pub. 'Well, Dicky, let's see.' It was clear that General Alford (himself connected, in some fashion he wasn't quite certain of, with the Boy Scout Movement) was disposed to take young Howland's meritorious efforts seriously. 'Just forget about us, and try again.'

A shade reluctantly, Dicky Howland retrieved the match-box. He was slender, dark-haired, black-eyed, and there was something wary, almost feral, in his sidelong glance. He might well have been a gipsy child. One could imagine him as an odd-boy-out in the little bucolic community around Thorley. His movements were nervous. He was gathering twigs, rapidly but a little fumblingly, from the litter around him. The Alfords watched silently, having cast themselves in the role of examiners of the rehearsal now in progress. Dicky made a small tent of twigs; it tumbled once, twice—and then at the third attempt seemed stable. He struck a match and inserted it with a trembling hand within the structure; it went out at once. He tried again. There was a little upward drift of smoke this time. A tiny flame climbed up one of the twigs, only to extinguish itself a moment later. Suddenly Dicky gave a yelp of pain and jumped to his feet. He had burnt his fingers on the match end.

'It won't do at all, you little duffer.' General Alford said this good-humouredly and indeed almost affectionately, but was at once aware that it hadn't been quite right. Even in the half-light it had been possible to see the child flush darkly, as an offended adult might have done. 'Will you let me have a go?' the General went on quickly. 'First there's the twigs, you see. It's not their size that matters, so much as that they should be dry. Don't use them if they bend. Use them only if they snap. Cast around, Dicky.'

The boy obeyed, captured by this brisk expertness. In no time there was a little pile of dry twigs to the General's hand.

'And now try it another way,' the General went on, standing back. 'Not a tent or pyramid, Dicky. That tumbles in no time, and out goes your fire. Criss-cross and four-square—as you've seen timber stacked when the men have been felling it. Leaving a little square chimney in the middle. Carry on, boy.' General Alford was enjoying himself. He might have been a young subaltern again, rapidly and lucidly explaining some simple operation to his platoon. Dicky was not so much enjoying himself as keyed up. His hands had steadied. He went to work on this new structural principle with the concentration another child might have put into building a house of cards, and this time with complete success. The fire required not the three matches allowed but only one. Had the Alfords been Dicky's real examiners, he would have passed his test triumphantly. And now he was enchanted. Rigid and oblivious, he stood gazing at the tiny blaze as if it had been a vast combustion. Then suddenly he sprang into life, darting here and there about the hut to gather further twigs, placing these—first carefully and then in careless handfuls—amid the flames, so that presently the whole place had become a flickering *chiaroscuro*. The boy halted once more, froze, stood staring into his achievement entranced, his hands thrust deep into the pockets of his shabby khaki shorts.

'So there you are,' General Alford said, laughing. 'We must be getting home now, Dicky. Good luck with your test.'

'Thank you, sir.' It was almost as if Dicky Howland had jerked awake in order to produce this surprisingly well-mannered response. 'Just one match! I won't forget how easy it is.'

'And you had better cut along home, too. Otherwise, darkness will catch up with you.'

'I like the dark.' Dicky spoke decidedly. 'You can see things then.'

'I'd say that's just what you can't do.'

'You can if you try. You can see things that don't come out in the day-time—or hardly ever. Like the badgers.'

'Perfectly true, my dear lad. But don't forget listening as well as looking. Listening's the key to quiet movement in the dark.' The General produced this military lore in an approving tone. It was evident that he thought well of this budding field naturalist. But Mrs Alford appeared to have been affected differently.

'Arthur,' she said during dinner, 'do you know I much doubt whether that boy is a Scout at all? He didn't *look* like one.'

'In his rig, you mean?'

'Yes—or that chiefly.'

'I rather agree with you. It wasn't very trim. Wouldn't do on parade—if they hold parades. But he knew about the tests and things. What they call proficiency badges, and so forth.'

'The Howlands must be quite well off. If they really had a son in the local troop, they'd see that he was properly dressed.'

'Perhaps so. Yes. He may be pretending a bit. Dug an older brother's abandoned togs out of the rag bag.'

'Possibly some enquiry should be made.'

'My dear old girl!' The General was a little given to this sort of indulgent address. 'If the boy isn't a Scout, but wants to dress up and dream of himself as a Scout, good luck to him. It would scarcely make the worthy Baden-Powell turn in his grave. And you couldn't call it a case of masquerading in the King's uniform.'

'I think Daddy is quite right,' Anne Alford said importantly. Anne had lately been promoted to the dinner-table on domestic occasions, and was a shade uppish as a result. 'After all, Dicky was getting fun out of it, wasn't he? He was tremendously excited by his silly little fire. Just like when he danced in the stubble.'

'When he did what?' the General asked, puzzled.

'It was when they were burning off the twelve-acre. I found it rather exciting too. Little licking lines of fire moving across the field, like waves on a beach. And Dicky Howland danced among them. He danced like a wave of the sea.' Anne had lately been turning away from the nursery bookshelves with their empty jingles and digging grown-up poetry out of the library. It was mostly incomprehensible, but thrilling all the same.

'Burning off!' Abruptly, General Alford quite ceased to be interested in Dicky Howland. 'There's another instance of its being high time I took matters in hand. It's a beastly practice—and I don't doubt brought in from America. Dangerous to property, for one thing. And destructive to no end of harmless and interesting insect life. It has to happen in war: the snail crushed by the felloe-rim, and all that.' (It was the General himself who had put most of the modern poetry in the library.) 'But peace and scorched earth don't go together. I'll have something pretty stiff to say about it. Laziness at the bottom of it, if you ask me.' General Alford was quite clear that, as a landowner now to be much around his own properties, he was going to see that his word would be law.

The Howlands were not very favourably regarded in the village—a fact which didn't greatly perturb either the publican or his wife, since theirs was the only licensed house within five miles of Thorley. Behind this lack of esteem there may have lain nothing more than the petty xenophobia characteristic of rural communities. Howland was a foreigner from somewhere in the Midlands, shoved into the job by the brewery company; his wife might almost have been a foreigner in the more authentic sense of the word, since she was dark and exotic-seeming like her son Dicky. So the villagers were no doubt prejudiced against them. But Mrs Alford, too, had not taken to the Howlands, and had once briefly remarked to her husband that they were 'perhaps not wholly desirable'. All these circumstances were to have some bearing on Richard Howland's history.

The Apperley Arms was not the kind of pub into which it would have occurred to any of the surrounding gentry to drop for a drink. The vicar however paid the Howlands an occasional visit, pastoral care being a duty which he discharged in a conscientious although untalented manner. Dr Ayliffe was a scholar, now of advanced age, and he had been presented to the living a long time ago by an Oxford contemporary, Sir Digby Apperley of Chesney Lodge, when it became apparent that a college fellowship wasn't coming his way. Dr Ayliffe, as the phrase is, 'kept up his scholarship', and was understood to contribute to theological journals of the learned sort. He had never quite got the feel of village life.

Mrs Howland was a complaining woman. She was this so preponderantly that a tone of grievance accompanied her speaking voice whether or not she was referring to any identifiable cause of discontent. On his visits to the Apperley Arms the vicar listened with much patience to the dismal woman. This was the more difficult of achievement in that he felt patience to be not enough; that he ought to be admonishing Mrs Howland to that resigned and even cheerful acceptance of daily trials and small adversities incumbent upon one who would lead the active Christian life. But in fact he shrank from this, compromising upon a resolve to work something of the kind into his sermon when Mrs Howland next came to church. She didn't come very often.

Among the circumstances occasioning Mrs Howland's vexation of spirit it sometimes appeared that there had to be numbered the mere existence of her son Dicky. Dr Ayliffe, although he wasn't very sure that he liked the look of this particular juvenile parishioner, found the attitude peculiarly disheartening. He was a bachelor who kept a large photograph of his dead mother on his writing-table in the vicarage, and he judged it quite dreadful that a woman should ever speak other than in terms of warm affection of her son. So sometimes he simply didn't listen to Mrs Howland when the shortcomings of Dicky were her theme. The boy often stayed out later than he should at his age. He'd even get up in the middle of the night at times, just to go fooling around with owls. He could hoot at owls so that owls would hoot back at him. Now, what was the use of that? The vicar reflected that it might get you into a poem by Wordsworth. But as this thought would not have conveyed much to Mrs Howland he held his peace, and perhaps a little removed his mind to other matters. Then one day he became aware of this tiresome female as complaining that Dicky was also far too fond of playing with matches. It was right dangerous, she said, and there might be a fatality—which was something you couldn't afford in a licensed house.

Dr Ayliffe didn't see that fatalities were to be less afforded in a public house than anywhere else. Nor did he quite understand what Mrs Howland was worried about. Dicky was at this moment on view through an open door, scowling over his homework at a table in the pub's back parlour, and he was surely past the age when striking matches is commonly considered dangerous in the young. Not having heard from any of the Alfords about the little episode in the lambing hut, the vicar was unable to connect the behaviour complained of with any honourable ambition connected with Boy Scouts. It occurred to him that in some obscure way Mrs Howland was not being quite frank with him, and had some more substantial occasion for anxiety than she had avowed. The notion remained with him after he had left the Apperley Arms, and later that afternoon he retailed the incident to Miss Nott, the District Nurse. He knew that she frequently visited the pub in a professional way, the senior Howland being much afflicted with boils. She might keep an eye on the boy, and judge whether there was anything wrong with him.

Unfortunately Dr Ayliffe (who had a fine carrying voice) made this communication to Miss Nott upon running into her in the village post office—a signal instance of his innocence in face of the *mores* of rural society. In no time the news was all over the place that young Dicky Howland was a detected—or at least suspected—fire-bug.

Perhaps prompting the swift spread of this intelligence was a circumstance which in a vague way may have been in the vicar's own head. Only in the next parish there had recently been several cases of petty incendiarism in farm buildings and the like. As setting a match to this or that item of another man's property in requital of injuries actual or supposed is a fairly common feature of rustic life these sporadic incidents had occasioned no great remark, and rated only a brief paragraph in the local paper. Yet they did probably lend some impetus to the spread of this agreeable information, or misinformation, about the Howlands' boy.

Then, on the very next day, occurred the incident of the school's waste-paper basket. It was a very large basket, full of inky English compositions and grossly erroneous arithmetical calculations, and it was put out in the yard to be emptied perhaps a couple of times a week. On this occasion, and just before afternoon school, it was found to be blazing, and the schoolmistress had been so alarmed that she employed a fire extinguisher to deal with it. Perhaps because conscious that this had been to over-react, and that a bucket of water would have served equally well, she then took somewhat precipitate action. She might have reflected that it had been Mr Elcox's morning (Mr Elcox came to conduct Swedish drill on one morning a week) and that Mr Elcox was known to be careless with his cigarette butts. Instead of this, and with the previous day's news filling her head, she roundly accused Richard Howland of the deed. Dicky, at once scared and sullen, said he knew nothing about it, he didn't. At this the schoolmistress, who didn't like Dicky anyway, declared that he had yet further darkened his atrocious deed by telling a very very wicked lie. She then whipped Dicky—not only on the bottom but also, and equally painfully, on the calves as well. At the end of this performance Dicky managed to suspend his howling and blubbering for sufficiently long to spit at the schoolmistress copiously and with entire accuracy of aim. Whereupon afternoon school broke up in confusion. All the children ran home (in great glee about the spitting, which made Dicky something of a hero) and piously told their parents that a very bad boy had got the stick for trying to burn down the school.

The schoolmistress, who knew that she ought not to have beaten Richard Howland on the mere strength of an arbitrary suspicion, reported the incident to nobody, and even went into the local market town and bought a new waste-paper basket with her own money. So the children's lurid version of Dicky's delinquency passed uncontradicted into history. General Alford heard it, and retailed it to his schoolfellow Sir Charles Apperley, at that time a vigorous and youngish landowner like himself. Neither of the gentlemen judged it a very probable story, and they agreed that if that hideous little Victorian school-house *had* been burnt down it would have been a capital thing. The General however did tell his friend about Dicky's activity in the lambing hut.

Even the stoutest proponent of corporal punishment could not have maintained that young Richard Howland's flogging had done him any good. He swaggered among the other children in a new way, and was at times inclined to adopt the pose of a very wicked fellow indeed.

He treated the schoolmistress with thinly masked contempt and ridicule, intuitively aware that, for some time at least, she would be frightened to wallop him again. Whether justifiably or not, he resented what had been done to him, and it might have been said that the hurt to his pride was lasting longer by a good way than the hurt to his backside. One wouldn't, somehow, have expected a son of Mr and Mrs Howland to be a sensitive plant. But he was certainly touchy. He hadn't liked being called a little duffer by the General, even in a genial way. Still less had he liked being reduced to squealing and blubbering by an old woman with a cane. An uncharitable observer might have declared him to be the sort of person who is determined to get his own back one day, perhaps by some random outrage against society at large. But this would only have been a guess, and it was possible that Dicky's resentments didn't go deep. Nobody really knew much about him. Nobody had bothered to find out.

A few weeks after this something much more substantial than a school waste-paper basket went up in flames at Thorley. But on this occasion the school was again at least in the picture, or not far off it. Its playground lay next to the rick-yard of the home farm, and it was there that a large haystack was suddenly seen to be on fire round about eleven o'clock in the morning. There was quite a strong wind blowing; wisps of burning hay were floating all over the place in no time; the schoolmistress, perhaps rendered particularly nervous by her recent experience, judged it wise to evacuate the school until the fire-engine arrived. The only result of this precaution was to put her charges at some risk as they tumbled into the rick-yard to view the conflagration. There was naturally a good deal of excitement—more than there had been since a small and rather mangy travelling menagerie had set up in a neighbouring field a couple of years before. The children pranced around, shouting and singing, much as they might have done on Guy Fawkes night. Dicky Howland was of course among them, but few could honestly have maintained that he was more excited than many of his companions, much less that he had in any way been hinting that this was in some peculiar degree his show. But by this time Dicky was a marked man—or a marked small boy, and by that evening it was widely believed that he was a dire menace to the King's lieges in their lawful beds. Dr Ayliffe was extremely perturbed—so much so that he thought it well to call both General Alford and Sir Charles Apperley into conference. They were magistrates—Sir Charles, indeed, had recently become chairman of the local bench—and might find some means of obviating painful court proceedings.

'This is all nonsense,' Sir Charles said at once. 'So far, I mean, as the lad Howland is concerned. The police ought to be hunting for the fellow who had been up to these games over at Little Treby.'

'Quite right, Charles.' General Alford nodded vigorously. 'I've spoken to Miss Powney.' Miss Powney was the schoolmistress. 'She's most upset by this talk about the lad. She feels she set it going with that hullabaloo over the waste-paper basket. Made the kid tip an arse, you know, in a most unwarranted manner. However, she's a decent woman enough, and anxious to get this quite clear. The boy hadn't been out of her sight since the school clocked in after breakfast. Hadn't so much as asked to be excused—which it seems is what they say when they want to go out and pee. So he could have had nothing to do with it.'

'I devoutly hope it may be so.' The vicar spoke on a desponding note. 'But if the boy eluded Miss Powney's notice for five minutes it would have been enough. Or he may have employed some ingenious device. Some sort of slow-burning fuse.'

'Good Lord, padre!' Sir Charles exclaimed. He was at times an impatient man, and could even forget what was owing to one whose cloth had, so to speak, been draped on him by his, Sir Charles's, own grandfather. 'What notions you learned fellows can get in your heads. This lad isn't a professional anarchist, you know. Consider his years.'

'I would be very willing to give him the benefit of every doubt, Apperley. But there is abundant testimony that fire holds a morbid fascination for him.'

'Oh, come!' the General said. ' "Morbid" pitches it a bit high, you know. Say "unusually strong". Anybody can get a bit excited by a fire. It's one of those odd psychological things.'

'I have hesitated to mention it, Alford. But there is one report that is really disturbing. Howland ran about shouting and so on like the other children. But then—if old Ritchings is to be believed, and you will both know him as a most respectable labouring man—the boy suddenly went quiet; withdrew, as he thought, from public observation; and then behaved in what I must term a sexually reprehensible manner.'

Neither of the landowners addressed ventured to betray amusement at this vocabulary; they probably reflected that the vicar belonged to a generation in which boys were taught that only instant insanity could succeed upon such behaviour as Dicky Howland had now been indicted of. But General Alford, at least, was a little shaken by what he had heard—and perhaps spoke out the more firmly as a result.

'It may have been so, Ayliffe—although old men like Ritchings sometimes think they see something their minds have been running on. In any case, it would be no proof that it was this wretched boy who set the confounded rick on fire. More things can prompt to a bout of masturbation, you know, than the sight of a wench in her shift. It's all part of our being fearfully and wonderfully made.' The General had produced this thought of the psalmist by way of making amends for the perhaps too robust expressions that had preceded it. 'But the practical question is: What can we do?'

'I can preach a sermon against malicious gossip, I suppose.' Dr Ayliffe, although a serious man, was by no means incapable of humour. 'But if the boy is as innocent as I am anxious to believe—and I *am* quite as anxious as either of you—the fact won't help once the village people have a down on him. He'll be a black sheep—just as a matter of giving a dog a bad name.' The vicar frowned, conscious that a certain confusion attended these images. 'The lad would be better elsewhere.'

'Aren't those publicans shunted around by the breweries?' Sir Charles asked. 'It ought to be easy to find the top man in this particular concern. Likely enough we were at school with him—eh, Arthur? The place reeked of malt and hops, as I remember it. We could ask him—just as a favour to an old chum—to promote those unappealing Howlands. It shouldn't be difficult. The Apperley Arms is a pretty miserable pot-house, if you ask me.'

'Unworthy of the family name,' the General said with a chuckle. 'But it's an idea, Charles—distinctly an idea.'

'The boy could start again with a clean sheet,' Dr Ayliffe said.

'That's the state of his sheet already, in my opinion. Call it just a fresh start.'

But benevolent plans of the kind these three gentlemen were perpending take time to mature. This one was overtaken by events.

The village school had shut down for the Christmas holidays, and the schoolmistress, who felt it had been a trying term, had gone off to spend the festive season in the household of a married sister in another part of the country. The children fooled around, hoping for snow and ice. There had been another fire, this time at Great Treby: it was much more serious than the last, since a church hall had been destroyed. This spectacular incendiarism was generously reported, and naturally kept arson well to the fore in Thorley heads. Nobody was made more aware of this than Dicky Howland, and its effect was to enhance in him that nocturnal habit deplored by his mother. It was no season for hooting-matches with owls at midnight, but when Dicky was not to be found in his bed it was presumably activities of that sort that he was up to. By day he either skulked or went about in an ostentatiously defiant manner. Had a psychiatrist been around (only in those days there probably wasn't one within a hundred miles of Thorley) he might have declared that an identity crisis was confronting this boy; that in face of such group hostility—but also, perhaps, gratifying attention—he was uncertain what role to assume. The person who came closest to this perception about Dicky was Anne Alford, whose own holidays had begun. She was rapidly becoming an articulate girl, and she had the advantage of being very much Dicky's age. When she heard of Sir Charles Apperley's plan for promoting the innkeeper she didn't at all approve of it, and she rebuked her father for lending countenance to anything so unconsidered.

'If those Howlands are sent away,' she said, 'even if it's pretended they deserve a better pub, everybody will know that it's because of Dicky that they've had to go. And the story will follow them, too. So there will have been a kind of confession of guilt where I just don't believe there has *been* any guilt. And neither do you, Daddy. So I don't know how you can have been led into such a plan by that stupid Sir Charles.'

'Anne, dear, you must not call Charles Apperley stupid. He is a very old friend of mine, and if you wish to criticize his ideas—which I consider you have a right to do—it must be in terms of proper respect.' If General Alford spoke thus severely, it may have been because he knew that his daughter was dead right. 'Perhaps'—he added without sarcasm—'you have a better idea yourself.'

'Of course I haven't. I know I'm only an ignorant child.' Anne had lately become fond of this irritating remark. 'But I think they should catch the man who has been burning things down at Treby before he manages to roast some wretched old couple in their hovel. What's more, I think he may have made Treby too hot to hold him.' Anne didn't pause to invite appreciation of this bizarre joke, although she hadn't produced it inadvertently. 'He has started casting around more widely—and that's what explains our haystack.'

'I think that may well be true.' It was becoming one of General Alford's pleasures to be able at times to treat his daughter as a grown-up. 'And if an end were put to his activities, all this village interest in fire-raising would fade away, and the boy would be all right again.'

'He certainly isn't all right now,' Anne said with decision. 'I saw him yesterday, and it quite shook me.'

'Ah.' General Alford, too, had been shaken—chiefly by the disagreeable allegation preferred by old Ritchings: something that couldn't possibly be mentioned to Anne. At the moment he was a little struck by his daughter's enlarging vocabulary. 'The boy looks under the weather, would you say?'

'I think he may be beginning to wonder whether he ought to give people a run for their money.'

'Live up to his reputation, you mean?'

Anne Alford did take a moment to grasp this expression.

'Yes,' she then said vigorously. 'That might be it.'

The greater part of Thorley Park was destroyed by fire that night. The blaze had started in, and been detected while still confined to, the cluster of miscellaneous offices contiguous with the mansion. These included much disused stabling at ground level, with numerous equally disused small chambers, once the quarters of grooms and stable-boys and other humble persons, ranged in two stories above. A good deal of this was tinder-dry, and the construction of the roof-spaces was such that the flames were quickly funnelled into the upper ranges of the house itself. The local fire brigade, although not a professional and full-time organization, was mustered with commendable speed, and yet more remarkable was the rapidity with which enormous mechanical monsters appeared from Great Treby. Not much could be done, all the same.

Something—perhaps a falling tile or the splintering of glass—had awakened General Alford almost before anybody else was alerted to the disaster. He at once set about checking his domestic staff out of the house, with strict orders not to attempt to enter it again on any account at all. By the time he had done this the entire village had assembled, and he made it his next business to get the children out of the way. So Mrs Alford, who knew all about being a commanding officer's wife and setting an example to married quarters, firmly led off the protesting Anne to Chesney Lodge, and then returned (accompanied by Sir Charles) to add her authority to the carrying out of similarly prudent action by the other Thorley mothers.

So at least there was going to be no loss of life—unless, indeed, on the part of a fireman—and firemen were at risk by their own choice, after all. Assured of this, and with Charles Apperley beside him, the General was able to take a reasonably dispassionate view of the destruction of his ancestral home. Or he would have been, could he have been assured that confronting him was what the lawyers— rather oddly—call an Act of God. He very much wanted it to be an Act of God, since the notion of some individual malignity at work, even if it had been directed against him quite at random, disturbed him greatly. When the village constable, a stupid and good-natured man called Curley, came up to him with some muttered remark about collaring the bastard this time, he shut the man up with a sharpness that surprised himself.

It was a very cold winter night, and the fire was very hot. The flames were a lurid red and now seemed to stain the sky and the smoke rising up to it; but at play upon the mansion at the same time were arc lights from the monsters which somehow seemed as chilly as the north wind fanning the flames.

'It looks as if they may save the west wing,' Apperley said to the General. His voice was carefully matter-of-fact rather than designed to be heartening. 'Did they manage to get much out?'

'The silver is in what's supposed to be a fire-proof safe. Bullion by now, I expect. Burford'—this was the General's butler—'seems to have managed to pitch out a good many paintings. Competent chap, Burford. There will be things of my wife's that I'll be sorry about. And the books. Something nasty about the idea of books burning. Good show by the fire brigade, wouldn't you say? Fellows well on their toes.'

Thus were these two gentlemen sparely conversing according to their order when they were disturbed by a woman's scream from close behind them.

'Dicky—it's Dicky!' the woman screamed. She was Mrs Howland.

Other people were now yelling too, and it was certainly Dicky they were excited about. Even as a diminutive and blackened figure now vanishing behind a pall of smoke and now luridly lit by a flicker of flame, there was no mistaking his identity as, high overhead, he scrambled frantically to and fro on the very ridge of the fast-collapsing stable block. And, now that he could be seen, his own faint cries, terrified and despairing, could be heard above the roar and crackle of the conflagration.

'My God!' Apperley exclaimed. 'It was that boy, Arthur. And now he's done for—the poor crazy kid.'

Dicky, however, was not done for—although he too undoubtedly believed he was. Miraculously, a great red ladder with a helmeted man at the tip of it extended itself in air, swung, dipped, hung for a moment over a sea of flame, and then rose again with Dicky in the fireman's arms. It had been like the sort of legend in which an eagle swoops down and carries off an infant exposed on a rock.

A minute later Dicky Howland stood in the centre of a circle of hostile or merely curious and gaping villagers. Suddenly there were murmurs, angry shouts, and Constable Curley thrust hastily forward.

'Quiet, there!' Curley called out with all the majesty of the law. 'Hold hard! Hold hard, I say—I have my eye on you!' He had been only just in time to stop an ugly rush at Dicky. And it was upon Dicky that he himself advanced now. He put out an arm as if to grasp the boy. Then he paused and glanced towards General Alford. The General was a magistrate, which meant a good deal. For miles around the General owned every acre not owned by Sir Charles Apperley, and this meant a good deal more.

Dicky too looked at General Alford. The boy was cowering, trembling all over, as black as a sweep. He was not, it seemed, burnt—or at least not badly—but he smelt as if some demon barber had been singeing him all over. For a moment he looked fixedly at the General. The General looked fixedly back—but how sternly, with how condemnatory a regard, he perhaps didn't know. Suddenly young Richard Howland appeared to brace himself, square himself, plant himself less insecurely on the ground. He had stopped trembling—yet his whole body seemed to vibrate, all the same. His voice, which during this horrible episode had been the vehicle of nothing except the howling of a frightened child, now rose up in abrupt command of articulate speech.

'All right, then!' Dicky shouted at General Alford. 'It was me, just like you all thought it was. Do you hear—all of you?' And he glared wildly and defiantly round the assembled villagers. 'It was me, I tell you, *me!*'

There was a moment's utter silence—or what would have been that but for the continued roar of the flames. Again Constable Curley glanced uncertainly at General Alford. For a bare second the General hesitated. Then he gave a curt nod. Constable Curley led Richard Howland away.

More than a couple of days went by before the searchers—firemen still, but now also the insurance people as well—found the charred body of the fire-bug in the ruins of Thorley Park. There could be no doubt about his identity. The police at Great Treby had already guessed who was the man they were looking for. Intermittently insane or near it, he had served a term of imprisonment for arson ten years before.

While this strange dawn of knowledge had been heaving up slowly towards the horizon things had been happening at a different pace to Dicky. Mrs Curley had given him hot milk and biscuits while her husband had made rather agitated telephone calls. Just occasionally, Constable Curley had to lock up a drunk in a little place at the bottom of his garden, but he was unaccustomed to juvenile offenders guilty of such heinous crime that they must clearly be held in custodial care from the start. He didn't like it at all. So he contrived to get Dicky into the presence of the chairman of the local children's court shortly after breakfast next morning—remembering to take Dicky's father the publican along with him. Within twenty minutes of this formality Dicky was on his way to something at that time called a juvenile remand centre, there to await due processes of law.

Although the county was proud of its remand centre Dicky didn't find it a nice place at all. He believed it, indeed, to be what his schoolfellows called bad school: an institution in which he was liable to be confined for years, and get the stick every day. What he got straight away was a certain amount of unwelcome attention from some rather bigger boys who had settled in, grasped the hang of the institution, and perfected numerous varieties of instant torture to be deployed whenever the screws (as they precociously expressed it) relaxed their surveillance. Dicky was soon wishing very much that he hadn't, in his moment of extremity, told that rash and boastful lie. He was also frightened by his own complete lack of knowledge as to why he had done so. And he didn't, of course, have Anne Alford to enlighten him.

General Alford, on learning the truth, was appalled by his own behaviour. With a single nod he had in fact denied his own intuitive conviction about the pub-keeper's unfortunate son. Being thus furious with himself, he quickly became furious with other people, even ringing up the remand centre and demanding Richard Howland's instant release in a very high-handed manner. Being politely informed that these things took a little time, he drove up to London accompanied by Sir Charles Apperley, organized perhaps excessive legal assistance around him, and by that afternoon arrived before the portals of Dicky's prison accompanied by the elder Howland and armed with a brief but sufficient document obtained from a judge in chambers. So there was no fuss at all, and he drove the liberated child and his father straight home.

Dicky gave an account of himself on the way. It wasn't very coherent, but it certainly began with owls. There was a species of owl pre-eminently likely to be discovered in abandoned stabling, and he had gone in search of that. What he had found was a maniac busily engaged in burning the place down. With some rashness in the circumstances, Dicky had expostulated with this person, who had promptly pursued him through the building—this in nearly pitch darkness—with murder plainly in his mind. Dicky had fled to its upper regions, and there the maniac, taking a rash leap at him in the murk, had gone clean through a gap in the decayed flooring and fallen into what was already a lake of flame below. Dicky had then managed to find and climb down a loft ladder, and had done his best to haul the man clear—partly from a confused notion that, not himself having been murdered after all, he might be accused of murder on his own part if his adversary perished, and partly because he understood that a Boy Scout (he still aspired to be a Scout) was expected to behave in a heroic manner on occasions of the kind. But the fire had defeated him, and he had been obliged to retreat to the roof.

Such was Dicky's entire story. General Alford listened to it in silence, and ended by accepting its substantial veracity. He had of course other things to think of besides this unfortunate boy's strange history. He would have to find time for the whole business of getting the insurance settled and building himself a new house, and he would have to do this without docking ten minutes from his labours on the Imperial General Staff. But of course the boy was a decent boy, just as he had always supposed, and something would have to be done for him. Preferably, it ought to be on the estate, so that in an unobtrusive way secure employment could be ensured for him as he grew older.

Yes, that was it. Whatever was appropriate to his abilities and ambitions it must be put within Richard Howland's power to achieve.

A READING IN TROLLOPE

THE BALMAYNES SUDDENLY realized that they knew almost nothing about Roland Redpath. He had begun by coming around the place as one of their son Ronnie's numerous quite casual acquaintances. Ronnie had nothing to say about him, and although Redpath himself appeared to be a frank and conversable young man his talk had never happened to turn upon any personal past. This was entirely in order, or at least the elder Balmaynes contrived to accept it as being that. Neither Ronnie nor his sister Claribel reacted favourably to any question of the investigative sort about contemporaries whom they sometimes introduced to their parents. 'What does he do?' and 'Is she related to the QC?' and even 'Are they fond of tennis?' received answers which, although civil, carried some faint suggestion of tolerance or irritation in their tone. It wasn't that Ronnie and Claribel took up with any raffish crowd. They were both thoroughly sensible, thoroughly sound. They were merely subscribing, perhaps unconsciously, to one of the minor taboos current in their generation.

On several occasions, however, Redpath, without appearing to have become really intimate with Ronnie, spent a weekend with the Balmaynes in their country cottage. Lady Balmayne wrote the invitations, but Redpath was essentially her son's guest. That there were written invitations at all showed that the younger Balmaynes accepted certain antique ways unconcernedly enough. But when a young man joins you at tea-time and takes his leave of you after breakfast three days later it is usual and natural that you hear a word or two about his people and his school and so on in the interim. This still didn't happen. And it wasn't that Roland Redpath was buttoned up all round. He expressed opinions in the most forthright way on all manner of topics. He was incisive without being assertive and well-informed without being overwhelming. His manner with Sir Bernard in particular was just right, combining the deference properly owed to a senior man with the confident freedom of address customary between social equals, regardless of any disparity in age. At one point Sir Bernard inclined to the conjecture that Redpath must have had a spell in the Guards, and resigned his commission to begin a career with some family concern in the City. Sir Bernard didn't in fact know much about soldiers, or about the City either. He was an architect of some distinction in a specialized field, and his professional connection was mainly with the Church Commissioners.

The weekend occasions had all taken place before the elder Balmaynes became aware of a significant and disturbing switch in the young man's relations with them. He was now less the friend of their son than the admirer of their daughter. Neither of them could have said clearly why they were bothered about this. It was true that when they took a fully considering look at Roland Redpath they saw that the picture was that of a clever boy and able young man who had arrived from nowhere in particular, and who was of an assimilative temperament which absorbed almost unconsciously at least the superficial habits and obvious assumptions of the people among whom his talents had taken him. It was by no means an unattractive picture. Moreover the Balmaynes regarded themselves as being of a liberal cast of mind, and insured against vulgar snobbery by the security of their own position in society. They immediately told one another that facts of character—integrity and kindness and constancy and so on—were more important than family origins. They were confident that Claribel knew this too.

A little further information would have been agreeable, all the same. And by this time it would have been natural as well. Were Roland Redpath again coming down for one of those weekends at Graziers Lady Balmayne felt the position to be now tacitly such that she could properly seek some enlightenment about the young man's background, and that equally Bernard could briskly acquaint himself with the broad facts of his present position and prospects. This might be done without any 'square' stuff (as the young people would say) about Redpath's intentions and a natural parental anxiety and so forth. But Redpath declined two invitations running on the score of engagements he couldn't escape. It was almost as if he were deliberately turning elusive. Yet in the same period he came three or four times to the house and whisked Claribel off to a concert or theatre. It was worrying.

Ronnie didn't help. It was his attitude that he and Roland had rather lost interest in one another in a perfectly normal manner, and that he had never known much about him anyway. But he was a perfectly respectable chap, with brains enough for two, and he held down a more senior job as a psychologist in some university or other than might be expected of so young a man. If Claribel was taking it into her head to marry Roland Redpath he didn't see that there would be anything against it.

This was reassuring up to a point, but Sir Bernard continued to feel misgivings and to communicate them to his wife.

'Not a very regular profession, I'm afraid,' he said. 'I was lunching the other day with John Ormerod, whom I think you've met once or twice. He's a good deal older than I am, of course, but said to be still the best brain surgeon in London. He happened to say that no patient of his would get into the clutches of those fellows except over his dead body.'

'But we don't know, Bernard, that the young man is that sort of psychologist. If he were, I think he would be Dr Redpath.'

'Claribel says he is a doctor, but sees no occasion to use the title in private life. Perhaps that means that he holds a degree of the outlandish sort which some American colleges peddle for straight cash down.' Sir Bernard frowned, as he did when not pleased with himself. 'But, no—that's unjust and extravagant. Taken all in all, he seems a very decent lad. So I can't think why he's being a little less than straightforward now.'

'I'm not sure, Bernard, of that being altogether just either. I believe he feels some awkwardness about his suit'—Lady Balmayne smiled at her use of this archaic expression—'and is hanging back with us because of it. And I'm not wholly able to acquit Claribel of all blame. She must know more about Roland than we do. But she has almost nothing to say about him. It's her attitude that it's no business of ours. Of course, she doesn't express that in any crude or pert way. But it's vexatious, all the same.'

'I don't myself blame Clarrie at all.' Having made this firm declaration, Sir Bernard steered his thought in another direction. 'There are Redpaths in Bedfordshire, you know. Julian Redpath and I were in the same election, and went up to Corpus together later on. An extremely nice fellow, Julian. But—do you know?—he pronounced his name not Redpath but Rippeth. All that family do. Early in our acquaintance with this young man, I actually addressed him in the wrong way. It was mildly embarrassing. I had to say I'd come across his name, but remembered it as slightly different. Something like that. He seemed almost startled for a moment.'

'Young men can be sensitive in matters of that sort. Particularly if it is suggested that their own Joneses are not the Joneses who alone count.'

'Good heavens, Mary! You can't imagine I hinted anything like that.'

'Of course not, dear.'

'He's a nice enough boy, as I say, and may suit Clarrie very well. If he does, I shan't care twopence if he's an entirely new man. The career open to talent is one of the great strengths of our society. It's an immensely stabilizing thing. Without it, our sort might all be dangling from lamp-posts by now. And the conception ought undoubtedly to be extended to—well, the domestic sanctities, and matrimonial alliance, and whatever grand name one cares to give the thing.'

'I am sure that is the wise view, Bernard. And we must just wait and see how the matter develops.'

'Exactly. And we must make another attempt to get him down to Graziers. Meantime, my mind is quite at ease about it all.' Sir Bernard, who had taken a second glass of port during this after-dinner colloquy, nodded confidently. He was a little silent, however, during the rest of the evening.

Lady Balmayne was accustomed to this. It was the way her husband often behaved when he had a difficult professional problem on his hands. Usually it was how to make a new church, however designed, look like a church at all. But sometimes, she knew, it was a problem even more difficult than that. An architect nowadays frequently finds himself involved in, or at least on the fringes of, enterprises that strike him as of a morally dubious character. Sir Bernard's own ethical standards were very strict; there had even been times when this had made things hard for him; ultimately it had contributed to the high regard in which he was held by his colleagues. Here he prized his standing very much—and the more because he saw his instinctive and untroubled honesty as a matter of upbringing. He was proud, indeed, of what might fairly be called ancient lineage—which, paradoxically, was the very circumstance that would have rendered him of an open mind about a prospective son-in-law from among the most simply bred. But at the same time he was more proud of his father than of all his other progenitors put together.

That father, Raymond Balmayne, was a seventh son, and when no more than a boy fate perched him on a high stool in the counting-house of a large mercantile concern. It was the sort of position celebrated by John Davidson in the poem called 'Thirty Bob a Week', and if young Raymond didn't quite have to make do on that he had a lean time of it, all the same. It ought not to be said of him, in the common phrase, that he 'fought his way up', since this suggests a tooth-and-claw attitude from which he was constitutionally aloof. But he *made* his way. It was a way which, but for the stimulus of family tradition, might finally have established him as a much respected head clerk, honourably devoted to an employer's interests. As it was, he did better. He did better because he took risks—just as earlier Balmaynes, it might be claimed, had taken risks in battle or on the hunting-field. Nobody had ever so much as hinted that they were other than honest risks. For quite a long time, and after he was in the enjoyment of a substantial prosperity, there had been difficult corners to turn: the last of them when his eldest son, Bernard, was already a young man. He had no desire to see Bernard succeed him in what would thus have become a family business; he would much rather have had the boy make a career for himself in the Army or the Church or at the Bar. Nevertheless he was content with the choice Bernard eventually made. Had he insisted otherwise, Bernard would probably have obeyed, even to the extent of getting into a dog-collar. For Bernard had been (as people then said) strictly brought up, and he accepted his father's wisdom as unhesitatingly as he did his rigid moral code.

On this particular evening, and with the weighty business of Roland Redpath before him, Sir Bernard Balmayne may have been turning over aspects of this past history in his mind. He may have been a little wondering about Ronnie—a good-hearted lad, but one in whom family pieties and the duty of strenuous endeavour were not prominent. But much more he was wondering about Claribel, and what awaited her with an almost unknown young man. Sir Bernard had been lacking in candour when he told his wife that his mind was quite at ease in the matter. What troubled him was not the now patent fact that Redpath's background was undistinguished; it was simply that this aspirant to his daughter's hand (as he was certainly going to turn out to be) had disclosed no background at all. A family tradition declaring generations of labour on the soil would have been accept-able in its fashion. A mere taken-for-granted blank was not.

Sir Bernard and Lady Balmayne went to bed. Sir Bernard was not so preoccupied as to neglect the closing ritual of their day. It consisted in his reading aloud to his wife for an hour before they turned the lights out. They were both fond of biographies and memoirs, but for this nightcap occasion (as Lady Balmayne called it) they generally chose fiction: sometimes recent novels, but more commonly the 'standard' sort. In this way they had read, and sometimes re-read, many of the major Victorians, and Trollope had recently become their favourite. On this night, as it happened, a new novel had to be begun. They had decided on *The Prime Minister*, which Sir Bernard had read long ago but which was unknown to his wife. He collected the volume from his library now, and as he made his way upstairs he opened it and glanced at the table of chapter headings. 'Chapter I: Ferdinand Lopez,' he read, and was instantly appalled.

A moment before, he would have said that the story was all about Plantagenet's difficulties as First Minister of the Crown, and how they were increased by the impulsive and indiscreet behaviour of his wife, now Duchess of Omnium but still known to her intimates as Lady Glen. Nothing of the sort. Ferdinand Lopez (an unpromising name) starts the story. And when the fifth chapter is headed 'No-one knows anything about him' the reference is to Lopez still. Recalling this and much else, Sir Bernard was prompted to return the book to the shelf and choose another Trollope instead. What about *He Knew He was Right*? It was doubtful whether the old boy had ever written a better book. But, in a way, *He Knew He was Right* would be almost as bad. It was about another nice girl landed with an unknown quantity as a husband. He is, indeed, a man of family, but spends the greater part of the book playing Othello to his wife's Desdemona, and then goes slowly and tediously mad. So Sir Bernard abandoned the idea of a switch, entered his wife's bedroom, and explained what was in prospect for her with as much lightness of air as he could assume. Lady Balmayne was amused.

'But, Bernard,' she said, 'Trollope abounds in girls who make disastrous marriages and then face up to them quite idiotically and with enormous courage. And I'm sure this Ferdinand Lopez isn't in the least like Roland Redpath. I expect Trollope thinks of him as a Portuguese Jew.'

'I'm not certain about the Jew—but Portuguese, certainly. Only the point is that his origins are totally unknown. Listen.' Sir Bernard opened the book. 'Here's page three. "Though a great many men and not a few women knew Ferdinand Lopez very well, none of them knew whence he had come, or what was his family." '

'I don't see it need have mattered in the least.'

'And this.' Sir Bernard turned the page, unheeding. ' "It was known to some few that he occupied rooms in a flat in Westminster,— but to very few where the rooms were situate." And the girl's father, a widower and a respectable barrister of West-country stock, has to blame himself bitterly for weakly permitting her to marry a totally unknown man. Lopez moves in good society for a time, you see, because the Duchess foolishly takes him up. But he turns out to be a most atrocious scoundrel.'

'Bernard, dear, we don't know much about Roland, and I have agreed that it's rather worrying. But we can be as sure of his not being an atrocious scoundrel as we are that he doesn't live in a flat in Westminster. So do get into bed and begin the book.'

Sir Bernard did as he was told.

' "Chapter I: Ferdinand Lopez," ' he read. ' "It is certainly of service to a man to know who were his grandfathers and who were his grandmothers if he entertain an ambition to move in the upper circles of society. . . ." ' As Sir Bernard read on he began to find Trollope as soothing as he commonly did. But he was conscious that the little fuss he had made betrayed him as obstinately feeling that there was trouble ahead for Claribel—just as there was for Emily Wharton when Lopez made her his bride.

'I'm bound to say that I've been studying your father a little,' Roland Redpath said.

'Studying Daddy? You'd do much better to talk to him.' Claribel had lately become a little disenchanted with Roland's studious habit. They were in a pub now because he was going to write a paper on people in pubs. He didn't seem to be getting any fun out of it. Claribel, who (under his escort, it was true) had discovered herself to be quite good at actually conversing with unknown people in public bars, enjoyed these occasions much more. 'And I don't see,' she went on, 'that lately you've been giving yourself much chance of studying him, anyway. He must feel you're avoiding him.'

'He has said that?' Roland asked quickly.

'Of course not. Daddy wouldn't say such a thing to me, although of course he might to Mummy. I just have a sense of it.'

'Does he think I want to seduce you, without being bothered by your family?'

'There have been one or two young men about whom he did feel that, I know. But you're not one of them, Roland darling. I suppose it's humiliating, but you have to face it honestly. You're rather nice.'

'All right, all right.' Being much in love, Roland found all Claribel's jokes wonderful. 'But it is dodgy, all the same. You can't deny it. There's nothing more natural than that your parents should take it for granted you'll marry a man of their own class.'

'You and my father are of precisely the same class. You are both well-regarded professional men.'

'That's just an evasion, Claribel dear.'

'It's you that's evasive, Roland. We've only to go head on with a simple no-fuss announcement, and there can't possibly be any trouble at all. I'd agree that I'd be rather upset if Daddy did come down on the thing in a weighty way, and I know that you're being so cautious because you want to spare me any risk of that. But it's a misconception of my father's character. I'm almost inclined to tell you that you haven't studied him quite enough.'

'I believe you're right.' Staring into his pint pot, Roland said this with the brisk decision of the competent scientist he was. 'It's true there's nothing to be gained by delay. But I rather favour the old-fashioned thing.'

'What old-fashioned thing, darling? I don't believe I know her.'

'Don't be silly. The modern custom, of course, is just for the girl to tell her parents—probably on the telephone. But I think that, in the circumstances, I ought to have a go at your father first.'

'And seek his permission to kneel at my feet? Roland, what an old funny you are.'

'You know perfectly well I shan't make a stilted fool of myself. But, as I say, in the circumstances—'

'Jesus, Roland—*what* circumstances? Have you a dark secret?'

'I have, in a way.'

'Is it about your people? You have been rather cagey, you know. Nothing except that joke about being late-risen from the people, like the nobleman in Mr Wopsel's *Hamlet*.'

'Your memory's pretty good. I could make a first-rate research assistant of you, if it came to a pinch.'

'Stick to the point. Your father was—or is—what used to be called a common working man. Right?'

'Well, no—I don't think he'd have seen himself as that. He'd have seen himself—for he's dead, of course—as a cut above it. Or two cuts above it, for that matter. Unfortunately your father, and this is what really worries me, will instinctively see it precisely the other way round. My father was a menial, Claribel.'

'A menial? What an absurd word!'

'It's not an absurd idea. A ploughboy is of greater dignity than a buttons, and a navvy than a flunkey.'

'Was your father a flunkey, Roland?'

'He was a butler—and that's worse. A young flunkey, or a buttons, can run away, join the army, and become a Field Marshal. A butler is fixed in his little pantry for good, rinsing the decanters and counting the spoons.'

'Roland, this conversation is completely mad! It simply doesn't belong to this age at all.'

'Oh, doesn't it?' The butler's son checked himself, conscious of an unduly sardonic note. 'Shall I get you another lager and lime?'

'No thank you, Jeeves.' This joke came from Claribel a little uncertainly. It was only just dawning on her that Roland saw this nonsense as very serious indeed. 'Do you have dreams,' she asked (remembering her lover's profession) 'in which you are a butler yourself?'

'No, I do not. The thing doesn't haunt me, and I can promise not to bore you with it in future. Still, it's a legacy aspects of which do irk me from time to time. My name, for instance.'

'Your Christian name?'

'Oh, that! Well, no. Roland, I believe, was the name of a hunter belonging to one of my father's employers and much admired in the servants' hall. No—it's my surname. I oughtn't to be Redpath. I ought to be Hedgepath.'

'Hedgepath? There's no such name—or at least there's no such thing. There are hedgerows and foot-paths and bridle-ways, but—'

'It's a rare but genuine rustic surname in Herefordshire and round about. I suppose my father thought it odd, since he made the change, it seems. I'm sensitive about Redpath, as if it was a kind of theft. How bloody irrational we can be.'

'Yes, can't we? And even my father, I suppose. I do think it may give him a jolt—but not more than that. Do you know what he'll profess to be curious about? It will be whether your father was a *good* butler. "If the fellow was a good butler," he'll say, "he was a rare bird. And there's all the more chance his son will be a good psychologist." Mark my words, that's how Daddy will carry it off.'

' "Carry it off" is about right, no doubt. And he ought to be able to find out easily enough.'

'What do you mean by that?'

'Oh, nothing.' For the first time in Claribel's experience of him Roland Redpath was suddenly confused. 'Darling, let's forget the whole thing for a bit. Are you sure you won't have another drink?'

Claribel shook her head slowly. But her mind worked quite fast, and it seemed to her that there was a mystery here that ought to be cleared up at once.

'Roland,' she said, 'is there something more to this than you've told me? I don't mean that what you *have* told me is important at all, or need ever have been mentioned. But is there something else; something a little odder, which produces all this caution about my father —and that you really should, perhaps, have told me about, but haven't?'

'Yes, there is.' Roland was self-possessed again, and his main disposition appeared to be to admire Claribel's clarity. 'My father wasn't just anybody's butler. He was your grandfather's butler. It's as absurd as that.'

If it was an absurdity it yet wasn't, to Claribel's mind, an absurdity to keep under one's hat. She hated the thought of Roland's concealing it from her during their brief courtship, and equally she hated the thought of his considering it 'dodgy' in relation to her parents. Perhaps it was—just a little. But, even so, Roland ought not to have hesitated to present his small piece of family history to them in a perfectly matter-of-fact way. There was something almost servile in an impulse to be prudent and contriving about disclosing such a thing.

But Claribel was her father's daughter, and alert to the danger of allowing injustices or even petty unfairness to harbour in the mind. The notion that Roland's circumspection represented a kind of hereditary taint—equating him, in fact, with a groom who awaits a favourable moment before disclosing that he has neglected a horse— would be an aberration more shocking than she had ever fallen into before. Roland was quite blameless in being a little hesitant before the situation in which he found himself. Marrying into the family in which your father has been a servant can't be at all common, and when it does happen it is probably the consequence of some antecedent sexual misconduct. It was perfectly sensible in Roland to feel that he must mind his step.

Claribel didn't at all mean, however, to do this herself. She regarded the ball as now being in her court—she had told Roland so at once—and she proposed to bang it straight back over the net. She did so the following morning at breakfast—sitting between her parents and while passing her mother the toast. She had become engaged to Roland Redpath and intended that the marriage should take place quite soon. When he returned to his provincial university in a few days' time she was going to go with him and they'd look for a house. And a curious fact had turned up. Roland's father's original name had been Hedgepath, not Redpath. And he had been Grandad's butler long ago. Perhaps Daddy remembered him.

This was all a shade bald, and might have produced a silence longer than it did. Lady Balmayne would have spoken at once had she not felt able to rely on her husband's doing so with only the briefest pause.

'Clarrie, dear,' Sir Bernard said, 'we have been expecting this, so it's no surprise and we are very happy about it. We have seen enough of Roland to know that he's an excellent young man, and I don't doubt that his father was an excellent butler. But my memory of the senior Redpath, or Hedgepath, is quite vague. His being with the family was, as you say, a long time ago. Which is perhaps just as well, on the whole.'

'Just as well, Daddy?'

'Come, come, Clarrie—be a wise girl. It would be a little awkward if we were grand enough to have a butler ourselves still, and the senior Mr Hedgepath was standing behind my chair at this moment.'

Claribel felt that this thought, although just, need not have been so soon obtruded. But she had been right to take the bull by the horns. Roland was accepted, and all would be well. It would be unfair—again she was alert to this—to say that her father had capitulated before adroit shock tactics. He meant what he said, or at least he hoped that he did. And although her mother was quietly weeping, that was just one of her generation's curious forms of behaviour. After a great deal of marriage, Lady Balmayne was really contriving to be overjoyed that her daughter was taking on the same stiff assignment.

So now there were kisses, and some rather random talk about plans, and then Claribel was sent to the telephone to find out whether

Roland would come to dinner. It was with a slight trepidation that she picked up the receiver. She had of course told Roland what she was going to do, but now she wondered whether she had been right to jump the gun. Roland, she suspected, had been building up in his mind the pattern of a little confrontation scene with her father, and perhaps his male vanity would be offended that she had done the job herself. She knew about male vanity, having frequently bumped up against it in her brother Ronnie and been aware of its subtler operation in her father from time to time. But Roland reacted very favourably to her news. In fact he sounded uncommonly grateful and relieved. He would certainly come to dinner. But meantime Claribel must join him immediately. They would find the right shop and buy an engagement ring.

'Why don't men wear engagement rings?' Claribel demanded. She was extremely happy, and wanted to talk nonsense to Roland at once.

'They just don't. It isn't the custom.'

'What a feeble reply from a psychologist! They do wear weddingrings now, and they didn't use to.'

'Quite a lot do. I shall.'

'But not an engagement ring? One that's all dainty little diamonds?'

'If you order me to, I'll do it without turning a hair. But in all right-thinking minds dark suspicions will be aroused.'

'You mean it must be a cigarette-lighter, or a barometer, or something like that?'

'Gold cuff-links, darling. They're more personal, and just the same as a ring. The bonding symbolism inheres equally in both.'

'Roland, shall I ever keep up with you? The depth of your thought!'

'It won't be necessary. Now, stop chattering, woman, and catch the next bus.'

He had never addressed her as 'woman' before. She thought it quite enchanting.

Later that morning, and when they were alone together, Sir Bernard and Lady Balmayne held a less light-hearted colloquy.

'I'm sure it's perfectly all right,' Sir Bernard said. 'Only we must expect from time to time—well, little things like this. Obscure birth, indifferent breeding: they're bound to show up now and again, wouldn't you say? It would be unfair, it would be quite ungenerous, to expect otherwise.'

'Yes, dear. But just what little thing like this?'

'The chap's having left it to Clarrie. He ought to have tackled me himself. Strictly speaking, that is. Instinct of a gentleman, and so forth. I don't say it's important. In fact, I'm saying there will be a number of things we shall be well advised to think of as quite trivial.'

'Yes, Bernard, I'm sure that must be so. But perhaps Roland did fully intend to speak to you himself, only Claribel was a little precipitate.'

'I very much doubt it. He has had plenty of time.'

'He would *take* his time, Bernard. Because he'd think of interviewing you in quite a formal way. A man inclines to be formal if his manners have come to him rather late.'

'Ah, that's true! Yes.' Sir Bernard quite brightened at this sage remark.

'And we must be glad that Roland has overcome his disadvantages so well. It must partly be a matter of high intelligence. But he must be sensitive to quite little things—social nuances, you know. He always pleases me. And you may count your own blessings, dear.' Lady Balmayne had judged it time to be firm. 'He's not a man you would hesitate to take into your club, is he?'

'Good heavens, no! Sometimes, Mary, you seem to have the weirdest ideas about me.'

'Then there you are. And we had better forget all this business about Mr Hedgepath the butler.'

'Well, now, that brings me to a funny thing. The name rings a faint bell with me, but I simply remember nothing at all about a butler called Hedgepath. I can't see him in my mind's eye, or anything of that kind. And it even occurs to me that his son may find that offensive. It won't be flattering to have to say I can't recall a con-founded thing about his father. A butler is normally quite somebody in a household, after all—and positively a figure of awe to its children. So the chronology of the thing puzzles me. I must get it sorted out.'

'I don't think, Bernard, that Roland will very much want to have chats about his father. And I do think he might be offended if he formed the impression that you were poking around in his family's past.'

'My dear Mary, am I likely to do that? Of course Mrs Corler is almost sure to know, and I shall be going to see her quite soon, in any case. Yes, I'll ask Mrs Corler about Hedgepath.'

When Roland came to dinner all went as well as Claribel could have hoped. Ronnie was away from home for a few days, so there was just the old couple and the young. And the young couple were obviously so happy that their elders warmed to them. Sir Bernard had arranged with his wife that, although the occasion was so very domestic, he and Roland should remain for a little at the dinner-table after mother and daughter withdrew. The resulting conversation was entirely friendly. Contrary to Lady Balmayne's expectation, the young man actually introduced the subject of his family history himself. Not much, it was true, emerged, and Sir Bernard was careful to ask few questions. What did become clear was that Roland knew little about Raymond Balmayne or his household, for the simple reason that he had been born several years after his father had left the Balmayne service. In fact Horace Hedgepath could have been at Cray Hall only for a few years all told, and as a man comparatively young for his position there. And this must have been during a period at which the future Sir Bernard had been first in the army and then studying architecture abroad—years, in fact, in which he had seldom been with his parents except in their London house. He must have heard about the young butler down at Cray, and even seen him and talked to him from time to time. But nothing except a vague memory of the man's name had stuck in his head.

Sir Bernard again felt that there was perhaps something slightly injurious about this blank in his mind. He was, indeed, relieved that his future son-in-law's connection with the Balmayne family was so tenuous, was in fact non-existent. But he felt that he must offer some explanation of his ignorance.

'I was studying hard in Munich,' he said, 'and for some years was a bit vague about affairs at home. Moreover, and to tell you the truth, Roland, I hadn't been getting on too well with my father. My respect for him never faltered—but that quite common kind of father-and-son friction must have been there. I dare say you can recall something of the sort yourself.'

'Well, no—I can't, as a matter of fact. My father died when I was three. I was never given more than scraps of information about him. The business of his having been your father's man came to me only by chance from an aunt.'

'Is that so? Well, well!' It is possible that this additional piece of information was satisfactory to Sir Bernard in its way. It seemed further to distance what might be called the whole buttling connection. 'The trouble didn't last with me, of course. My father and I became great friends again later on, and I shall always account him as the prime agent in forming my character, such as it is. But those German years of mine coincided with a period of considerable strain in his career, and perhaps he became a little distanced from all of us.'

This exchange of confidence, although circumspect and slender, was to the satisfaction of both men, and hard upon it they rose and returned to the drawing-room. They were not, they probably felt, ever going to be very intimately acquainted, but a reasonable basis of understanding had been established between them. It was a point at which Sir Bernard would have done well to take his wife's advice and leave the long dead Horace Hedgepath in his near oblivion. That he failed to do so may be seen to some extent as a matter of bad luck. Had Mrs Corler passed from his ken long before, it is doubtful whether he would deliberately have sought her out for the somewhat invidious purpose of checking up on the antecedents of a prospective son-in-law. As it was, he owned the entirely laudable habit of paying regular visits to this ancient retainer of the family, treating her much as if she had been his nurse, although her actual position had been for many years that of his parents' housekeeper. It may be that there was a small element of vanity in Sir Bernard's thus maintaining contact with a person recalling the consequence and material prosperity which his father had won. But he was doing no more than act as his father would have acted—a decent regard for servants retired after long service having been in Raymond Balmayne's view among the minor obligations of life.

Mrs Corler was in no degree a financial liability, since Raymond (to whom she had been singularly devoted) had bought her an annuity when she left his employment. So Sir Bernard when he visited her two or three times a year was able simply to take along a suitable present chosen by his wife: a shawl or bed-jacket, perhaps, or alternatively some delicacy judged suitable for degustation in extreme old age. Each Christmas, however, Sir Bernard departed from this rule, sending the old lady a ten-pound note, together with a card saying 'With gratitude and best wishes from the entire Balmayne family'.

The recipient of these bounties lived in Pimlico, in the attic quarters of a small house owned by an elderly married niece. Although in no sense enjoying anything that could be called this niece's services, Mrs Corler was felt to be fortunately placed, since were anything to go seriously 'wrong' it was probable that the circumstance would be remarked within twenty-four hours or so and some appropriate mea-sure taken. Meanwhile Mrs Corler did for herself and her cat; took an interest in the Royal Family, sensational crime and the Nine o'Clock News; and was as yet free from culpable accident with her gas fire or her electric kettle. Sir Bernard had on several occasions expressed his willingness to make arrangements for her transfer into institutional care. But this had not been well received, and he had come to judge that matters were best left as they were.

On the present occasion he took a taxi to Pimlico, with an unusu-ally bulky present, a quilted dressing-gown, in a box on the seat beside him. He was not at all easy about his mission—about, that is, the particular aspect of this routine visit to which the term could be attached. Perhaps he would do well to drop it out of the programme. Was there not something demeaning in the proposal to extract from one former servant information about another—whose son was going to marry one's daughter? There quite clamantly was! Sir Bernard actually wondered at himself, and from this wonderment a small and fresh perception grew. To that faint bell which the name 'Hedgepath' sounded in his head, some unsatisfactory—or even sinister—timbre attached. Had he then suppressed some actively displeasing memory in the fashion that Roland Redpath's colleagues were fond of talking about, or had he sensed a withholding from him of some unfavour-able, if unimportant, information concerning the man which it would have been natural for him to receive? Something of the sort, although he had no idea what, must be prompting his present behaviour.

He had no idea what. But then suddenly, and as his taxi swung into Lupus Street, he *had*. Very definitely he had. Lupus . . . Lopez: perhaps the association of these names gave a fresh jolt to his obsti-nate sense of the inconveniences that may lurk within so untoward a parentage as Roland Redpath's. Hadn't some burglary taken place during the period about which he felt himself to be imperfectly informed? He could now remember his father referring to it, although briefly, as having been quite a serious affair. All the silver—and there was a lot of it—had been taken from Cray, and so had a good many other valuables as well. Moreover, unless he had got the story wrong, none of the booty had ever been recovered. His father, characteristi-cally, had made no tragedy out of it; the firm was beginning notably to prosper, and everything was no doubt soon replaced with interest. But wasn't it possible that the theft had been what the police call an inside job? As he asked himself this question, Sir Bernard admitted to his dismayed consciousness a further possibility that followed upon this one. It could only be for two or three years that the man Hedgepath had been his father's butler, and for a fairly young man to leave such good service so soon was surely something out of the way. *And he had changed his name!*

The fellow had changed his name to that which the Balmaynes' prospective son-in-law now bore. Confronted by this, Sir Bernard experienced a strong revulsion of feeling. He almost rapped on the glass in front of him and instructed the taxi-driver to turn back. Wasn't he in danger of discovering about Hedgepath something criminal that Hedgepath's own son possibly didn't know? Indeed, something that he *certainly* didn't know. For, consulting his sense of the young man, Sir Bernard saw that just this must be the case. Roland, indeed, had a little hung back about his parentage. But if such a grim fact as had now to be suspected harboured in the situation, Roland would have concealed it neither from Claribel nor from her parents. He was not that sort of man.

So here was a dreadful situation developing—and it wasn't one to which he could simply call a halt. A dishonest servant was something beyond the pale. It might be irrational and wrong, but he would never himself feel comfortable about his daughter's husband if this suspicion inspissated the uncomfortableness of his lowly birth. And it might be a suspicion merely. This meant that, having started it, he owed it to both Roland and Claribel to determine the truth.

The taxi had turned towards the river and was approaching the half-derelict little street, ignored by developers, humbly neighbouring Dolphin Square. He had to make up his mind, and it seemed to him that he must persevere with Mrs Corler, distasteful as this seemed. She was his only ready means to acquainting himself with the small obscure domestic event which had assumed such shocking proportions in his mind. But he rather hoped that Mrs Corler would recall nothing material about Hedgepath. It would quite probably be so. Her memory, as often in people of great age, was frequently vivid but as frequently patchy. The period she particularly liked to dwell upon was that of Bernard Balmayne's boyhood, which coincided with the earlier years of her occupying a station of responsibility and even grandeur at Cray. She hadn't, of course, been what was later to be termed a 'working' housekeeper, but neither had she been at the start 'superior' in any very definite way, let alone a member of the tribe of gentlewomen in reduced circumstances. She had worked her way up (as her employer, indeed, had done). Since retiring she had, it could not be denied, a little slithered down again, and you might never have guessed that she had once found no difficulty in controlling flighty housemaids, or even in holding the cook herself at a respectful distance. Sir Bernard had lately learnt, with high indignation, that the niece downstairs was disposed to regard her aunt as 'common'.

What Mrs Corler remembered, then, was what might be called the period of her apogee, and she had comparatively little to say of the years in which Master Bernard was 'Master' no longer, and had become first a 'varsity' man and then largely an absentee and a citizen of the world. Moreover she had an odd touchiness at times, and would obstinately refuse to recall matters which were plainly not really eluding her memory. Sir Bernard, as he rang the door-bell to gain admittance from Mrs Corler's snobbish relative, indicted himself of considerable confusion of mind in face of all this. He seemed to be proposing to conduct a catechism to which he hoped to receive no answer. It wouldn't do; he must get his purpose clear before entering the old woman's presence. And to this he was at once assisted, as it turned out, by Mrs Peglin. Mrs Peglin was the niece, and she claimed at one time to have held some connection with the legitimate stage. She had at least carried away from this an extravagantly accented speech and an addiction to what must be thought of as grease-paint rather than mere cosmetic aid. Her figure was flabby and shapeless but her features were cragged and deeply lined; her hair was a dirty chaos and nothing else. Much more, if it were useful, could be said in dispraise of Mrs Peglin's person, and Sir Bernard disliked it only less than he did her personality. He thought her a horrible old gin-sodden wretch, although in fact she was probably no more than an inadequate and defeated woman perpetually on the verge of cracking up. As on numerous previous occasions, Sir Bernard told himself that Mrs Corler ought not to be even remotely in the charge of such a creature, and that he was much to blame for not having taken some firm action in the matter long ago. Nor ought he to have failed to consider how much Mrs Corler's annuity from his father had probably been hit by inflation.

His immediate reaction now, however, was rather different and not particularly logical. Here was what used to be called low life, and he would not, when within its miasma, put on a low turn himself. To say that it was only fair to Roland Redpath to discover whether or not his father had been a scoundrel was, if not humbug, at least sheer muddle. Roland's father was Roland's business, and he himself ought to keep out of it. During this brief visit to his father's former house-keeper he would make no reference whatever to his father's deceased butler.

The sense that this was an oddly belated resolution, and that he had betrayed himself into a marked infirmity of purpose, didn't improve Sir Bernard's manner with Mrs Peglin. He even asked her—very absurdly—whether Mrs Corler was at home. But this expression—belonging, as it did, to high rather than low life—didn't offend a lady who recalled herself as an ornament of the West End stage, and she waved her hand towards her narrow dusty staircase with the air of a court chamberlain according the *grande entrée* to a person only of lesser consequence than himself.

'She never goes out,' she said, 'despite my utmost endeavours when it's a nice day. It would do her good. It would freshen her up—a thing needful to my mind, Sir Bernard. She may be nigh losing the use of her feet, for aught I know.' Mrs Peglin's idiom had always been a little peculiar, perhaps as bearing traces of 'period' parts she had sustained in youth. 'The shadows lengthen and the scene darkens—which is only the sad legacy of eld, after all.'

'No doubt it is, Mrs Peglin. But you will recall that I have particu-larly asked to be informed should there be any marked change in your aunt's health. Please remember that.'

'Go up and look for yourself.' Mrs Peglin did now show some sign of taking umbrage at this stiff note. 'Her physician has attended her, and at my own behest. On account of her rambling chiefly, although incontinence looms ahead. We end as running brooks, do we not? But it's her speech at present. She prattles like a shallow stream over the pebbles. "Confabulation" is what the doctor says.'

'Does he, indeed?' Sir Bernard was not quite sure of the force of this word when used in a technical sense, but reflected that it must be familiar to Roland. If it indicated, as he conjectured, persistent and pointless fibbing, it was just as well that he had abandoned the thought of putting Mrs Corler in a notional witness-box. 'I'll go straight up,' he added abruptly. And he gave Mrs Peglin a nod more dismissive than was wholly accordant with the fact that he was standing in that lady's hall.

*　　*　　*

The staircase was lined with photographs of male and female theatrical celebrities of a former age, each stepped a little above the last, so that one felt one ought to be moving past them on an escalator. All bore the appearance of signatures and even affectionate messages, but these had already been printed on them when they left the shop. Sir Bernard doubted whether there was any longer a lively trade in such naive deceptions; they were as outmoded as horse-brasses and bogus warming-pans in a pub. Mrs Peglin belonged to a discarded age, and Mrs Corler to an age before that. Mrs Corler must be nearly ninety, and entitled to confabulate if she wanted to. Sir Bernard had probably been insufficiently alert to degenerative processes going on in her during the last few years. It was something that made the idea of interrogating her additionally inapposite. He would simply hand over his gift, make kindly inquiries and remarks, and come away.

Her little living-room (it was both parlour and kitchen, although her dwelling did run to a bedroom as well) was unchanged since his last visit—only perhaps a trifle stuffier, as Mrs Peglin had hinted. The gas-fire, economically constructed so as to operate either on two little burners or on four, produced an innocent smell, not to be taken exception of. There was also a fish-like smell which was disturbing until one noticed, strung up across the closed window like gardening gloves put to dry, a couple of kippers that had probably been forgotten about. Before the fire Mrs Corler's cat sat on the mat, surrounded by the heads, tails and vertebrae of further fish. Sir Bernard had to make no additional inventory, nor recall in detail the starched and chintzy propriety of the housekeeper's room at Cray, in order to conjure up reflections of the *tempus ferox, tempus edax* order. He was given little time, however, for this indulgence, since Mrs Corler had instantly risen from her chair to greet him. She had risen and then at once appeared to stumble, so that Sir Bernard started forward to save her, and even the cat was alarmed. But—was it possible?—what Mrs Corler had been minded to contrive was a curtsy. She had always— and even then it had been an antique usage—performed this reverence before either of Sir Bernard's parents, but certainly not before the younger members of the family. She must be confusing father and son now. So strong was her visitor's persuasion of this that he involuntarily exclaimed 'I'm Sir Bernard,' before realizing the mild absurdity of the statement.

'I'm very much honoured, Master Bernard, I'm sure.' Mrs Corler invariably produced these words, and invariably accompanied them with a gesture of restrained elegance in the direction of a chair. It was Sir Bernard's mother's gesture, and it always touched him on that account.

'I hope you're feeling fit, Mrs Corler,' he said. (Honesty forbad 'I'm delighted to see you looking so well'.) 'And I've brought you a small present which my wife and I hope you'll like.'

The quilted dressing-gown was a success. Mrs Corler, although too refined to don such a garment even over day-clothes in the presence of a gentleman, was certain that it was what she had desired for a long time; prompted to an enhanced hospitality by the gift, she turned on the two additional jets on the gas-fire and made proposals for brewing tea. But presently the kettle was steaming away unregarded, the old lady having discovered a great deal it was incumbent upon her to say. Sir Bernard couldn't remember her ever having been so talkative before. Disconnected fragments of Balmayne family history seemed endlessly at her command, and she recounted them with a surprising vividness but in a complete chronological confusion. It was some time before Sir Bernard realized that what he was listening to was matter and impertinency mixed, although the effect was not so apocalyptic as in King Lear's case. It was quite amiably for the most part, indeed, that Mrs Corler was making things up, and her motive was perhaps a harmless desire—shoved into this shabby corner as she was in unregarded age—to render herself interesting to a distinguished visitor. Probably, Sir Bernard thought, *that* was what confabulation was. So he listened to the old creature patiently enough, although at times his mind wandered. He felt relaxed and not a little pleased with himself, if the truth be told. He had come to a wise and honourable decision, worthy of his father, in deciding not to pump Mrs Corler about her long-since deceased fellow-servant, Hedgepath later Redpath.

'My little niece read it to me out of the newspaper,' he suddenly heard Mrs Corler say.

'I beg your pardon?' It was a moment before Sir Bernard realized that 'my little niece' must be Mrs Corler's rather grand way of referring to Mrs Peglin downstairs. But what the woman had read out of the newspaper had escaped him entirely.

'Miss Claribel's engagement, Master Bernard. I hope she has found a nice young gentleman, fully worthy of her, and proper to enter into your own family in a manner of speaking, sir. A Mr Redpath, my little niece read out.'

'Yes, Roland Redpath. An excellent fellow, I am glad to say, Mrs Corler.' It was astonishing, Sir Bernard thought, how the old soul had suddenly come bang up to date. It was also—but how irrational this was!—a shade alarming.

'And what is Mr Hedgepath's profession, sir?'

'Not Hedgepath—Redpath.' Sir Bernard's eyes had rounded on Mrs Corler. It was almost as if she were threatening to reveal herself as endowed with some sinister and sibylline power. 'He's a psychologist—a kind of scientist, that is.'

'The one name must have reminded me of the other,' Mrs Corler said—so prosaically that she at once seemed no more than a commonplace old woman again. 'You'll remember Hedgepath, Master Bernard?'

'Barely, if at all.' Sir Bernard got to his feet with some notion of taking his leave at once. Perhaps only his sense of the ludicrous nature of this reversal prevented him. He had resolved not to pursue Mrs Corler with Hedgepath. Now she seemed to be showing every sign of pursuing him.

'A regular rascal, Mr Hedgepath was.' Mrs Corler appeared not to have noticed her visitor's desire to depart. 'But at least they put him where he deserved.'

'Do you mean he went to gaol?' This was an unnecessary question. Sir Bernard knew very well that Mrs Corler meant just that. Out of the blue, his worst fear had been confirmed. His daughter was going to marry the son of a convicted criminal! 'It was over the burglary?' he added weakly.

'Of course it was over the burglary.' Mrs Corler had been surprised by this question. 'You were in foreign parts at the time, I remember. But your father must have told you all about it.'

'Very little, as a matter of fact.'

'Well, he did say he wanted no great sensation made, and the whole thing soon forgotten about. I believe he was quite glad that Hedgepath got off lightly. It was because they said he was a minor figure—a dupe, they said—who supposed he was only helping with some petty theft. He was out in two or three years, I believe. But I never saw him again.'

'It may have been just as well.' This was an almost meaningless remark, and witnessed to the extent of Sir Bernard's perturbation. There could surely be no question of Mrs Corler romancing now, for her speech was coherent and her manner matter-of-fact.

'Only I did hear that he had changed his name, and so got into respectable service again. Would you know about that, sir?'

'No, nothing at all.' It was with astonishment that Sir Bernard Balmayne heard himself thus utter a blank lie to a faithful old family retainer. 'I am afraid that I must leave you now, Mrs Corler. Unfortunately I have an appointment with a client.'

'You must be a busy man, I'm sure, Master Bernard. And that's just as your father was. But it was wonderful how, with all those great concerns on his hands, he could take thought about everything at Cray. Like that time with the silver and all those other valuable things.'

'What time, Mrs Corler?' It seemed to Sir Bernard that the old woman must be beginning to ramble again. But he asked this question patiently enough. In fact he sat down again. His agitation was subsiding. He now knew the worst about Roland Redpath's father, and it was knowledge he must learn to put up with. There seemed no reason why he should ever share it with anyone. 'Do you mean,' he added suddenly, 'the time of the burglary?'

'There we were, you see, just the master and myself, hard at work all through the small hours.' Mrs Corler had ignored Sir Bernard's question as one to which an obvious reply need not be given. 'The thieves had been surprised or alarmed, you see, and had got away with very little. And, of course, only Hedgepath was ever caught. I can see the master now.' Mrs Corler paused in order to emit, quite suddenly, a shrill cackle of laughter such as Sir Bernard had never heard from her before. It was so senile in suggestion that he had to return to the view that nothing she said was to be relied upon in the slightest degree. 'I can see him now,' she repeated, 'the most handsome man in England, to my mind—'

'My father?' Sir Bernard asked, momentarily surprised as well as bewildered. It had never occurred to him that Mrs Corler's devotion to her employer might have included a strong romantic component.

'Of course. There he was, working as hard and carefully with newspaper and straw and the like as if everything had been crystal, and himself from Pickfords or Carter Patterson.'

'Good heavens, Mrs Corler! Whatever are you talking about?'

'He didn't trust the police, he said. Not even to protect Cray from another and more successful burglary straight away.'

'This—this nocturnal activity you shared with my father was just after Hedgepath and his accomplices had made their attempt? I simply don't understand you in the least, Mrs Corler.' Sir Bernard was shocked by the dismay in his own voice. 'What were the police saying about it all?'

'I don't know.' Mrs Corler was momentarily doubtful. 'I think they mayn't have been called in until the morning. We'd got everything out to the barn by then, ready for the master to take to his bank later. Of course we had to keep quiet about it, he said—himself and me. Otherwise there might be a misunderstanding by the insurance company.'

'I see.'

This was true. Sir Bernard could scarcely believe that he saw. But he did.

'Mrs Corler,' he asked, 'have you ever told this story to anybody else?'

'No.'

'Not even to your niece, Mrs Peglin?'

'Certainly not, sir. But I remember it well enough. The master ended in such high spirits, you see. He even made a joke before sending me off to bed.'

'A *joke*?'

'He said, "Corler helps to turn the corner". I didn't understand it, sir. But the master did seem to find it very funny.'

Sir Bernard Balmayne spent a night as sleepless as that which Mrs Corler had called to mind—or had invented. The crux of the matter lay there. She was a dotty old creature and utterly unreliable. A good deal that she had said earlier in that dreadful interview had been demonstrable fabrication—and some of it of a sensational sort. But that purported joke of his father's carried a horrible suggestion of authenticity, and he doubted whether the decayed mind of Mrs Corler could have made it up. Moreover the story, fantastic though it was, seemed coherent in its way—and to cohere with other things. Raymond Balmayne had always taken risks, and they had sometimes left him with awkward corners to turn quite late in his career. It was conceivable that what the insurance company had paid out, together with some subsequent criminal trafficking in the spoils of Cray, had provided a bridge which, although comparatively slender, had carried him safely over a financial chasm.

But it was all in doubt. That, surely, was the truly terrible thing. He had been telling himself that he couldn't live comfortably with an uncertainty as to whether his daughter's husband was the son of a crook. Now here was the same uncertainty about his own heredity!

What could he do about it? What could he do about it without starting a scandal that would be only the more intolerable if it turned out to be wholly unfounded: the mere fantasy of a crazed old servant? His only course, he saw, was to sound Mrs Corler again—and then perhaps, in the most confidential fashion, bring in physicians who could assess her state of mind. As preliminary action, indeed, this was his only feasible course.

He was in Pimlico once more before noon. For some reason there was a little knot of idle persons staring up at the house from the other side of the street. Suddenly full of a wild misgiving, he rang the door-bell violently, and was confronted by Mrs Peglin at once.

'Can I see Mrs Corler?' he demanded abruptly.

'That, Sir Bernard, you can not.' A sense of high drama clearly possessed this beastly woman. 'The final curtain has fallen on that blameless life. My poor aunt has passed away.'

Sir Bernard stared at Mrs Peglin unbelievingly. He felt a little dizzy. Was it possible that the excitement of her yesterday's disclosure had been too much for the aged housekeeper and that she had failed to survive it?

'Dead?' he said.

'It was that dressing-gown, Sir Bernard. She went too near the gas-fire in it. The doctor from the police says it must have been all over within a minute. We must be thankful that no foul play can be suspected.'

So Sir Bernard was never to know. Without danger of publicity impossible to contemplate, there was nothing he could do. He had to live with the doubt, and he lived with it alone—saying not a word even to his wife. Claribel's wedding took place quite soon. Roland Redpath (who clearly had never heard of his father's felonious behaviour) had been modestly dissimulating the fact that he was a very up-and-coming young man indeed. In fact he knew that he was about to be appointed to a Chair at Cambridge, and that no house in a provincial wilderness would be required. So quickly did all this happen and transpire that the Balmaynes were still involved with *The Prime Minister* when the couple returned from their honeymoon. There

were several chapters to go before Ferdinand Lopez, that unspeakable son of an unknown Portuguese father, should precipitate himself
under a train.

THE CHOMSKY FILE

It was some years since Herbert Humbert had published anything, even an article in a journal. He was beginning to be worried by this. More and more in England—as for long in America—you had to keep in print if you were to hold your place in the academic rat race. A man must 'contribute to his subject' in a manner immediately apparent on a library shelf. It was no good being a brilliant lecturer, or a tutor whose talk had fructified whole generations of young minds. It no longer even much helped to be known as a nice chap, guaranteed not to rock the boat, and always ready to lend a colleague a hand. Print it had to be, followed by decently respectful even if somewhat astringent notices in periodicals with titles like *Modern Language Notes* or the *Journal of English and Germanic Philology*.

Humbert had to think and count for a minute before being sure of when the *Review of English Studies* had published a paper of his with the challenging title, 'The Yale Formalist Fallacy'. That had looked like something of a break-through at the time. But nobody—or certainly nobody at Yale—had paid any attention to it, and somehow he had failed to follow it up. To follow it up in print, that is to say, for he had done plenty of thinking about the subject, and about the Theory of Literature in general, since then. And indeed literary aesthetics (if the term were still an admissible one) had been his single passion since he was an undergraduate. He had filled scores of notebooks with his enquiries in this supremely fascinating field. But he hadn't yet, somehow, managed to sort out the complexities, ponder and resolve the contradictions, establish a systematic approach to the grand problems.

Significantly as it was to transpire, this unsatisfactory state of the case was particularly troubling him on the day he ran into Vivian Cardwell. It happened in the London Library, the *habitués* of which, on the whole, may be said to cough in ink and each to know the man his neighbour knows. An erudite homogeneity is the rule. Yet in this instance you could have told at once that here was an encounter between two scholars inhabiting substantially different worlds. Cardwell, only the more certainly because so unobtrusively, betrayed himself as one who might have stepped out of a club in St James's round the corner. This was a matter of his bearing rather than of his clothes, although these would have declared themselves—at least to a stray emissary from the *Tailor and Cutter*—as having started off in life in the same superior quarter of the metropolis. Humbert, in a way, would have been harder to place. His garments, of a marked antiquity, had certainly come from off the peg at Marks and Spencer, and there was something badly wrong with his shoes. But in the London Library there is nothing out-of-the-way about this, since an honourable disregard of sartorial nicety frequently characterizes members of the learned classes. Humbert's singularity lay elsewhere.

It lay partly in his limbs and head, which appeared always to be in tentative movement in a clumsy and uncoordinated way. His features exhibited a similar mobility and, as it were, irresolution—his forehead and mouth and eyebrows, and even his insignificant and rather stubby nose, being inclined to dispose themselves simultaneously under the influence of what could only be read as quite unrelated emotions. His articulation was at times indistinct and halting, as if he were uncertain which of two speeches he had embarked upon, and he had a slight tendency to spit or slobber. People sometimes said impatiently that Herbert Humbert was like a great baby. And then somebody might add, almost resentfully, that he had uncommonly striking eyes. This was certainly true. Mysteriously yet unmistakably, Humbert's eyes spoke of something a little beyond a common scholar's capacity.

'Herbert—God bless me!' This apostrophe reached Humbert as he had his nose buried in one of the lower drawers of the author-catalogue—which meant that he must have been recognized more or less by the cut of his backside. He may have judged this to be the more remarkable when he straightened up and turned round, since here was a man who hadn't set eyes on him for years—but who now touched him affectionately on the shoulder, nevertheless.

'Vivian—well, well!' Humbert's slight stutter accompanied this. It was almost as if he had said, 'Sir Vivian—well, well!'—which might have been proper to a person only slightly known to him. In fact, he and Sir Vivian Cardwell had in youth been close associates for two or three years. They had seen one another quite frequently after that—perhaps for two or three years more. Then the relationship had faded out. Since they continued to have common intellectual interests this ought not to have happened. It hadn't been the intention of either man in particular. Men do drift apart. Awkward train journeys, crowded engagement-books, possessive wives and exacting children, covertly conflicting social assumptions may all be at work. In this particular instance Cardwell had to shoulder the main burden of fault—this even although Humbert was a difficult man and he himself would have been universally described as eminently an easy one. Cardwell was rather wealthy as well as rather grand, and Humbert was a poor devil of a lecturer in an obscure corner of the University of London. So if the present encounter was something that had to be 'carried off' it was primarily up to Cardwell so to carry it.

He did this with no appearance of effort at all, making a merely whimsical business of those disregarding years. Nor did Humbert fuss over them. Long ago he had regretted that Vivian owned a country house and a substantial estate—and some sort of hereditary position in a merchant bank into the bargain. He had regretted this, foreseeing that the various cares and responsibilities involved would be likely to distract his friend from the pursuit of those purely intellectual interests for which, as an undergraduate at Cambridge, he had shown himself to be so exceptionally well-endowed. Humbert felt this loss to scholarship and learning more strongly, perhaps, than he did the severance of a personal relationship. He was a bachelor, who had taught himself to get along fairly well without much in the way of friendship or the domestic affections; in fact it might have been said that other people scarcely came into his head at all except as having made some contribution—inevitably quite small, more often than not—to the sum of human knowledge. This temperamental slant had ensured his accepting without resentment Vivian's having drifted out of contact with him for so long, and he envied him nothing except, conceivably, the elegance rather than the power of his mind—that and his ability to do without effort what he also did well. For Humbert, although a dedicated scholar, was not without a streak of personal ambition. He would have liked fame. He would even have liked—he would very much have liked—the mere academic advancement that had failed to come to him.

'I don't often run up to town nowadays,' Cardwell said. 'They've turned me out of that weekly meeting at the bank, you see—telling me to look to my acres. The Funds are all very well. But a score of good ewes may be worth ten pounds at Stamford Fair.'

'I'm sure they may, Vivian.' Humbert dimly remembered how Vivian and he had played some sort of primitive quoting game out of Shakespeare. 'But it must give you more time for *Concrete Universals in Literature.*'

'In what? Oh, yes! I do remember. But I don't think I'd call the book that now. It's not much of an affair, and I wouldn't want to weigh it down with an ink-horn term on the title page.'

'It exists? It's finished?' Humbert's features lit up—nearly all over. 'What splendid news!'

'Yes, it is finished—so there's no question of now having more time for it. Although I do take it out of the drawer and glance over it now and then.'

'You don't mean you're not going to publish it?' Humbert asked. His tone indicated bewilderment and dismay. 'Why, Vivian, it's bound to be a masterpiece!'

'Come, come, my dear chap.' Cardwell's answering tone was designed to be whimsically tolerant, but a note of something like irritation sounded through it. 'Masterpieces don't occur in that line of business. Books about books are all a matter either of graceful gesture or clever concoction. Don't you think?'

At this juncture something slightly untoward happened in the London Library. A young man had paused hoveringly beside these two elderly ones, with a momentary air of feeling entitled to listen to their conversation and even perhaps to join in it. He was an unnoticeable young man, so pale and pinched and bespectacled that he looked very like an ink-horn term himself. Humbert and Cardwell had, in fact, both failed—again for the moment—to notice him, perhaps because they were more concerned than they realized to sound out the revived relationship between them. And it so happened that Cardwell's last remark to his friend, which had been an appeal for concurrence in a mildly humorous view of things, had the appearance, through a casual turn of the head, of having been directed challengingly to this new-comer on the scene. The new-comer's reception of the small infelicity was scarcely urbane. He scowled contemptuously, muttered something to Cardwell that sounded distinctly rude, and marched quickly off into the nearest book-stack.

'Do you know that young man?' Cardwell asked.

'Oh, yes—very well. And he seemed upset.' Humbert gazed in perplexity in the direction in which this uncivil person had vanished. 'I wonder why? His name is Bernard Hinkstone, and he was one of the best pupils I've had in years. We don't often talk about "pupils", as a matter of fact. We just say "students", as if nobody in particular was responsible for them. It's not as in Cambridge, you see.' Humbert said this a shade wistfully. 'Hinkstone came to us from Christ's Hospital—the Blue-coat School, you know—and I've tried to help him along. He has rather a dreary job in a polytechnic now. But his real interests are close to mine—and yours.'

'I see.' Cardwell didn't feel very drawn to the unmannerly young Hinkstone. And he was aware that it was now up to him to do something definite about this encounter with one who brought a strong claim in the way of former friendship along with him. 'Herbert, do you by any chance have time to lunch with me?'

'Certainly I have.' Humbert sounded as surprised as if luncheon were something hitherto unheard of, which Cardwell had now invented on the spot.

'That's capital! We have all sorts of things to talk about, wouldn't you say? If we want to be quiet, we can go to—' Cardwell had been about to say 'my club', but a glance at Humbert's outward man made him change his mind. 'We can go to that little Italian place, just round the corner in Duke of York Street. I dare say you drop in there yourself from time to time. It's not half bad.'

'It needn't be even that, Vivian, so far as I'm concerned.' Humbert spoke with a sudden warmth, and those remarkable eyes flashed as if the mind behind them had abruptly dredged up from memory days of golden association long ago. 'If we can really talk, pulse and tap-water would do.'

'So it would!' Sir Vivian Cardwell rose manfully to the pitch of this. 'But we can have a bottle of tolerable chianti, all the same.'

They had come together as freshmen at Trinity, in the first place simply as having rooms on the same staircase. Trinity was Vivian Cardwell's natural college from the moment it had been decided that he was not to follow his father to Christ Church at the other university. For Herbert Humbert, contrastingly, it was as is the non-watery world to a fish—or it was this in every regard that didn't directly concern gaining in a Tripos the hall-mark of a first-class mind. Neither of the young men had any athletic interests, so they weren't going to meet in a boat on the Cam. Cardwell belonged to a kind of secret college society so intellectually distinguished that it held even the most brilliant examination performances in slight regard; Humbert had possibly not so much as heard of this elite coterie. For some weeks they had just failed of physical collision on emerging simultaneously from their sets, or while respectively dashing upstairs and down. Then there had actually been a bump, in consequence of which Cardwell had let fall a recently published book called *Seven Types of Ambiguity*. Within minutes this treatise (which they were quite soon ungratefully to regard as mere chicken-feed) had revealed them each to each as kindred spirits. Or perhaps not quite that. It might have been more accurate to speak of similarly orientated intelligences. They sat up with one another regularly until far past midnight, planning a radical reform of the principles of literary criticism. Humbert proposed to write an epoch-making book to be called *The Literary Mind: Its Place in an Age of Science*, and was discouraged upon discovering that somebody had incubated the same idea in New York. Cardwell was the first into print, with a contribution to a high-brow undergraduate journal which he entitled 'A Critical Exposition of Croce's *La Teoria dell'arte come pura visibilità*'. Locally in Cambridge, all the running in criticism was being made by F. R. Leavis, an English don at Downing, who took a rather pulpit-thumping view of his function. But more esoteric matter poured in from elsewhere in sufficient abundance to keep both budding scholars in an almost febrile condition. Humbert, in particular, could get almost drunk on the discovery of an essay with some such title as 'Psychical Distance as a Factor in Art and an Aesthetic Principle'. Bliss was it in that dawn to be alive. But to be young was very heaven.

Vacations separated them, since it never occurred to them either to try travelling together or to visit one another at home. They corresponded copiously, as undergraduates often do, but it was almost entirely without any approach to personal intimacy; indeed without any substantial exchange of information on personal matters. Humbert believed that Cardwell had been at Eton whereas he had really been at Rugby; Cardwell would have conjectured—vaguely if quite accurately—that Humbert's earlier education had been at 'one of those rather good grammar schools they go in for in the Midlands'. Neither knew whether the other had brothers or sisters, and such problems as those of sexual initiation (upon which young males are commonly at least obliquely informative with their closer companions) were never perpended between them. There was something old-fashioned, almost Victorian, about their relationship, which contrasted oddly with their addiction to the newest of New Criticism. Here were two serious reading men, not caring to be curious about one another's social background, but bound together by a common commanding interest in a severe branch of literary study.

It was on this level that their association continued until their final undergraduate year. Then it happened that Cardwell's mother, recently widowed and as a consequence increasingly vigilant in her son's affairs, decided that a presumably respectable young man whose letters on learned matters arrived so punctually at Chantries whenever Vivian was at home ought at least to be invited to turn up in his own person. The new baronet (who was continuing to do what his mother told him while looking round at leisure for a wife) agreed at once, and the visit took place. Lady Cardwell (the parent from whom Vivian inherited his brains) found no difficulty in liking Herbert Humbert. Naturally he couldn't know some of the ropes, but the fact didn't tiresomely embarrass him; and it was creditable that Vivian, whom she thought of as preparing himself for a distinguished career in politics, should have thus all in his stride attached to himself the interest and respect of a patently impressive if uncouth young scholar. Nevertheless Humbert's week at Chantries, superficially at least, was no great success. Intelligent though he was, he had never given time to reflecting that in Vivian there must certainly harbour Cardwells unknown to him. These were only the more apparent now because his host, out of consideration for his guest, tried to tuck them away a little. It wasn't really possible. Girls turned up and Vivian got meekly into flannels and played tennis with them—betraying evident enjoyment in an activity which, at Cambridge, he classed with rugger and rowing as sweaty futilities. Men came and paced up and down the terrace, smoking cigars and talking about the constituency: one thing, they would decide, might be chattered about at the local Conservative Association but another must be arranged quietly through the Central Office; what was important was that the seat should be safe as houses when young Cardwell came along to collect it. It appeared that young Cardwell was showing signs of being very decent about the Hunt, although everybody knew that his own interest was entirely in shooting and fishing.

All this had surprised and disturbed Humbert, but at an obscure level it pleased him as well. Yet this very sense of pleasure disturbed him too, intimating as it did possibilities of personal relationship which he had taught himself to regard as a distraction from the life of the mind. He was glad to get away from Chantries. Yet he was to look back to it with what he knew was a hint of affection. He would always now be to some extent Vivian Cardwell's man. At a pinch he would even do whatever Vivian told him. Which was only to say—what he knew very well—that, unlike Vivian, he packed a good deal more intellect than will.

Cardwell on his part was quite glad when Humbert took his leave of Chantries. The visit had made him realize the extent to which his college friend was (in the words of a contemporary poet) not a bus but a tram. For poor old Herbert life would be all a matter of determinate grooves. It was impossible to think of him getting married—or even getting drunk. He was going to be hopelessly unpractical. It was hard to imagine him holding down a job—unless, of course, he was lucky enough to land a fellowship at one of the obscurer colleges. Perhaps it would be possible to do something for him. Cardwell wasn't certain that he didn't actually have a duty that way.

In the succeeding few years, when they were still seeing something of each other, Cardwell did nothing of this sort. He had a wholesome feeling that it would be impertinent to patronize Herbert—in addition to which Herbert had landed himself quite a decent teaching appointment after all. Moreover he had published several interesting papers, so something like *The Literary Mind: Its Place in an Age of Science* might be expected sooner or later. Such was Sir Vivian Cardwell's feeling in the matter when he eventually lost sight of Herbert Humbert altogether. He had the excuse of being much occupied. Alike as a landowner, a banker, and a member of parliament he was endlessly busy. In addition to which he still found time for his interests in literature and scholarship, and his name had become well-known in the learned as well as the political world. He had never, it was true, produced anything which could quite be called a major work, although the slow maturing of such a thing on his writing-table was sometimes rumoured. But he wrote with wide authority and great charm on a variety of topics, so that knowledgeable people would say 'That must be by Vivian Cardwell', when they ran across a particularly graceful and scintillating major review in the anonymous columns (as they still were) of the *Times Literary Supplement*. Humbert's name in such a context would have come into nobody's head.

* * *

The two men hadn't been long in the Italian restaurant in Duke of York Street before Cardwell was recalling two facts about Humbert: one with the effect of recovering something quite forgotten, and the other as the kind of thing one doesn't really ever forget. Humbert was that sort of person, unrewarding to entertain, who is totally unconscious of what he either eats or drinks. It was the more irritating now because, on a mere freakish impulse, he devoted to the actual choosing of his meal the concentrated attention, and the dialectal elaboration in colloquy with the waiter, of a Frenchman at the most solemn moment of the day. But then he had at once appeared to forget that he was at table at all. And although food did disappear down his throat it was impossible to understand how it could have done so. For Humbert never stopped talking. This was the unforgotten, the unforgettable thing. Yet one has to be precise. Only a tape-recorder could have caught, and stored up for analysis and eventual comprehension, the actual burden of his discourse. Without such an aid, one could follow him from clause to clause, even from sentence to sentence—and this to an effect of constant illumination of the most recondite recesses of literature and art. But what might be called the discursive whole was more elusive, was evanescent, faded like Burns's snowflakes in the river. It was possible to believe that in this quarter of the intellectual field Herbert Humbert could have given a fair run for his money to Samuel Taylor Coleridge himself.

And then—quite suddenly—Humbert was stammering and mumbling again. He had been saying something about a formalist fallacy, and it had appeared to upset him. It was a moment before Cardwell caught up with this, although he ought to have remembered at once. 'The Yale Formalist Fallacy' was something that Herbert had printed somewhere some years before. He must be talking about that.

'You gave it to those chaps good and hard,' Cardwell said at a venture.

'Of course I did.' Humbert had no doubts on this point. 'But nobody paid any attention to it. More and more, you see, it's a matter of status. People won't listen to a lecturer.'

'It was a lecture?' Cardwell was puzzled. 'I thought—'

'No, no! I'm saying that if you've donkeyed away for years without getting to the top of one of their silly academic trees you're treated as a harmless drudge who's not worth attending to.'

'Oh, but surely not!' There had been something disconcerting about Humbert's thus suddenly plummeting from the most abstract (and elevating) level of literary discourse to this disconsolate personal note. Yet at once it came back to Cardwell as characteristic of his friend. Herbert was at times a distinctly chip-on-the-shoulder type, and when in that mood not easy to deal with. Cardwell doubted whether what he had just said was true. Although no academic himself, he dined from time to time at high tables, and he had gained the impression that on the whole it was professors who were regarded as harmless drudges, while the real advances in knowledge were achieved by bright young men. But then although Herbert wasn't a professor he certainly wasn't a bright young man either.

'Well, that's how I see it.' Herbert was looking sullen—or at least bits and pieces of his face could be read that way. 'All because I haven't produced a great tombstone of a critical edition of Mark Akenside or Thomas Shadwell or somebody.'

'Very well.' Cardwell decided to speak robustly. 'You'll have to produce a book, Herbert. Not a thing like that, of course, but a real book. A regular block-buster. You must have masses of material.'

'That's what Bernard says.'

'Bernard?' Cardwell was at sea.

'Bernard Hinkstone—who ran into us there in the London Library. *He's* always on at me about it too.'

'Is he, indeed?' It didn't greatly please Sir Vivian Cardwell thus to be lumped together with that briefly-glimpsed unmannerly young man. 'I hope he doesn't bully you, Herbert. But from the point of view of professional advancement he's probably quite right.'

'I distrust books. There's something too final about them.' Delivering this odd verdict, Humbert drained his glass—which Cardwell hospitably filled again. 'And it looks as if you feel the same way, Vivian. Where's *your* big book? Put away in a drawer, it seems—and just occasionally taken a timid peep at.' Humbert took another big gulp of chianti. 'You're a bloody great pot, old boy, calling the kettle black.'

It was at this point that the dangerous notion of a rescue-operation came into Cardwell's head. He didn't at all see how it was to be achieved, but he felt strongly that he would like to achieve it. He was himself a temperate, although by no means a drearily abstemious man, and there was something about the speed with which Herbert had raised that glass which alerted him for the first time to a disturbing possibility. He didn't actually see himself in a custodial role: a

Theodore Watts-Dunton, say, devoted to keeping a Swinburne off the bottle. There was something ridiculous in that image, and Cardwell was a man very sensitive to ridicule. Moreover he had only the most slender ground for suspecting that drink was an important factor in the situation. What seemed certain was that Herbert was in a state of impaired confidence as to his own powers and prospects. Could means be taken, for a start, merely to boost his morale? In what way could a very old friend address himself to being a bracing influence?

'But Herbert,' Cardwell said, 'I haven't got a big book—put away in a drawer or anywhere else. Occasional pieces, yes. Beyond that, I simply have nothing that I could honestly call my own.'

'Just what do you mean by that?'

'Come, come, Herbert! No need to be modest.' Cardwell was inwardly delighted at the adroitness, as he conceived it, of the man-oeuvre he had hit upon. 'Remember what our relationship was, back in that wonderful time. You gave me pretty well every idea I ever had. And what have I done since? Elaborate one or two of them, and doll them up a bit. *Il miglior fabbro*, old chap—that's you.'

As he produced this version of things (which, of course, he didn't believe in a bit), Cardwell wished that at the start he hadn't so stiffly played down the quality of his unpublished book. What he had then said didn't quite square with this sudden assertion that he had produced something which somehow enshrined the fine essence of Herbert Humbert's thought. But Humbert himself appeared uncon-scious of this point. He had flushed with pleasure and confusion, like a schoolboy who has unexpectedly been commended in extravagant terms for work which he had supposed would earn him a wigging. Or was it quite like that? Although Humbert at once exploded into a stammered 'Vivian, what utter nonsense!' was there a flicker of something else apparent, which his friend might have remarked had he not been congratulating himself on his successful employment of what somebody has called the psychotherapy of warm praise? It is possible that what Cardwell had produced as a novel and just poss-ibly persuasive fiction already lurked in Humbert's mind as the all-too-probable fact of the matter.

However this may have been, the meal ended pleasantly enough, and with a distinct implication that the revived relationship between the two men was to continue. The will to this was perhaps more Cardwell's than Humbert's. At last, and after all those years, Card-well had set about 'doing something' for his friend. Or at least he had taken a first step that way, obeyed an impulse in the matter which it was now incumbent upon him to take means to further. A laudably charitable intention was at work in Sir Vivian Cardwell, but it was also true that an element of intellectual curiosity had its influence with him. He had moved much among men and affairs, and had developed in consequence an interest in the character and conduct of actual men and women in a way unknown to Humbert, who viewed nearly everything through the spectacles of books. Just how could one persuade, coax, edge, prod a chap like Herbert in one direction or another—always, of course, entirely to his own benefit? The question was a complex and challenging one, Herbert being the very gifted and exceptional individual he was.

As they left the restaurant, Cardwell secured his friend's address. It may have been significant that he felt this to be a slightly tricky operation, even although it was clearly essential if they really were going to keep in contact with one another. There was a certain wariness about Herbert, which no doubt went along with the sense of being an unsuccessful man. Obvious and honest as was his admiration for his former intimate, he had what might almost be called an impulse to elude capture if he could. And so it came about that, if only ever so faintly, Sir Vivian Cardwell felt much as he did when, following his favourite recreations at Chantries, he was out with a gun or casting a still fly over a pool.

The present Lady Cardwell had never met Herbert Humbert. It turned out, indeed, that she had never even heard of him, and it was this circumstance that appeared particularly to strike her when her husband reported on the encounter in the London Library.

'Has Mr Humbert ever been to Chantries?' she asked.

'Oh, yes. He stayed here—I think it was for about a week—when we were both still at Trinity. I don't know that he greatly enjoyed himself. He must come of very simple people, I suppose. My mother liked him.'

'Because he was extremely clever?'

'It would have been partly that.'

'You used to tell me quite a lot about your undergraduate days, Vivian. It's odd that you never mentioned this close friend.'

'Herbert wasn't exactly that. But it is odd, all the same, and requires accounting for. Do you know? I think that by the time you and I met I may have developed some unconscious sense almost of guilt about the chap. About having rather dropped him, that is. Perhaps that's why I never told you about him. I ought to have—if only because he was an enormously interesting man. He still is, in a way.'

'Is it true, Vivian, that you got a great many of your ideas from this Mr Humbert?' Lady Cardwell asked this in some amusement. Her husband had confided to her the means he had taken to cheer up his former associate.

'Well, as I told you, darling, I wasn't being quite honest there.' It was with a certain discomfort that Cardwell reiterated this. 'It was all give-and-take between us, really. Or that's how I remember it.'

'At least it wasn't the other way round? Mr Humbert, that's to say, didn't get nearly all his ideas from you?'

'No, no—nothing like that.'

'If he had, I think it might have been he who dropped you. His spirit would have felt rebuked by you, as they say.'

'What an odd idea, darling.'

'It isn't odd at all.' Lady Cardwell, who was quite as intelligent as her mother-in-law had been (and had, indeed, been courted by Vivian Cardwell on that account) was seldom slow in speaking out like this. 'If one knows in one's heart that someone with whom one is expected to live on equal terms is in fact very much one's intellectual superior, it's quite likely that one day one will unobtrusively pack one's bags. And you say there is something a little elusive about Mr Humbert still. So that's it. The poor man knows he isn't quite up to you.'

'I wouldn't care to think of it in that way at all.' Cardwell made a momentary pause. 'Or the other way round, for that matter.'

'Are you going to see more of him?'

'Yes, I think so. I've a notion of looking him up at the address he gave me when I'm next in town.'

'Why not ask him down here? You say he has been to Chantries once. And I'd like to have a look at him—just as your mother must have done.'

'Later, perhaps, darling. I'll sound him out about it first. It's a question of finding just the best way to help him.'

'He needs help?'

'Well—encouragement, say. But, yes—definitely a leg-up.'

'Is he very poor, or something?'

'I'd hardly suppose so. It's true that a university lecturer is rather miserably paid. But Herbert's an unmarried man, and I'd imagine him to be of pretty simple tastes. What needs seeing to is his doing himself justice by means of publishing more. That kind of thing.'

'It sounds to me as if you'll have to be rather tactful, Vivian dear. Mr Humbert isn't a young man, and he may well be set in his ways. If you suddenly turn up out of a remote past with the evident intention of running him or treating him as a protégé—'

'My dear, I've spent a large part of my life, as you know, ladling out tact to all sorts and conditions of men. It's now next to second nature with me.' And Sir Vivian Cardwell laughed—gaily, but perhaps with a shade of complacency as well. 'Dear old Herbert Humbert has nothing to fear from me there.'

Nevertheless Cardwell didn't remain quite certain that, in proposing to drop in on Humbert unheralded and in a casual way, he hadn't begun on the wrong foot. The little street to the north of Dorset Square bore so run-down an appearance that to visit it felt like going slumming. But perhaps, he thought, Herbert worked at Bedford College, and it would no doubt be a convenient address for that. Still, he found himself rather hoping that his friend would be out (which seemed likely enough) so that he could effect some different approach. His wife had been right. An immediate invitation to Chantries might only have alarmed Herbert. But it would have been the gracious thing, all the same.

He came to a halt before a door badly in need of a lick of paint. On one side there was a row of small electric bell-pushes, like buttons on a grubby waistcoat. Most had names against them, either scribbled on slivers of pasteboard or punched out on a strip of metal tape. Humbert's name did not appear. But two of the buttons were anonymous, and the uppermost was one of them. Deciding that it was somehow in character that Herbert should inhabit an attic, and that there was an equal likelihood of his not bothering to intimate his tenancy to the world, Cardwell pressed this at a venture. Nothing happened, so he tried the door. It proved to be unlocked, so he went in and climbed several flights of stairs. Milk-bottles, some full and some empty but uncleansed, stood outside doors, and beside one or two of them lay newspapers of the more popular order. He was stared at disapprovingly by a woman in carpet slippers carrying a mop and bucket; he was similarly stared at by a cat which had the appearance of being in ill-health. These evidences of unimproved life were dispiriting, but he pressed on. On the top landing somebody stood in an open doorway, as if expecting him, so that he concluded the bell to have effected some sort of summons, after all. But this wasn't Herbert, and for a moment he supposed that he must have guessed wrong. Then he realized that here was the person, encountered in the London Library, whom Herbert had described as a former pupil. Cardwell, who had a well-trained memory for names, said 'Good-morning, Mr Hinkstone', in a proper tone of mild cordiality.

'Oh, it's you.' Hinkstone produced this singularly incontrovertible statement, contrastingly, on a note of distinct disappointment, much as if he would have preferred the appearance of a man to read the gas-meter, or even of a policeman with a summons for speeding.

'Is Herbert at home?' It seemed best to Cardwell to treat the unexpected encounter as having established itself on a basis of pleasing informality, which was the reason of thus employing his friend's Christian name.

'Oh, yes—he's at home. I suppose you'd better come in. Not that he's expecting you, I imagine.'

'Well, no. It's a call on the spur of the moment, actually.' Cardwell wondered why he should be prompted to a small untruth by this meagre and graceless person. 'Do you share quarters with him, Mr Hinkstone?'

'Of course not. I sometimes come in and do a bit of typing for him. He can't work a typewriter. Part of his general clumsiness.'

This remark, although doubtless true, displeased Cardwell, and he felt that he ought by now to have been ushered into his friend's presence. But he and Hinkstone were still standing in a gloomy little lobby, and the young man was looking at him rather as if he were an inconveniently dumped parcel which must somehow be got rid of.

'It's the hell of a climb up to this flat,' the young man said. He gave Cardwell an appraising glance. 'Particularly if one's a bit out of condition, I'd imagine. But it seems to suit Herbert. ὃς ὑπέρτατα δώματα ναίει.'

Although it was perhaps proper that one who laboured in a polytechnic should know his Hesiod, Cardwell was disconcerted by this unexpected command of an ancient tongue by so uncouth a young man. He was aware, at the same time, of having been given notice that he was dealing with a scholar, and he made a mental note that it would be prudent to treat Herbert's young assistant (as Hinkstone now appeared to be) with respect.

'But I don't want to hold up your work,' he said. 'Perhaps—'

Whatever accommodating remark was to follow upon this remained unuttered—being interrupted, from beyond a closed door, by a cry of dismay, a clatter as of overturned furniture, and sundry dull bumpings to which it was not easy to assign a cause. But Hinkstone appeared to be in no doubt as to what had happened, and now raised both arms in air with a gesture more of irritation than alarm.

'Oh, God!' he exclaimed. 'If Herbert hasn't gone and fallen off that library ladder again.'

It was a big room, and although on one side the windows scarcely came knee-high in the sloping roof, on the other there was a lofty blank wall clothed to the ceiling with books. It was here that the misadventure had occurred and that Herbert still lay sprawled on the floor with a dozen volumes on top of him. The library ladder seemed substantial enough; it was a solid mahogany affair, terminating in a stout pole with a knob for holding on to when you were on the top step. The trouble lay, it appeared to Cardwell, in the treacherous character of the terrain beneath it. The whole room lay ankle-deep in waste paper—or it might have been safer to say in manuscript material. Some of this looked freshly crumpled up but much was already yellowed with age. There were loose sheets, torn sheets, little bundles in process of freeing themselves from paper-clips, larger bundles tied up with tape or string. And since all this was deposited on top of slippery linoleum of an antique sort, any venture around the room could be undertaken only at considerable hazard. This was clearly the opinion of Bernard Hinkstone—who was picking up Humbert, dusting him down, and angrily chiding him, all at one and the same time.

'You're not safe!' he shouted. 'It's not just that you can't safely be let out alone. You can't even be left alone in your own room. How often have I told you to give over scrambling up that damned thing? I'll have to move in on you, Herbert. There's nothing else for it.' Hinkstone turned to Cardwell. 'They talk about being accident-prone,' he said, 'and of just that Herbert's the bloody mark and acme.' He picked up an enormous tome from Humbert's feet. 'Stunning yourself with quartos and folios is all very well. But one day he'll stroll out into the middle of the street and have a little chat with a bus.'

Sir Vivian Cardwell, although not a fussy man, liked to have everything neat and shipshape around him. The scene of disorder upon which he had intruded, therefore, distressed him a good deal.

While Humbert recovered breath and prepared to talk (for talk wonderfully he certainly would) his former companion took further stock of the situation. It didn't greatly trouble him that Herbert so clearly lived a physically comfortless life; that from the crumpled paper in one corner of the room there rose an iron bedstead with equally crumpled bedding, that the one-bar electric fire was dulled by a corroded reflector, that Herbert's notion of home cookery was evidenced by a single frying-pan perched on a primus stove. Herbert had always been like that, and there was nothing discreditable about it in a man devoted to unceasing intellectual toil. It was the coil into which the toil so hopelessly degenerated that was disheartening. All this litter perfectly epitomized Herbert's mind—a mind of which the thoughts were like a scattered pack of cards. It was easy to say that here in Herbert Humbert was a sovereign intellect but a subject will. The truth wasn't really quite like that. The intellect itself was imperfect, being incapable of ordonnance, of construction on any large scale. Another way of saying this would be to declare that poor Herbert was incapable of grasping his own fleeting conceptions and excluding other people's while he expanded and developed what was radically his own. He was, in a way, too open, too suggestible in his intellectual life. Perhaps he was that in his personal life too. If Herbert *had* a personal life. Meditating thus, Cardwell was perhaps coming insensibly to regard his old associate as an intriguing puzzle; almost, it might be said, as laboratory material. Nothing could be more interesting than to find out what, under just what circumstances and compulsions, so extraordinary a creature as Herbert would do.

'I can see you feel I live in rather a mess,' Herbert said cheerfully when Hinkstone had shoved him into a chair. 'I suppose it's true in a way, and Bernard would agree with you. Bernard tries to tidy me up from time to time, but I have to stop him. If you tidy everything up it means you can never put your hand on something when you want it, because it isn't where it was.'

'Which probably meant buried invisibly beneath something else,' Cardwell said with a careful lightness of air. 'It seems to me, Herbert, that you'll have to live as De Quincey did, migrating from one set of rooms to another when the first became too jam-packed to move about it. He simply flitted in what he stood up in and started the process of accumulation all over again. It was a simplification, but one couldn't call it exactly efficient.'

'It didn't prevent him,' Hinkstone said, 'from publishing no end of rubbish. Seventeen volumes of it, all sozzled in opium. Herbert is still seventeen short of that, but at least he keeps a clear head.'

'I don't doubt that,' Cardwell said brusquely. He didn't care to have this young man appear in the role of one defending Herbert against criticism. But at the same time he fleetingly wondered whether it would be possible to make an ally of Hinkstone. It might have to be either that or an enemy. For there was no doubt that this polytechnic person, so incongruously well-seen in Greek, was devoted to his old teacher.

'The same is true of Bernard,' Herbert said with a sudden cheerful splutter. 'About the clear head, I mean. Not that there aren't phases of obfuscation from time to time. The poor lad has got hung up lately on this chap Chomsky—*Syntactic Structures*, you know. And that reminds me, Vivian. I've put together a few notes on Chomsky that I'd like you to see. Irreverent, perhaps—but those outstanding fellows must put up with a little of that. Mind you, I've nothing against Generative Grammar in a general way. But when you begin to hear of Cartesian Linguistics it's time to ask a question or two, wouldn't you say?' As he offered these arcane remarks Humbert was already fussing around the room—turning over books tumbled on tables, peering at shelves and into cupboards, actually here and there stirring the silt of papers on the floor with his foot. Then he came to a baffled pause. 'Bernard,' he demanded, 'just where is that Chomsky file?'

'I haven't a clue, Herbert.' It was with a hint of impatience that Hinkstone made this reply. Here had perhaps been an appeal of a kind that reached him too often.

'You see?' It was triumphantly but without malice—in fact it was with the most genial of splutters—that Humbert had turned to Cardwell. 'Bernard has tidied the Chomsky file away, never to be seen again. Time will perform the same office by the man himself, of course. But it's a shame he can't even have a run for his money with me.'

Herbert Humbert couldn't have been called a witty man (except in an obsolete and superior sense of the word) but he was always pleased when he achieved some approximation to that character. He promptly forgot about Professor Chomsky now and talked about other things. With a little translation into his own fields of concern, it might be said that he talked about shoes and ships and sealing wax, and this without omitting cabbages and kings. Intermittently there was a hunt for appropriate documentation—for other files than the Chomsky one. More often than not, the search was again futile. But on half-a-dozen occasions either jottings in Humbert's hand or Hinkstone's typescript copies (or perhaps recensions) of similar material were placed in Cardwell's hands. He didn't make a great deal of them. (Perhaps he made less than he ought to have done.) In places the effect was momentarily dazzling, as if a flash of lightning had lit up some far territory not commonly seen. But what was the use of that when the total effect was of helplessness and confusion? Cardwell found that repeatedly asking himself this question was fatiguing, and he was quite glad when the moment came at which he could get away. This didn't mean that he was at all ditching Herbert. He was now quite clear that he was going to 'do something' for Herbert; was going to rehabilitate him by one means or another. Not that 'rehabilitate' was quite the right word, since poor old Herbert could scarcely be said ever to have been habilitated in the first place. Rather he was going to bring Herbert forward: that was it. And already he had a vague plan, a wholly benevolent plan, in his head. He couldn't, however, broach it in this messy room, and with young Bernard Hinkstone standing jealously by. Herbert must be got down to Chantries, and there softened up—or chatted up, as the young people said.

In the interest of this preliminary part of his plan, Cardwell went vigorously to work at once. Even Hinkstone couldn't take exception to Herbert's spending a weekend or a week on a visit to a very old friend. And eventually Herbert agreed. He was evidently alarmed, but when Cardwell fished out a pocket diary and fixed a date he submitted at once. Cardwell wondered whether, long ago, he had been able thus to give Herbert his orders, at least in the common affairs of life. He couldn't remember. What he did remember (now for the first time in many years) was that in intellectual matters it had been Herbert who held the lead. Perhaps he himself (despite all the prizes he had taken) had been rather a slow developer. It was commonly said that slow developers got furthest in the long run.

Rather to Cardwell's surprise, Hinkstone saw him not only to the door of the flat but politely down the staircase as well. This proved, however, to be only because he had something not particularly agreeable to say.

'He should be let alone,' Hinkstone said.

'I beg your pardon?' Cardwell produced this in a manner suffi-

ciently frigid, he supposed, to quell further impertinence. But Hinkstone was resolved to have his say.

'You may mean well, Sir Vivian. But you'll only mess him around.'

'My dear young man, I am prepared to give you credit for meaning
well too. But Herbert Humbert and I were close friends before you
were born. You will forgive me if I say that you speak a little out of
turn.'

'He's perfectly happy as he is.'

'I think not. Herbert has not been done justice to within his
profession, and he feels it keenly. He ought to be a professor by now.'

'Nothing of the kind. A reader, perhaps. Readers are more learned
than professors, but lack guile.'

'Indeed?' This facetiousness had seemed to Cardwell misplaced.
'Let us say that Herbert has not received proper recognition, and that
it is partly his own fault. He ought to have published more. He must
be encouraged to publish.'

'And you're going to encourage him?'

'He and I, Mr Hinkstone, used to work closely together. And the
thought has come to me that we might do so again. I confide this to
you, despite a certain acerbity in your tone, because I recognize that
you have Herbert's interest at heart. It has occurred to me that if he
and I were to collaborate it might . . .' Cardwell had been about to
say, 'bring Herbert forward'. More circumspectly, however, he said,
'help matters along.'

'Collaborate?' The two men had now reached the front door, and
Hinkstone opened it as he echoed the word. 'Herbert collaborate with
you? Don't make me laugh.'

With this fantastically discourteous speech (particularly shocking
in a Grecian from Christ's Hospital) Bernard Hinkstone virtually
thrust Sir Vivian Cardwell into the street.

Cardwell no longer played tennis with the daughters of the neighbouring families. But he sometimes played croquet with his wife, and
on the second day of Herbert's visit to Chantries it occurred to him
that this would be a reasonable diversion to which to introduce his
unathletic friend. He wasn't exactly finding Herbert heavy in hand,
but literary talk with him wasn't sufficiently easy to be a resource
right round the clock. As undergraduates they had frequently dis-
agreed with one another vehemently, but at the same time owned so
much common ground that the disagreements often proved fruitful as

well as being fun. Now in late middle age their interests didn't so exactly coincide. Perhaps it might be said that Humbert took the whole notion of a Theory of Literature more seriously than Cardwell; he certainly took more seriously (and commanded more familiarly) what Cardwell would have been disposed to call the current jargon in the field. Humbert had never been easy to follow, and now there were times when Cardwell simply didn't know what he was talking about. Cardwell had to admit to himself that he was still some way from even beginning to see how to sort poor Herbert out.

At the start the croquet was quite a success. Herbert insisted on calling it pell-mell, and he talked about flamingoes and hedgehogs in a manner Cardwell found perplexing until he remembered *Alice's Adventures in Wonderland*. (Sir Vivian had never much cared for Alice.) The processes of 'making a roquet' and 'taking croquet' pleased Herbert, and the discovery that he was allowed so to hit his own ball that it scarcely moved whereas his opponent's went hurtling into the gooseberry bushes delighted him inordinately. But he couldn't be brought to realize that, by way of scoring, more was required of him than to bang his ball at random through any hoop he chose. And every now and then he would recall *Alice* again, and either shout 'Off with her head!' or turn himself into a soldier pretending to be a hoop for Lady Cardwell's benefit. It was quite as much the croquet as the literary conversation that suggested to Sir Vivian that the unspeakable Hinkstone had been right, and that Herbert was simply not to be collaborated with. The notion of an impressive work by V. Cardwell and H. Humbert had to be ruled out.

In future years Cardwell would have found hard to remember either the point at which a bold new plan came to him, or the mingled (and even conflicting) motives that had gone to the framing of it. He may have begun from the perception that if anything were to be effected at all the first step must still be to gain some sort of ascendancy over Herbert of a kind not easy to define but the possibility of which he sensed as buried deep in their relationship. This was, in fact, the 'softening up' he had already thought of, and it didn't sound wholly agreeable expressed in that way. Cardwell was by no means blind to the possibility that the lure of power was here jostling with his benevolent intentions—and indeed that his benevolence might be less active than his mere curiosity. He certainly wasn't going to let Herbert return to London (and the clutches of Bernard Hinkstone) without exploring him a good deal further. He gave his friend the typescript of the book which at one time was to have been called *Concrete Universals in Literature*. It wasn't exactly that kind of book now.

Humbert took the book to bed with him, and had of course read it through by breakfast-time next morning. He was enthusiastic. He was enthusiastic—an informed spectator might have felt—in an almost curiously undiscriminating way. This ought to have irked Cardwell quite as much as it pleased him. But he felt nothing of the kind. He felt simply that Herbert was well on the road to where he wanted him.

'Vivian, you simply *must* publish it! It would be criminal not to.' Humbert was stammering and spluttering—something he had so far contrived not to do at Lady Cardwell's table.

'Let's go and talk about it on the terrace, Herbert.' Cardwell appeared to be making this suggestion out of consideration for his guest's embarrassingly over-moist condition, but may also have felt that he might get further in helping Herbert if both were out of his wife's eye.

'My dear Herbert,' he said as he began to stuff his morning pipe, 'we must be realistic about this. Or, rather, we must simply be honest.'

'Honest, Vivian?' Not perhaps surprisingly, Humbert was a little puzzled by this suddenly conjured up moral imperative. 'Honest about what?'

'Simply about whose book it is. And I've pretty well told you about that already. It's yours, almost every word of it. You alone can properly send it to the printer.'

As he produced this remarkable speech Sir Vivian Caldwell kept his friend held in a level and penetrating gaze. It had come to him that the softening-up process was something to be achieved not by slow and cautious habituation but—as now—almost at a stroke. The right technique, in fact, was something very close to the stage hypnotist's. It mightn't work. But it was as likely to work as anything else was.

'To the printer?' Herbert's features were more than commonly at sixes and sevens. 'What printer?'

'Whatever printer you please. It's simply time the book—*your* book—was published.'

'It's not my book, Vivian. It's your book.' Herbert said this in a strange small voice not habitual to him.

'Look, Herbert—you and I are philosophers in a fashion, and we can see this thing in its essence and not its mere appearance. Of course

I scribbled the book. But at a deep level I was nothing but your amanuensis. Of course there will be passages and turns of expression and so forth that you will improve in one way or another. But published your book must be.'

Cardwell, although offering this speech with all the authority of the gentleman in tails and a cloak who has just made passes over the face of the yokel from the audience, felt inwardly a little at sixes and sevens himself. He took a good deal of satisfaction in what he appeared to be getting away with. He admired his boldness and even a certain element of selflessness and sacrifice inherent in his design. It was true that the old manuscript (brilliant though it probably was) meant little to him. It was with rather different material that he had secured his position on the literary front—but that had come to mean little to him either. He had been a junior minister. If the next general election went as it should he had a good chance of winding up his career as a senior, although not particularly important, member of the Cabinet. And he would have the further satisfaction of numbering poor old Professor Humbert among his acquaintances.

So Sir Vivian Cardwell was rather pleased with himself. But there can be no doubt that, like most of us, he had two sides to his head, and was therefore aware that thus to make a monkey of an old friend was not an altogether amiable proceeding.

Varieties of Literary Experience by Herbert Humbert was published six months later and received with universal obloquy and disdain. An influential journal (which had always been eager to print any of the elegant essays which Sir Vivian Cardwell wrote from time to time) described it as mannered and largely devoid of substance; another declared it to be 'hauntingly *démodé*'; and a farouche young critic in an avant-garde weekly found it 'as toothsome and nutritious as expanded polystyrene'.

In the face of this unanimous censure it is necessary to conclude that Humbert's relationship with his friend had become in its final phase essentially pathological; that not only was his will impaired to the extraordinary degree evidenced by his accepting the bizarre and demeaning deception proposed to him but also that his critical judgement was so overlaid by a cloud of fatuous admiration for Sir Vivian Cardwell that he had misestimated the quality of the book (let alone its consonance with his own early thinking) in a singularly strange fashion.

Cardwell, naturally enough, didn't see the matter quite in this light. It was of course a great shock to him. But he was outraged as well. It staggered him that a work which would have been competently examined and justly praised had it appeared under his own name should be laughed to scorn when supposed to be the work of an unknown drudge in an obscure academic situation. Sir Vivian actually composed a long letter to *The Times* about this before he realized (with the help of his wife, to whom he had confessed the whole thing) that a certain inconvenience must attend upon any public denunciation of the monstrous fate his labours had met with.

Humbert, perhaps because he had long ceased to expect very much from the world, was not at first nearly so upset. He had certainly got himself involved in an odd situation, and with the peculiar patchy clarity that characterized his mind, he saw that it wouldn't have happened if that mind hadn't been affected by some degree of premature senescence. This discovery about himself interested him very much, and he would talk about it acutely to Bernard Hinkstone for hours on end. At other times he was increasingly abstracted and withdrawn. His clumsiness increased, together with an attendant liability to petty physical mishap.

Then something really worrying turned up on his horizon. He certainly was never going to be a professor now—and he began to doubt whether he would for long even continue to be a lecturer. His appointment in that academic grade would soon be due for renewal, and it seemed to him that, after the fiasco of *Varieties of Literary Experience*, there was a strong probability that the renewal would not take place. This was of course a totally baseless notion, as Hinkstone strove to persuade him. Only if that absurd deception were made public could there be the slightest risk of such a disaster and humiliation. But Humbert continued disturbed. He wasn't depressed. Hinkstone was to assert later that, in any recognizable clinical sense, Humbert was from first to last not under that sort of weather. But he did become more and more absent-minded. Then one day he went out to buy a box of matches, chose to cross the street at an injudicious moment, and was knocked down by a small motor-cycle and killed instantly.

Sir Vivian, although much distressed by the news of the fatality, also felt a certain measure of relief. His conscience had been pricking him over the freakish experiment (as it had been) with *Varieties of Literary*

Experience, and it had been striking him that the only thing to do was to return to the proposal of producing along with Herbert a collaborated work. His own name, carried on the title-page of such a better-conceived venture, would surely bring Herbert the enhanced reputation which was required. But he had also been conscious that there would be difficulties (Herbert *was* difficult) of a formidable order to be overcome if such a project were to be achieved. So perhaps what had happened was just as well.

It was nearly two years after this that there appeared in the bookshops, in two volumes, *The Chomsky File and Other Literary Remains of Herbert Humbert,* edited by Bernard Hinkstone. Than this monstrous collection of *disjecta membra*, of the outpourings of waste-paper baskets, of sweepings-up from a littered floor there had been, in the highest literary and academic circles, no such sensation since the turn of the century. To the roll of the great English critics—Dryden, Johnson, Arnold, Eliot, Leavis—a new name had been added overnight. Humbert's former employers in a corner of the University of London were appalled at the little regard they had paid to the genius in their midst: a spectacle that could only have been paralleled had, say, Richard Bentley been constrained to vapour away his days in a private school. So they touted around and found a millionaire—the owner of some chain-stores—who approved of education, and from him they got enough money to endow their college with a Herbert Humbert Professorship. The first incumbent of the Chair was, very rightly, that sound scholar, Bernard Hinkstone. When, a good many years later again, the distinguished belletrist and littérateur Sir Vivian Cardwell was given an honorary degree, Professor Hinkstone made an urbane little speech about him.

THE REAL THING

I

OLIVER RUSSELL AND David Read had been at school together. They were in the same house, and they became full prefects on the same day, sharing the joys and cares of suddenly being in a position to exercise despotic authority over forty or fifty other boys. It was a civilized school as schools went in the early 1930s, but you could be pretty Draconian if that amused you. Russell tackled the job more robustly, more in his stride, than Read. Read was inclined to be now hard and now soft, to be ashamed and even guilt-ridden over mild routine sadisms, and to bore the housemaster by over-conscientious endeavours. But it all really went quite well. The year ended with the house taking a creditable position in the school at one thing and another. Russell and Read were both popular. Both won scholarships to Oxford.

The achievement took them to different colleges, since when you are after an award you have to go, within limits, where the dons take it into their heads to send you. People seldom complained about the system, an open scholarship being a prestige affair: the equivalent, in the brainy world into which you were moving, of rugger caps and cricket colours. Being quartered on different sides of Oxford's High Street didn't much affect the friendship of Russell and Read, who had long before (and even in those formal days) become Olly and David to one another. But it brought Timothy Merton into their joint life and companionship. Tim was at Olly's college, and it thus came about that, although all three were pretty thick together, Olly and Tim were thicker on the whole. This continued to be so to some extent thereafter, and perhaps the more so because, paradoxically, it was between Tim and David that there existed a closer underlying temperamental affinity. Tim and David continued a little shy of one another, as if not wanting to pry. But for several years Tim, David and Olly were to continue a triumvirate, like chums in a school story.

Rather to the surprise of his friends, it was Olly who took a First in Schools, the other two just missing this tricky distinction. They then all found plausible reasons for continuing their education in Vienna: the Vienna of Chancellor Dollfuss (who was a midget) and the *Kreditanstalt* bankruptcy. They had thought of Berlin, which precocious writers a few years older than themselves had begun to celebrate in various curious ways. But Tim's father, who was in the Foreign Office, knew things about Berlin that he didn't at all like. So the young men closed with Vienna in the interest of a discreet solidarity. Besides, Vienna was a good deal cheaper than Berlin; you could live almost affluently for a year there on the allowance you had barely made do on at Oxford during three eight-week terms. And that wasn't quite all. They were clever youths, all three; they came of good families, traditional in feeling and cultivated after a fashion; the instinct for rebellion proper to their age didn't extend to sympathy with, or even tolerance of, anything like a riff-raff, raggle-taggle society. None of them would have been—or at the start would have been—much at home among people whom it would have been impossible to introduce to a sister. Vienna was understood to conduct its affairs with a certain eighteenth-century refinement unknown to Berlin, which was unashamedly vulgar. Olly had been to Berlin with his family, and he said it was quite unbelievable. It was true that on the banks of the Havel at Potsdam there had been naked youths chucking javelins and discuses in an amusing neo-Greek fashion (and even, he swore, picking up chunks of rock and hurling them at each other like the warriors before windy Troy). But the Palace itself was sick-making to anybody who knew Versailles: it would be just the place for this howling maniac Adolf Hitler. Neither Tim nor David had been to Versailles, let alone Potsdam, both happening to have Italomaniac parents, who had dragged them through the Uffizi and the Brera from their tender years. So they had to receive these judgements with respect.

David, who had in fact become first resigned to and then a lover of those artists referred to by his mother as the Old Masters, looked forward to spending a good deal of time in the *Kunsthistorisches Hofmuseum*. And since he had played the recorder at school he believed himself all agog to hear Vienna's principal orchestras other than on his old portable gramophone.

Olly, who affected philistinism although he was the best-read of the three, said that you could ride very decent horses for next to nothing

156

in the Prater, skate all winter at the *Eislaufverein*, and play tennis there for the rest of the year when on a fixed date the ice miraculously vanished and the place turned into dozens of tennis-courts instead. You could still dine at Sachers: if you wanted to, in one of the private rooms in which the Grand-dukes had industriously seduced ballet-girls after tanking them up with the imperial Tokay.

Tim was the only one of the three booked for any academically respectable activity in Vienna. His Second in Schools had perplexed and for a time outraged his tutors. But having discovered through a family grape-vine that it had been the consequence of some private disaster too delicate to be discussed, they had rallied round in a big way, securing for him various introductions to influential and even exalted persons such as would enable him, he believed, to advance as a diplomatic historian and set Metternich in a clear light once and for all.

This serious purpose apart, what were they chiefly thinking about, all three, as they thus exchanged a familiar Oxford (then an enlarged public school) for an unknown continent? It is a question hard to answer, and which they would have found hard to answer with any seriousness themselves. Olly professed to view their situation in terms of the Grand Tour. Here they were, sent abroad to improve themselves as ornaments of society, but fortunately without that superintendence by a bear-leading tutor which had been prescriptive even when Grand Tourists had been little younger—if younger at all—than themselves. Olly even averred that his parents, worldly-wise as became their station in life, had packed him off to sow his wild oats in regions conveniently remote, and had chosen David and Tim for his companions as discerning in them youths ripe for similar profligacy at the drop of a hat. So time and occasion must be found for low pleasures were the old folks at home not to be let down.

Tim and David played up to this sort of nonsense effectively enough, although each was inclined to wonder why the other could be detected as not terribly liking it. None of the three would very readily have admitted much thinking about sex except when talking about it in a routine bawdy way that grew boring if it went on for long. Had they been questioned on the subject by somebody who must be given an answer, they would have produced a common front on reticent and defensive lines. Sex lay within a category of activities that must definitely be got round to soon. The behaviour of their bodies (including their heads when their heads swam at a mere glimpse of one thing or another) told them that. But the thing required to be slotted in with other activities, physical, intellectual and even aesthetic, which it was taking a good deal of energy to get the hang of. Beyond this—even if so far—they wouldn't have been communicative. Young American men, of whom there were plenty around Vienna at the time, seemed perpetually absorbed in, and prepared lavishly to discuss, plans for laying this woman or that in a fashion that struck Olly, David and Tim as highly ludicrous and mildly contemptible. The Americans on their part, confronting an attitude so perplexingly compounded of the half-baked and the immature, were inclined to declare that so protracted a latency in the three Britishers simply betrayed the fact that they couldn't be too well hung. But this, as well as being coarse, was untrue. Otherwise, there wouldn't be any story.

II

OLLY AND TIM had made the railway journey to Vienna together, and David followed by himself a few days later. He'd had to be at home for a sister's wedding. The event had been vaguely upsetting—which was silly in the light of the fact that his new brother-in-law seemed a thoroughly nice man. But during the marriage service (in which certain tremendous things were said, so that he had felt the tears in his eyes) it had suddenly occurred to him that he might lie awake that night, imagining the very private consummation that must follow upon this very public solemnity. He would visualize the couple's caresses, their kisses, the disposition of their limbs—the lot. And it seemed to David that this almost involuntary or compulsive voyeurism would mark him out as an extremely depraved and degenerate person. He had, of course, read the appropriate books, and knew that the most disgraceful phantasies generated themselves occasionally in other heads besides his own. But there was a kind of incestuous slant to this impending indulgence that would surely make it totally unforgivable.

Needless to say, when he got into bed the horror didn't happen. He even saw that he wouldn't be a monster if it did. And from this he went on (for there was a certain boldness in his nature) to try to *make* it happen. But this immediately seemed quite foolish, and he fell asleep. Next morning, his memory was very little perturbed by the whole thing. Yet a little uneasiness remained. Here he was, with his twentyfirster behind him. And he wasn't being at all good at coping with the whole area of experience that ends up, presumably, with your getting married yourself.

At Calais he got into his second-class sleeper, which was the way one travelled in those days even when still living on one's father. One side of the little compartment made up into two beds or bunks for the night. But it turned out that there wasn't going to be another passenger. So he had it all to himself, including a privy and wash place through a sliding door. It was as good as travelling first— although it would be rather solitary in effect, except when he went along to dinner and breakfast in the *Speisewagen*.

The train was called the Orient Express, and if you moved up to the front you would be in carriages that went on to Constantinople, and that advertised the fact by saying so in Turkish characters on boards slung below the windows. David, although not so widely travelled as his own children in their nonage were to be, had been here and there about the continent—usually with his parents in Italy, but sometimes with friends, or even on his own, in other places. So he wasn't particularly keyed up by his present situation. Still, it was something of a milestone, or at least it ought to be. He was off and into something in a way he'd never been before. It was a pity, the more sagacious side of his head opined, that it wasn't something a bit more definite.

David settled down in his encapsulated and gently wobbling condition to read *The Autobiography of Alice B. Toklas*. This and *The Orators* and *Words for Music Perhaps* constituted the reading-matter with which he had provided himself for the journey. At the bookstall at Victoria his father had spent a well-meaning but futile seven-and-six on buying him an Agatha Christie detective-story. It had to be admitted that he and his father (although in general agreement about Giotto and Masaccio) weren't all that close to one another. He hadn't even owned to his father that he wanted to be a writer—an unnecessary reticence, since his father would have regarded it as a quite ordinary thing to want to be.

But Gertrude Stein—although described facetiously by Olly Russell as a writer's writer's writer—didn't on this occasion hold David's interest, any more than did the Belgian industrial landscape (which was like souped-up Wadsworth) deploying itself along the railway-line. He put down the book and explored his little wash place and loo. It turned out to be shared with the neighbouring compartment, but when he locked the door on his side a door on the other side locked automatically too. He wondered whether his neighbour was also travelling alone, and might prove to be a beautiful and accessible (but not promiscuously accessible: accessible, really, only to a masterful David Read) girl. When he had peed and washed his hands and returned to his seat he remembered that he hadn't entered the word 'loo' in the pocket notebook he kept for brand-new words, and he made good this deficiency before withdrawing into an introspection controlled at the outset by his shamelessly sanguine and sadly unrealistic fancy. He had to admit—owning, as he did, considerable intellectual clarity—that if such a neighbouring girl there were, and if she now came to him all warm and breathing and so on, the result would simply be to scare the pants off him, although not in a literal and apposite way.

So far, he hadn't been much good with girls. Once in a taxi coming away from a dance (he hated dances), he had put his hand on a girl's leg just above the knee—prompted, possibly, by the memory of Léon's successful performance with Emma Bovary in a cab. But he hadn't himself been successful. The stocking had felt unexpectedly harsh and grainy, so that he had taken his hand away with a mumbled apology, pretending that the contact had been accidental. On another and similar occasion he had suddenly grabbed a girl and kissed her. She had been surprised and upset, and on the following day had told her best friend about it, so that in no time the story was all over the place. This could only mean that she had interpreted his action as merely oafish—*une grossièreté voulue* would be the French for it—and in this she had no doubt been far from astray. He hadn't really wanted to a bit! It was a humiliating recollection, and he still sometimes woke up in the middle of the night with it. In fact it was the climax of a recurrent wet dream. Which was very mysterious indeed.

He knew he wasn't homosexual: hadn't ever been so even in a schoolboy way. Olly, that extravagant liar, was fond of expatiating on the enormous secret lust that had possessed him whenever he had walloped a small boy for burning his toast or failing to get the mud off his rugger boots. This was incomprehensible to David, who was convinced that Olly had simply picked it up from a school-story of the modern spuriously emancipated, now-it-can-all-be-told sort. David had worked it out that his own embarrassingly retarded condition had something to do with his mother. Again with the aid of the appropriate books, he had seen that, although not father-eclipsed, he did go in for mother-refuge in a big way. In fact he was rather like Paul Morel in *Sons and Lovers*—this much more than like Léon or Rodolphe in *Madame Bovary*. No Miriam would be any good to him until his mother was dead, probably after a long and agonizing illness. What an appalling condition! David was still brooding over it when the Orient Express expressed itself into Germany, and horrible *Polizei* were clicking their heels at him and arrogantly demanding to see his passport. Soon, however, he began to look forward to his dinner. He would call for *Löwenbräu* in a knowledgeable way. And what had been going through his head he would put behind him. It was stuff he would never dream of confessing to Olly and Tim, now waiting for him in Vienna.

But before he got there a strange, and strangely upsetting, thing happened. It was in the middle of the night. He had wakened up, he supposed because the train seemed to have slowed down a little. Leaning out of his bunk, he pulled up a blind and looked out. He had no idea where they were, and now there wasn't much to enlighten him. A crescent moon was in the sky; there were clouds over most of the stars; a vague impression of forest and mountain was something he was perhaps merely making up. Then the train's speed dropped further, and there was a rattle and slight swerve as if it was passing over points. A few faint lights appeared, then a low building, and he saw that they were running through a station. On the platform he glimpsed a uniformed man standing stiffly at attention in the solitude of the night. They did things like that, he remembered, in Germany. The chap probably took pride in thus turning out and going on parade for the benefit of perhaps nobody at all. David himself couldn't even wave to him.

They were through the station and in complete darkness again. But not quite. There was a house, close to the line, in which there was a single lighted window. In a moment David was abreast of this. And in the window, apparently looking out at the train, stood a young woman. She was quite naked.

The train hadn't yet gathered speed; nevertheless, what David ought to have seen was no more than a blurred impression of something barely to be identified. But this hadn't been the fact. The vision had been as clear, as detailed in every way, as if he had been standing before a frontally posed nude by Ingres. Only Ingres' nudes aren't real; aren't meant to be. This had been real.

David dropped the blind and lay back in his bunk, trembling and with his heart thumping. He'd never before seen a naked girl. No, that wasn't quite true. He remembered a girl cousin, straight from her bath and with her dressing-gown hanging open, smiling at him from the top of a staircase. But she'd been about three, and he hadn't been much older. So here was yet another measure of inexperience. He was astounded by the instantaneity and pitch of his excitement. It was quite a long time before he went to sleep again.

III

TIM, THROUGH WHAT might be called diplomatic channels, had found them accommodation. It was in a large apartment-block in the Ötzeltgasse, not a particularly august locality. The proprietrix, Frau Weber, had received numerous young Englishmen in her time: polite boys proposing a little to improve their German before undertaking to serve their country in embassies and legations in one or another part of Central Europe. Lately she had been finding such agreeable and remunerative boarders hard to come by, and she was quite as hard up as almost everybody else in Vienna. So she had put considerable cordiality into her welcome.

'*Alles, alles was Sie wünschen!*' she had exclaimed to the first two arrivals, and had accompanied the words with an expansive gesture comprehending indifferently her enormous Dresden stoves, her equally enormous feather quilts, and her two ill-favoured and not precisely young daughters.

'Thank you very much indeed,' Olly said formally—and then remembered that he was in a foreign country. So he made a kind of stage bow to the daughters. '*Es freut mich sehr*'—he said to them firmly and as if imperfectly remembering something from a phrase-book— '*Sie kennen lernen zu dürfen.*'

This, whether or not it was idiomatic or even grammatical, went down quite well. But with it ended, for the time being, any further attempt at communication in an alien tongue. Frau Weber explained in English that she provided only *Frühstück*, but that Herr Naumann ran an excellent restaurant in a cellar in the next street. And when a look of some dubiety betrayed itself on Olly's face she informed him with asperity that a very good society dined regularly at Herr Naumann's. It was evident that, despite her abject need of money, Frau Weber was a woman who stood no nonsense. Tim smoothed things over by venturing to inquire whether her late husband (she was understood to be a widow) had belonged to the same family as the musician. As the Webers had been officers and gentlemen as well as fiddlers and so forth, Frau Weber's reply was gratified as well as affirmative. Baron Franz Anton von Weber, she reminded Tim, had never declined to acknowledge his cousinship with the much humbler family of the Mozarts. After this cultivated exchange the Weber ladies withdrew, and the new boarders considered their situation.

Olly was not very favourably impressed by it.

'It's all going to be bloody stuffy,' he said.

'It had better be, with nothing to warm us but those great porcelain mausoleums, and the outside temperature heaven knows how many degrees below zero. A good fug will be our only hope.' Tim didn't seem in too good spirits. Every now and then, Olly reflected, Tim looked like a man remembering some defeat he'd rather forget. Olly never fished for this. Although by nature unscrupulous, he observed the taboos in which young men of his sort believe.

'I mean figuratively stuffy,' Olly said. 'That old woman will think it her business to keep an eye on us. And all the *hochbürgerlich* proprieties will have to be toadied to.'

'I don't think there's such a word as *hochbürgerlich*.'

'There is now. You ought to have found us something more in the Bohemian line. Students with their wenches and sausages and puddles of beer. That sort of thing. Particularly wenches.'

'I thought the woman was practically offering us her daughters.'

'It would be useless to offer them to a goat or a tom-cat. Do you realize that apartments like this are as good as gaols?'

'A pretty spacious gaol. The Webers must have about a dozen rooms. And apparently several of the attics as well.'

'Yes, of course. But don't you know that not a soul in a single one of these flats is so much as allowed a latch-key? You may have lived in one of them for twenty years. But when you come home you still have to ring a bell and be scrutinized by a nasty old woman in a glass box in the hall. It's rather like returning to an Oxford college at night. Except that a good simple kick at the door wouldn't be too well regarded.'

'It does sound a bit over the odds.' Tim plainly hadn't thought of this aspect of the matter. 'I expect it goes back to the paternalism of dear old Francis Joseph. Liked to feel every *Wiener* and *Wienerin* was tucked up and accounted for.'

'Better decide how to tuck up ourselves,' Olly said. They had been allotted two bedrooms, which faced each other across a broad corridor at its far end. They made their way to them now. 'Reasonably secluded,' Olly pronounced. 'And well away, one hopes, from Sin and Death.' It appeared that the Weber daughters were to be thus referred to. 'But we'll have to draw lots, I suppose.'

Each of the rooms held one very large double bed. They poked around the first of them.

'A *Nachttopf* each,' Tim reported. 'That's quite refined. But drawing lots it will have to be—unless, of course, the passions are involved.'

'I don't know about you and David. But, as for me, I'd rather have Sin herself than either of you.' Olly didn't pause on this obligatory pleasantry. He was preparing three slips of paper. 'Longest is me,' he said. 'The second is you, and the shortest is David. First out of the scrum gets solitary.' They devised a method of drawing the slips with meticulous fairness. David got solitary.

'Just what he'd like,' Olly said. 'David's not sociable in what you might call a *Nachttopf* way. I sing of a maiden that is makeless, wouldn't you say?'

'Don't be disgustingly profane, Olly.' It sounded as if Tim was actually serious in this rebuke. 'Look, the other room has a glimpse of the *Stephans-Dom*. Let's bag it and leave this one for our wandering boy. No reason why he should make all the going.'

'We'll let him do that with S. and D.' Olly said. 'And now we'll unpack.'

IV

ALMOST DAVID'S FIRST act was to ration the Sin and Death joke. His authority didn't extend to banning it, but he could cut down Olly's producing it to a maximum of once a day. It was a curious fact of their relationship that, when the chips were down, the rather diffident and misdoubting David had the confident and extravert Olly substantially under his thumb. On the other hand with Tim (who, as has been recorded, was akin to David in some ways) David's authority was nil. This seemed to be because Tim was in some mysterious fashion grown-up and David was not. Not that Tim's adult condition seemed to be much good to him; he was often tiresomely withdrawn and occasionally hard and cynical. In fact he was no longer quite the Oxford Tim.

David's point about Sin and Death was quite clear. They were decent girls—or women rather—and evident non-starters in the highly competitive Viennese marriage-market which their wretched mother probably insisted on as their only hope. It was apparent that family pretensions of some sort had precluded their being brought up to earn a living in a telephone exchange or as dentists' receptionists or something like that, and you could take a bet that their future was entirely drear. It wasn't necessary to look at them too often if the effort was over-taxing in an aesthetico-erotic way. But God's creatures they were, and Sin's name was Lotte and Death's—incredible though it seemed—was Pfiffi. So there.

Olly accepted this homily and Tim humoured it, so they all three fell to saying Pfiffi and Lotte like mad. The Webers seemed a little surprised, and Tim expressed misgivings. Wouldn't it be more proper just to say *Fräulein* every time? That wasn't in the least like addressing a young English gentlewoman as 'Miss'—a usage undeniably under-bred. But David said that Lotte and Pfiffi liked a little warmth, and responded to it. This was undeniably true. Quite soon Frau Weber's daughters were adoring their three guests. They would have liked to run for their slippers: that sort of thing. Olly, Tim and David didn't quite tumble to the depth of the enamourment they were occasioning. But by Frau Weber herself it was doubtless remarked.

The young men weren't much bothering about the Webers at all. They quickly had a great many activities in hand. Tim presented his introductions and was admitted with gratifying ease to certain archives of minor importance. David went to see a Professor of *Anglistik* with the idea of favouring him in the role of a superior research student. But not being instantly received (as an Oxford tutor would have received him) as a fellow-scholar and social equal, he was puzzled and offended, and abandoned his inquiries in that direction. Olly hired a bank-clerk to teach him what he insisted must be 'conversational' German. He was a nervous little man, miserably undernourished, but proud of his own 'conversational' English, and saying 'Please take place', when he meant 'Do sit down'. Olly made fun of him, grew ashamed of doing so, and resolved the matter by sacking him. Olly had discovered that the thing to have was the sort of girl that American students called a sleeping dictionary. They must each of them find a sleeping dictionary, and all would be well. But the hunt for this compendious convenience hung fire, partly because it wasn't easy to see how three sleeping dictionaries could come and go unchallenged by the *Pförtnerin* in the glass box, and partly because of the competing claims of skating and riding: the outdoor skating-rink was enormous, and in the Prater there were whole avenues so lavishly laid with frost-resistant bark that you could ride and jump however hard the ground. Olly had found a retired NCO, with very grand officer's airs, who was teaching him an Austrian cavalry seat with which one could cut quite a figure at home.

They also did a great deal of simple tourist's sightseeing, but engaged in all the proper cultural exercises as well, frequenting the galleries, the *Oper*, the *Burgtheater*, the *Theater an der Wien*, the *Volkstheater*, and the Spanish Riding School—and indeed everything else they could get to hear of. Impecunious Russian painters—all of them, oddly enough, aristocratic *émigrés* as well—got wind of them and sold them pictures. Bouvard and Pécuchet, liberated by that legacy into whole new worlds of experience, were pale shadows to them. They changed ten pounds each into an absurd currency expressed in *pengos*, and did a stupendous weekend in Budapest on the proceeds.

Social life—or the first social life to which they attained—proved, although at first intriguing, not quite so satisfactory. Tim had been written about to a Gräfin Somebody, actually an Englishwoman whose family manufactured torpedoes, who was understood to represent in Vienna the exiled Court. An invitation arrived, and they all went to tea. The Gräfin (like a female Arion, Olly said, straddled securely on one of those naval projectiles above the dark waters of Viennese penury) owned an apartment about six times the size of Frau Weber's. But even this miniature palace seemed a little run-down, and its menservants, although no doubt to be thought of as feudally devoted to a fallen nobility, looked as sullen as if they were minded to cut your throat or hang you heels-up from the nearest lamp-post.

The young men did quite well, and were in consequence accorded the regular entrée. The *corps diplomatique* wasn't supposed to frequent the Gräfin's salon with any obtrusiveness, but some of them were always there and their hostess insisted on everything being *en règle*. It didn't matter when you arrived, but you could take your leave only in strict order of precedence. This was awkward for Olly, Tim and David, who would have preferred to be allowed to take French leave in the original sense of the term; as it was, they were condemned always to be in the dusty rear. Most of the guests were old women of the Gräfin's sort, toting round daughters or grand-daughters who they hoped might catch the fancy of some eligible young attaché from the American Embassy or the British Legation. Because of this ambition, the girls, although frequently in the next thing to rags, were exquisitely groomed, their mothers' assuredly starveling maids having made sure that not a hair was out of place. They were extremely pretty; they sat without moving hand or foot; their conversation was limited to asking whether you knew A, B, or C—which invariably you did not. For a time they quite amused Olly and David, who passed them little cakes and imagined taking their clothes off. Olly was always in hopes that one or two of them would prove to be married already, and to unfaithful husbands, since in that case they would be licensed to take lovers galore, as in the world of *Les Liaisons Dangereuses*.

On Tim, however, the fillies from this stable had a quite different and rather perplexing effect. He ought to have been easier with them than the others were, since his family had been in the diplomatic line of business for several generations and he acknowledged that occasional hob-nobbings of this sort had made part of his holiday and vacation life almost since he was a kid. In addition to which he possessed excellent French, a language which these aristocratic Viennese liked to talk almost as if they were Russians in Turgenev or Tolstoy. But every now and then Tim would fix his regard on one or another of the doll-like creatures in an intent and strained way. It was clear that he wasn't just wondering whether the clothes came off and there was something anatomically complete underneath; it was part of Tim's annoying maturity that it wasn't like that at all. When he and his friends came away he would put on his withdrawn and brooding turn. This was coming to annoy Olly excessively and almost as if he were jealous of it. David felt that he ought to tackle Tim and in some way lend a hand. Only he didn't know how to begin.

Superficially at least, they all did better in less assuming circles. In one way and another they got to know quite a number of Viennese girls who were gay and friendly and pleasure-loving—and also (one had to guess) good Catholics and virginal as well. The young men skated with them and took them to cafés and restaurants and concerts and cinemas—places of diversion in which they wouldn't have had a penny to pay their way themselves. They were frank about their families' post-war poverty, treating it as a kind of game in which they had become involved, and which looked like lasting for an indefinite time ahead. In Austria, unlike Germany, there wasn't much *Umbau* going on. Vienna was a great capital city suddenly bereft of any economic hinterland.

The three Englishmen didn't much like this aspect of their situation, and Olly even said that it got in the way of making love to these young women as they deserved. Offer one of them so much as a cup of coffee with a lot of whipped cream slobbed on top of it, and you felt like an Edwardian rake seducing a chorus-girl with a pair of diamond ear-rings. This seemed a surprising delicacy of feeling in one who believed in low pleasures as a kind of contractual duty, but his friends knew what Olly meant. Deep in their hearts these feather-headed but courageous girls dreamed of marrying you. It was either you or—and even this would require luck—somebody like the little man who said 'Please take place'. It was difficult for them not to be designing in a way that wounded their pride. David, whose lucidity sometimes got the better of his modesty, said it wasn't as bad as if he and Olly and Tim were a trio positively unattractive in themselves. At times when shaving he had happened to notice that he himself wasn't at all bad looking, and that went for Tim and Olly too. And didn't they all have nice manners? At least a girl needn't suppose that she was trying to sell herself in exchange for a wedding-ring from a pig.

These observations, although defensively offered on an ironic note, were basically true. But they didn't mean that David took any unalarmed pleasure at the thought of one of these girls being after him. A girl after him, rather than he after a girl, would be a most uncomfortable thing. And he *wasn't* after a girl. Some of the girls undoubtedly excited him, and all sorts of amorous visions came and went in his head. But he was pretty sure that the mother-refuge thing still operated. He looked forward with anxiety to every letter from home, in case it should bring the news that his mother had been run over by a bus, since he'd then have felt like an Australian aborigine who had successfully pointed a bone at somebody. Fortunately Mrs Read remained in excellent health.

v

IT WILL BE seen that problems of sexual comportment were gaining on the boarders in the Ötzeltgasse. There would be occasion for surprise had it been otherwise since, despite a daily flurry of activities, they were leading thoroughly idle lives. Skating and riding, and long snowy walks in the Wiener Wald scarcely stopped their putting on weight to an extent that might have impaired David's estimate of their personableness. When they felt hard up they dined at Herr Naumann's as Frau Weber had advised. More often they went to the Rathaus Keller, where enormous quantities of food were served in dining-rooms severally appropriated to different classes of society. Sometimes they went to more expensive restaurants, including one in which you could point to a fish swimming happily amid its fellows in a tank, and be eating it ten minutes later. This was a refinement of polite life they'd none of them happened to meet before, and they permitted it to amuse them very much. But sometimes they felt rather silly, just arsing agreeably around. Even Tim felt this, although managing a short bout with his archives every now and then. Of course it was their *Wanderjahr*, which was—or had used to be—a perfectly respectable idea for young men with passably industrious *Lehrjahre* immediately behind them. Nevertheless they were conscious of being in a bit of a muddle. They were quite genuinely active and high-spirited and pleased with themselves; but at the same time they acknowledged (although barely to one another) that elsewhere there was heat and dust and a race going on, and that they had rather feebly dropped out of it. But they weren't exactly ready to pack up, and the advancing Viennese spring was very delightful. Perhaps they could at least end up with a bang rather than a whimper? And oughtn't it to be a bang in an incoming sense of the word? A mood of irresponsibility was seeping into all three of them. And all this meant that, in their several ways, they were in a mood for Elsa when she turned up.

Elsa came from a place called Mistelbach. All Viennese policemen were facetiously supposed to come from there, apparently because the name meant something like 'dung-heap'. But there was nothing of that suggestion about Elsa, who was as fresh as the May. She was a peasant girl, used to hard work, and her arrival in the Ötzeltgasse was a consequence of Frau Weber's enhanced sense of unwonted prosperity—which in turn flowed from the substantial weekly sums coming to her from the Herren Russell, Read and Merton. Hitherto Frau Weber had relied for domestic assistance upon a nameless old woman, perhaps a poor relation of the *Pförtnerin*, who had come in by the day. But now the Elsa, having been hired for heaven knew what pittance, was established in one of the low-hutched attics that went

along with the Webers' top-floor apartment dwelling. The enormity
of implication inherent in this fact came to the young men at once.
The wench was inside, not without, the ring-fence system of things
insisted upon by the paternalistic Emperor Francis Joseph. Unfortunately Frau Weber was far from unaware of the possibilities thus
opened up. The little internal staircase communicating with the attics
(learnedly described by Olly as the *aedes annexae*) was guarded by a
door which the mistress of the establishment simply locked at night,
so that the poor girl was incarcerated as if in gaol until liberated in the
morning. What would happen if there were a fire and she was forgotten about it wasn't nice to imagine. But David did sometimes dream
of a heroic and spectacular rescue effected by himself. The Elsa would
cling deliciously round his neck as he staggered downstairs with her
through the smoke and flame—this after he had kicked through the
door in a masterful fashion.

Certainly the locked door was a challenge; had it *not* been locked,
the young men might not have let their minds go to work as they did.
The door was fair game, and somehow made the girl fair game too.
Olly was the first to feel matters in this way. Tim held back for a time;
then, with a disconcerting abruptness as if something had snapped in
his head, became brutally predatory in everything he said. David was
a misdoubting partner all the way through—or at least until the
climax of the affair.

Had the Elsa been a modest girl, nothing might have taken place.
But she was something headier and different: at once virginal-
seeming and ripe for mischief. Back in Mistelbach, she must have put
in time imagining all sorts of shameless things about life in Vienna.

The boarders began flirting with her in various ways. Quite soon
they were snatching kisses (a good literary phrase) in corridors and
also in their own chaste sleeping quarters when she came to make the
beds. Even David kissed her, and she was certainly neither upset nor
surprised. They got round to spanking her, gamesomely and vulgarly,
as she leant invitingly out of the window in the standard Viennese
employment of disposing the voluminous bed *Decken* to air. The
atmosphere, like one's body under those mountains of feathers, hot-
ted up. They provided themselves with French letters from an auto-
matic machine they had discovered in a public lavatory.

Frau Weber seemed unaware of this scandalous course of things.
They weren't so sure about Lotte and Pfiffi—Sin and Death. The
daughters of the house were certainly less and less nice to their serf.

This produced a kind of ganging-up effect. The young men were on the Elsa's side, and were going to get her her due. An unedifying moral confusion thickened. It so thickened that Olly presently did a quite extraordinary thing. He abstracted the key of the attic door (which remained in place during the day) and had a copy expeditiously made by a local locksmith. This was real intrigue at last.

But there was now a real problem too—undreamt of at that remote time when lots had been drawn to decide who should share a bedroom with whom. The girl was prepared for almost anything—it had got to that—but not for receiving nocturnal visitors in her own narrow quarters. She seemed to think of the young men as enormous blundering creatures not to be trusted to achieve any cat-like tread along the marble-floored corridors of the Weber home. But she was quite ready to make her own way to an assignation downstairs. But where? And with whom?

This unreal and dream-like situation (it wasn't yet a nightmarish one) persisted for some time. Olly and Tim became rather secret together; they even whispered to one another in their room. David had a dim sense of their planning something attractively extreme, and was content himself to draw apart a little, and let be. Or almost content. If something really *happened*, and he was excluded from it, he would resent being relegated to the role of what his Italophil parents would call a *terzo incomodo*.

What did happen he didn't expect. He woke up abruptly in the middle of one night, aware of a strange weight on his bed. He thought of a cat: the Webers had several of these creatures, inconvenient though they were on a top-floor flat. He sat up abruptly and turned on his bedside lamp. A hand appeared on it and turned it off again, but not before he had seen that Elsa was perched beside him.

David was terrified. His knees trembled—which knees usually do only when you're standing up and about to be beaten or obliged to make a speech—something like that.

The girl was giggling in the dark. She was whispering, and he found that—amazingly—he had put an arm round her. There was only something very thin indeed between his hand and her flesh. She whispered that Olly and Tim were expecting her. Olly had given her the key. She'd had another idea.

The idea plainly was to slip into David's bed. But before she could do that he had pulled her there. He had read in his books of a misfortune called *ejaculatio praecox*, and he was urgently feeling the point of it. But all went well, most amazingly well. He was astounded, as the hours went by, at the reach of his own virility. The dawn—ah God!—the dawn it came too soon. But the moment the Elsa did depart David fell asleep.

He woke up in broad daylight to the staggering memory. He had done it! He believed himself to be blissfully happy.

VI

BUT NOT so on the following night. During the day he had kept mum, given nothing away. Olly and Tim were both in a bad temper, but they said nothing either. It ought to have been rather comical, this situation like a bawdy tale in the *Decameron*. But in fact it was uncomfortable. Why weren't they all roaring with laughter, why did they distrust looking straight at one another? Life isn't like the *Decameron*. Far from it at times. The three young men weren't on a collision course. But they were on a drifting-apart one.

The Elsa wasn't visible. Perhaps it was her day off or something. Or had he conceivably injured her? Things like that happen. This morbid notion, although David didn't know it, was prelusive of dire nemesis to come. A portentous chronicler might assert, indeed, that here was to be an instance of that favourite mechanism of the tragic poets whereby a more or less venial and trivial fault on the hero's part is disproportionately visited with titanic disaster.

David went to bed early, but of course he didn't go to sleep. Would the Elsa, so handsomely entertained twenty-four hours before, come to him again now? Or was it possible—

The obvious happened, as it so commonly does. A little after midnight David's strained ear heard a door softly open and close. He lay still for a time, feeling slightly sick, and trying to hear more. But no further sound penetrated across the corridor from his friends' room. He got out of bed, with the strangest sense of a physical struggle not to do so, and opened his door and crept out. At least the Webers couldn't come upon him shamefully employed; their rooms were far away on a branching corridor at the other end of the apartment. He tiptoed to the door beyond which he had to imagine Olly, Tim and the girl. Cautiously he located the keyhole with a finger. And then he put his ear to it and listened.

He heard what he deserved: the Elsa's giggle, the creaking of a bed, a kind of scuffling almost of a skylarking sort, smothered laughter, the slapping of hands on bare flesh. There then followed, very predictably, heavy breathing and panting at an accelerating pace. But these sound-effects ceased abruptly, to be succeeded by others which were odd and not easily to be interpreted. At this David straightened up and groped his way blindly back to his own room. He could hardly believe he'd done the demeaning thing he had.

In bed he calmed down. It would be absurd to be jealous of Olly and Tim—and, after all, he'd been there himself first. And fairly normal people probably give way to prurient curiosities from time to time. He'd tell them what he'd done. What he'd done both tonight and the night before. Nothing had happened not of a sort that they'd concocted cheerfully indecent chat about often enough. In fact hadn't they arrived, all three, at what might be a very snug little *ménage?* There seemed not to be any reason—or any rational reason, since perhaps it mightn't feel too nice—why a sleeping dictionary shouldn't be fixed up on a polyandrous system. But then was the Elsa unalphabetic? She almost certainly was. . . . Thus David Read under his *Decke,* having become quite the man of the world. He fell asleep imagining himself fondling the Elsa's breasts and behind.

On the next morning he expected Olly and Tim to be jubilant and assertive, and he looked forward to deflating them a little by revealing that they hadn't been first in the field—unless, indeed, they'd extracted this information from the Elsa already. But it didn't work out like that. Both his friends were in a much worse temper than they had been after the previous night when the Elsa had failed them. And now *they* had failed *her.* This (as their overall sense of the conclusion of the occasion) emerged at once as an amazing· truth that Olly was much too angry and confused to conceal. David's disgusting eavesdropping (which he confessed) had been delusive or too soon given over. His Elsa, it was clear, hadn't been the Elsa revealed to Olly and Tim. She had typed David, accurately enough, as romantic and innocent, and had played up to that. Quite inaccurately, and perhaps as a result of the other two young men having made it a joint enterprise, she had concluded them to be revolting *roués,* and had behaved accordingly.

Olly was utterly confused and incoherent about this. In a state of violent reaction from his proposed libidinous courses, he could only exclaim that the girl had turned out—had turned out in the end—a filthy little bitch. Mistelbach must be bloody well named, after all.

There ought to have been something comical in this picture of a hopeful young rake getting more than he'd bargained for. But David was at once merely horrified; was perhaps already obscurely glimpsing what was coming at him. He turned to Tim for explanations. Tim, although equally in a state of shock, was at his coldest and most cynical. He was also quite articulate.

'We just weren't on her wave-length,' he said. 'Not as the pleasant occasion developed, that is. Our imaginations were defective, Olly's and mine. Or utterly old-world. It never occurred to us, for instance, not just to take turns. *Sancta simplicitas!* The angel-child had other ideas about threesomes.'

David tried to say, 'It damn well served you right.' The thing was utterly beastly, but ought to be controlled and played down. He found himself, however, incapable of speech.

'The loathsome pox-ridden trollop!' Olly burst out. And he stormed from the room.

These had been fatal words. Before the door banged the terror had fallen upon David. He remembered reading in one of his authorities— Havelock Ellis, perhaps, or the translation of Krafft-Ebing—that it was maid-servants, hotel chambermaids and the like who were the prime dispensers of horrible diseases. Later he was to remember that Freud, here in Vienna, had discovered that half his psycho-neurotic patients had fathers who suffered from syphilis. Within an hour, David's phobia was fully established.

It was a hell extending beyond the reach of imagination, and so is not to be described. And it was his secret, for he simply couldn't divulge it to Olly and Tim. He seemed to live inside it as if it were a physical integument, with everything beyond grown shadowy and insubstantial. His only gleam of comfort lay in the intellectual perception that, if he ever escaped it, he would never be thus terrified by anything again. Should he die in old age, he would remember it as the worst thing that had ever happened to him.

A lot of time passed—or it may have been almost no time at all. An aunt of David's, an admirable woman, turned up in Vienna, with a vague plan for taking her favourite nephew on a short spring cruise down the Dalmatian coast. Seeing within minutes that something was very badly wrong, she put the proposal into operation at once. David was helpless. They took train to Trieste and boarded a Yugoslavian steamer. The change of scene didn't help David a bit. The food was very good, but he couldn't eat it. His aunt sat in the stern, making watercolour sketches. There was nothing to do but stare out at an

interminable barren coast, just here and there beginning to be dotted
with little pleasure resorts. Finally, David broke down entirely. At
Spalato, bang in the middle of the ruins of Diocletian's palace, he
wept, and told his aunt the truth. She said composedly that they must
return to England at once. David refused; he couldn't face up to his
parents with this shame upon him. So she took him back to Vienna by
train, and within hours he was in the presence of a specialist in
venereology. Examinations and tests happened. Time was utterly
hazy still.

'*Gott sei dank, Herr Read!*' a benevolent old gentleman was saying to
him. '*Keine Spur, keine Spur!*' And he added that marriage was the best
thing for a young man's *Gesundheit*.

Just as if the nice old man had been a mesmerist, David believed the
verdict implicitly. The phobia departed as it had arrived: instantane-
ously. David's aunt departed too. She had done her job. In her heart
she had been shocked and displeased by this aberration of late-
adolescence. As soon as she got to England she paid a visit to David's
home, but with no informative intention. She wrote David a prompt
letter, full of news about dogs and ponies. She had been to the
vicarage too. The vicar's younger daughter, just 'out', was prettier
than ever, and extremely charming.

VII

AMAZINGLY, LIFE IN the Ötzeltgasse resumed its even tenor. Olly and
Tim, if they knew or suspected anything, said nothing. David reported favourably on Spalato as a nice place for a holiday. He would
have reported favourably on anywhere short of Gehenna. He wasn't
even euphoric in an unstable fashion. He was simply happy. The Elsa
had vanished, being replaced by a second old crone. It was conceivable that David's aunt had enjoyed—or at least firmly undertaken—
some conversation with Frau Weber. Lotte and Pfiffi were more
devoted than ever. It was a pity that the whole thing would soon be
coming to an end. The tiresome business of adopting honourable
professions was now looming up before all three young men.

But the inconceivable seemed to have the habit of turning up in the
Ötzeltgasse. It became known to David that Olly had made Pfiffi his
mistress. Tim must have been aware of this rather earlier. It was, after
all, from the chaste bed he shared with Olly that Olly had to slip in

order to make his way to his charmer's chamber. Tim didn't appear interested. His reclusiveness was growing on him. David sometimes wondered whether he was next in line for a bout of madness. As for Olly's affair, David thought it horribly depraved. Freud came into his head again. He had read some severe critic of Freud who maintained that the lunatic pansexualism of psychoanalytic theory was a function of the pervasively corrupt society in which this undeniably great *savant* had formed his ideas. And it was very disgraceful to seduce a daughter of the house, particularly in quest of nothing but second-rate cold pleasure. It was worse than the Elsa business by a long way.

Olly began to insist that Lotte must be accommodated too. Lotte was madly jealous, and it simply wasn't fair on her. She was pretty well panting for a lover of her own. David didn't know whether this was true, although observation constrained him to the view that there was something in it. He felt the threat of nightmare on the horizon again. And, sure enough, they *all* presently went mad. It became established that there was only one humane and decent course for Tim and David to adopt. They must toss up for Lotte. It was like the affair of drawing lots for the beds again. Lots for Lotte.

Tim made no objection. He might have been Macbeth, resigned and indifferent before the necessity of one more murder. There really was something very odd about Tim's make-up. To David himself the thing came as a dare—and as a dare demanding heroism. He had decided, and without being unhappy about it, that what lay ahead of him could only be a celibate life. Get into bed with *any* woman, and an irrational guilt would take the form of landing him once more where he had been. He had given up the mother-refuge theory as half-baked. The thing would have been part of his constitution if he had been a creature spontaneously generated from the sea or the mud.

Lotte fell to David—Olly having meanwhile played some inconceivable Pandarus-rôle that fixed everything up. What sort of a female could Lotte be to submit to such a scheme of things? He remembered grimly that if Pfiffi was Sin, Lotte was Death. And if it didn't turn out to be death exactly, wouldn't it almost certainly be fiasco? Was there the slightest chance that, on his own part, the necessary physiological phenomenon would take place? What was ahead, at best, was a specific humiliation that no young man cares to contemplate. He lay in bed, imagining with all his might making gradual, or abrupt, or delirious love to Lotte. He awaited some result.

Nothing took place. Limp as a worm, he told himself—thus anticipating by some years the poet Yeats.

He went along. That was the only way to express it: he went along in total darkness to Lotte's room, having previously measured his path and located all the hideous objects—the Webers only went in for massively hideous furniture—that he mustn't blunder into. He wished with all his heart that Frau Weber would be alerted, and would emerge as with a flaming sword to banish him whence he had come. She seemed to be a mysteriously unsuspicious woman. Or was it possible—? He didn't let his mind dwell on this.

Lotte was expecting him, and Lotte was entirely kind. She took him in her arms and comforted him, nursed him; she was sublimely grateful for his simply being there. In the near-darkness she moved the hair back from his damp forehead and gently kissed it. He realized that he could have whipped her and she would have remained just the same. He made love to her instead—himself gently, and compassionately as she was compassionate. He was safe. It was a heavenly night. Neither during it nor over succeeding days did his former vulnerability so much as come into his head. It had gone for good.

Then one more unexpected thing happened. David and Olly received severally from Frau Weber written invitations to *fünf-Uhr Tee*. There was nothing for it; appalled, they solemnly wrote out formal acceptances. Nothing of the sort had ever happened before. Tim said icily that they were for it. They believed him.

In Frau Weber's ugly *Gesellschaftszimmer* a round table had been set out with a tea-run, and little napkins, and plates of repellent-looking sandwiches. On upright chairs placed severely around it quite a company was already present. It didn't include Lotte and Pfiffi. In addition to Frau Weber herself there were three old women exactly like her. There were also two old men, each balancing his hands on a silver-headed stick, with his bearded chin on his hands. One of them wore a decoration; he was clearly a *Geheimrat*, or something like that. Neither of them failed to bear a resemblance to their late beloved emperor.

So here was the Family: the Webers, in fact, putting their most terrifying feet forward, and showing that they were by no means humble people like the Mozarts. Introductions were effected, although neither the ladies nor the gentlemen moved other than to offer a frigid bow. Olly, with a desperate flicker of impudence that David judged not too well-bred, clicked his heels and said '*Servus!*'—which was undoubtedly Viennese but probably not quite right. Tea was dispensed, and sandwiches sparingly consumed. Conversation was sparing too, but did happen. Everybody in turn, that is to say, offered a single polite remark. After that there was silence. David and Olly supposed that this would be followed by the real thing: stern reprobation, probably by the *Geheimrat*. Or perhaps both gentlemen, although aged, would rise simultaneously and each tweak an English nose— after which the details of the duels would fall to be arranged by seconds summoned for the purpose. But the silence continued. And everybody was looking at David and Olly inquiringly.

It was clearly up to them to say something. And as they were about equally clever it is probable that they arrived at one and the same moment at what it was. They were expected to petition the Family for the hands of Fräulein Lotte and Fräulein Pfiffi respectively. The time had come—had decidedly come—for that.

Faced with this frightful situation, Olly did not too badly. At least he wasn't again impudent. He simply launched out on approving observations on the musical life of Vienna, and didn't let up for three or four minutes. David put in this interval imagining himself arriving home with a thirty-year-old Austrian *fiancée*, or even wife. He was very fond of Lotte, and at present grateful to her beyond measure. But he had a clear head, and he knew there was nothing in it for either of them. And, of course, he had behaved like a cad, etc. When he told his father about it (and this, rather oddly, he knew he'd have to do) he would be informed that it sounded to have been a pretty poor show.

They extricated themselves from the party as best they could, and returned to their own quarters. David felt he wanted to barricade the door. Olly made a half-hearted attempt to denounce Frau Weber who, with that utterly delusive hope of matrimony in mind, had pretty well acted as bawd to her own daughters. David lost his temper, and told him to shut up. Olly obeyed. They decided that the best thing to do was to pack. When Olly went into his bedroom to begin the process, it was to find Tim already doing the same thing. Tim had no doubts about Vienna. *Schluss!* That was it. As it damn well ought to have been long ago.

There were two horrible partings, and the young men set off for home next day.

VIII

ALMOST AT ONCE they drifted apart. They'd never had a reunion, and there wouldn't be one now. Even Olly and David, who had been at school together, never met for more than a drink and a quick word until, in the 1970s, they found themselves spending the night in the same hotel. It was in the small market-town on the outskirts of which their old school lay. They discovered that they both had grandsons there now: quite small boys in their first term. Being conscientious grandparents, they had both come down on a visit, just to see how things were going along. They agreed that it seemed to be not too badly. The school, Sir Oliver Russell said, had been humanized and liberalized in a most notable way since their time. Professor Read was of the same opinion. Every variety of civilized activity seemed to be encouraged; games, although vigorously pursued, were not the tyranny and fetish they had been; and their grandsons couldn't be told to tip an arse because they had burnt some great oaf's toast.

'But most of the proper things remain,' Sir Oliver said. 'Nice to see everyone in chapel, wouldn't you say? And all in surplices still. And the candles! Terribly jolly.'

Professor Read agreed that the scene in chapel was terribly jolly. The two old men reminisced together through a long evening, and after a second glass of port and some brandy following dinner each summoned the flickering attention of the other to the recollection of occasions not always particularly civilized or humane. Not unaware of their condition, they joked about being respectively Shallow and Silence. But it was a Shallow and Silence in form-rooms and dormitories and on playing-fields rather than as young blades about a town, pursuing the *bona-robas*. They took their time, in other words, about approaching Vienna.

'The fees at the confounded school,' Sir Oliver suddenly said, 'are turning outrageous. I've had to lend a hand with covenants and so forth. I daresay you have too, David.'

'Moderately, Olly. The academic life hasn't been a gold-mine exactly.' While teaching in a university, David had developed quite a profitable side-line in the production of literary biographies, carefully researched, and written in an urbanely formal prose that pleased old-fashioned readers. But he wasn't at all rich as a result.

'A gold-mine, David? There just aren't any—not now. I expect you know, by the way, that there are grandchildren of poor Tim Merton's of school age now? Boys, I believe. A pity they can't be with ours. Out of the question, I suppose.'

'No doubt.' David knew nothing about Tim, except that he had been killed while driving an ambulance around London in 1944. 'I almost believe,' he went on, 'that I never once ran into Tim again— not after our coming back from Vienna all those ages ago.' David sipped his brandy. 'In fact he disappeared abruptly. I felt he'd stopped approving of us.'

'Oh, I don't think it was that, David. Just then, he had a bad nervous breakdown, and that buggered things up a bit. Nasty thing to come on one, it must be. Never barged into that sort of trouble myself. Did you?'

'No—or never anything to speak of.' David gazed into his glass as he gently rotated it. He wondered whether if now, a dotard on the very verge of his confine, he was at last going to tell Olly, also a dotard, the story of that bad time that had climaxed in Spalato. It certainly remained with him vividly enough to be an effective story. But he rejected the idea. Close as Olly and he had once been, such a confidence would be unseemly now. 'Don't you seem to remember,' he asked, 'that Tim was a good deal under the weather during most of that time in Vienna? That's how it comes back to me, at least.'

'True enough—and I know what the trouble was.' Olly looked round for a waiter; he would have one more brandy before going to bed. 'I got it out of him not long before they killed him. He'd been married for only two or three years, you know. Sad. You must have got married about the same time, David?' Olly looked up, for a moment sharply curious.

'Yes, just about then.'

'Local girl, eh?'

'Oh, entirely.' As impudent as ever, David thought. 'Our vicar's daughter.'

'Good, good! Another brandy, please. We none of us went back to Vienna, did we, to collect a bride?'

'*Gott sei dank*, Olly. And don't be frivolous. But tell me what you got out of Tim. I'm curious. I always was. I used to wonder why he was grown-up.'

'Grown-up?' Olly was perplexed. 'We were all three that, weren't we? Or more or less.'

'We shaved, and had our adventures, I suppose. But go on.'

'Tim had been in love. Thank you—will you put it on my bill

please? Tim had been very much in love.'

'In love?' There was a note of perplexity in David's repetition of the phrase—rather as if its reference was to some dubious condition he'd once or twice heard of. It occurred to him that, back in that Tim-and-Olly time, they'd never used it. *Making love*, yes: it was the upper-class way of saying something denominated otherwise by the vulgar. But *in love*, no. It just hadn't cropped up. 'Do you mean,' he asked Olly, 'before our stay in Vienna?'

'Yes, of course. During Tim's final year at Oxford. It was what mucked up his Schools.'

'I remember about that, of course. But I never knew why it had happened.' David paused, puzzled. 'Do you mean that, all through that Vienna period, Tim was a heart-broken man because some love-affair had gone wrong?'

'Just that. It happens, you know.' For a moment, and as he said this, Olly was almost the old Olly again. 'Yes, it does happen. The real thing.'

'But he mucked in, didn't he, in those attempts—and successes—of ours at what our sons would call an easy lay?'

'Well, yes. He did—in a kind of cynical and half-hearted fashion. But all dust and ashes to him, I think. It *would* be—wouldn't it?—after something quite different.'

'Yes.' David wondered whether he wanted to hear more. He found he did. 'How did the crash come?' he asked. 'Was it before—'

'It was before *Tim* came—with the wench, that is.' Sir Oliver Russell paused, perhaps discomposed by this resurgence in himself of an ancient routine grossness. 'But that wasn't the point. Whether or not he'd possessed her—and he hadn't—was precisely not the point. For Tim had landed himself with the real thing, as I say. The girl had indeed lain in his arms, he said. Moaning. All that. But at the same time it was beyond sense. And then she was pretty well wrenched away from him.'

'What sort of a girl was she?'

'Austrian, as a matter of fact, and aristocratic. Her people and his people saw—or thought they saw—it wouldn't do.'

'Good God! Just because—?'

'No, no. Nothing of that kind. Not class stuff at all. The Mertons were quite in the right drawer themselves, so far as that went. It was some ghastly medical superstition of the time. The same sort of blood disease, or loopiness, or heaven knows what, imagined as running in both families. So a gaggle of bloody leeches blundered in and smashed the thing up. It was a bit morbid, in a way, Tim's coming to Vienna at all. The girl's grandfather had been something quite tremendous there, and her father had hung on in the Austrian Embassy in London. That's how they met. I believe Tim's father had a crazy idea that Tim might find another, and blamelessly hygienic, wench of the same sort on the banks of the Donau.' Olly paused on this. Something of his old idiom was returning to him. 'Perhaps Tim himself had dimly the same useless idea. Do you remember, David, that ghastly old party-giving *Baronin*?'

'*Gräfin*, not *Baronin*. *Baronessen* were two a penny. Like the wives of knighted quill-pushers or grocers.'

This was scarcely a tactful pedantry on Professor Read's part. But Sir Oliver, who nowadays only intermittently listened to what was said to him, ignored it.

'Remember the girls paraded at those bun-fights, David? I think Tim really was a little cracked at the time, and imagined things as he gaped at them. Certainly when he got home they had to shove him for a time into a shocking bin in Northumberland, or some such discreet back-of-beyond. But, of course, he came round in time. He had a perfectly lovely wife. Astounding kids, too. Too bad that he never saw them scramble out of their perambulators.'

Sir Oliver Russell—he had driven a quill to good effect in some respectable Ministry—fell silent, and Professor Read said nothing. It was time to go to bed in this not very comfortable hotel. They both rose and made their way, a little creakingly, to the staircase. Sir Oliver paused at the foot of it.

'I say,' he said, 'do you remember Sin and Death? My Sin, David, and pretty well your Death, eh?'

Chuckling softly at this aged witticism, Olly—who was inclined to stumble at times—cautiously led the way up to their rooms.